GAME OVER

Recent Titles by Cynthia Harrod-Eagles from Severn House

THE COLONEL'S DAUGHTER
A CORNISH AFFAIR
DANGEROUS LOVE
DIVIDED LOVE
EVEN CHANCE
HARTE'S DESIRE
THE HORSEMASTERS
JULIA
LAST RUN
THE LONGEST DANCE
NOBODY'S FOOL
ON WINGS OF LOVE
PLAY FOR LOVE
A RAINBOW SUMMER
REAL LIFE (*Short Stories*)

The Bill Slider Mysteries

GAME OVER

GAME OVER

A Bill Slider Mystery

Cynthia Harrod-Eagles

This first world edition published in Great Britain 2008 by
SEVERN HOUSE PUBLISHERS LTD of
Eardley House, 4 Uxbridge Street, London W8 7SY
This first world edition published in the USA 2008 by
SEVERN HOUSE PUBLISHERS INC of
595 Madison Avenue, New York, N.Y. 10022.

British Library Cataloguing in Publication Data

Harrod-Eagles, Cynthia
  Game over. - (A Bill Slider mystery)
  1. Slider, Bill (Fictitious character) - Fiction 2. Police
  - England - Fiction 3. Journalists - Crimes against -
  Fiction 4. Detective and mystery stories
  I. Title
  823.9'14[F]

  ISBN-13: 978-0-7278-6615-8 (cased)
  ISBN-13: 978-1-84751-056-3 (trade paper)

Typeset by Palimpsest Book Production Ltd.,
Grangemouth, Stirlingshire, Scotland.

For Peter Wright, as long promised.

One

Fame Shrewdly Gored

The habits learned in childhood tend to become ingrained, so that they operate on an involuntary level. With Detective Inspector Bill Slider, observation was second nature. His countryman father had taken him out to watch badgers' setts at dusk, to wait for deer to come down to the stream at dawn, to know by a flattened patch of grass, a scrap of hair snagged on a hedge, a broken spider's web, fallen feathers, or the crusty bits of a mouse left by a path-side, who had passed by, and when, and why. He noticed things often without immediately knowing he had done so.

So on his way to a call-out it was the second sighting of the black Ford Focus that impinged on him. Focuses were plentiful in West London and black had lately replaced silver as the most popular car colour, so there was nothing remark-able about it, except that it had tinted windows, and he was inherently suspicious of anyone trying to hide their face, and that there had been a black Focus parked just down the road from the back door of the police station the day before. It had had the same ding-and-scrape on the nearside rear quarter, but a different number plate. Slider's interest prickled. The traffic halted him along the Goldhawk Road, just after the car had passed him, and he whipped out his notebook and jotted down its registration while he remembered it. He didn't remember the number of the earlier car except that it had begun with LN, while this began with LR. It was probably nothing, of course, but he *had* noticed it, and the fact of noticing made him uneasy. If he was being followed, it was following of a professional order, to have bothered to change the plates. But anyone who had been in the Job as long as he had was bound to accumulate enemies, and he had had his share of high-profile cases.

The traffic was no better than crawling now, so he cut off to the right as soon as a gap opened and made his way through the back streets to his destination. Valancy House, Riverene Road was a handsome Edwardian block of flats: red-brick work, white stone trim, noble windows and an impressive door and entrance hall. It was an annoying address to Slider, replete with those names beloved of the Edwardians, which sounded almost but not quite like real words (its sister blocks were called Croftdene and Endsleigh), but it was not a cheap one. With the new rich of London moving ever westwards, these big, high-ceilinged flats were going for a million and upwards now – even in Riverene Road, a turning off King Street that pined under the shadow of the Great West Road flyover. The noise of it would be like a waterfall – a constant roaring driving out all else. But triple glazing took care of most of that, and it was still a tree-lined road that ran down to the river. The trees, he noted, were limes. In July the piercing sweetness of their blossom would overpower even the exhaust reek from the traffic above.

Riverene Road was closed now to traffic, and a uniformed constable, whose name Slider annoyingly couldn't remember, moved the barrier and let him through. Before the building, a further barrier of blue and white tape kept the spectators away from the entrance. Word had got out, he thought, noting the number of press hounds. Someone in the building who couldn't wait to be famous must have blabbed. The reporters shouted questions at him as he went up the shallow steps to the front door, but he did not distinguish what they were saying. He hated his enforced contacts with the news media, and blanked them out from his consciousness as much as possible.

Atherton, his bagman and friend, was waiting for him in the lobby: tall, elegant, fair-haired, incongruous in these surroundings, he lounged with his hands in his pockets like displaced minor royalty, or a refugee from Gatsby's circle. He offered the important information first. 'Mackay's gone for coffee. There's a Starbucks round the corner in King Street.'

'There's always a Starbucks round the corner,' Slider complained. He rarely drank coffee, and tea from places like that was never any good. 'Good job I had breakfast before the shout came in.'

'That was early.'

'Joanna's gone down to see her parents. She wanted to get away before the traffic got bad, so we made an early start.'

The brown smell of old-fashioned polish in the hall went with the brown of the panelling and the dim brown light: penny-pinching low wattage bulbs did little to mitigate the loss of daylight to the flyover. There was a printed notice, hanging by a string loop on the lift door: OUT OF ORDER.

'The security door's not working either,' Atherton said.

'Oh?' Slider queried.

'Could be,' Atherton answered elliptically. 'But these old lifts work on prayer and chewing gum anyway.'

'Thanks for that comforting thought.' They trod up the stairs. 'What've we got, anyway? I was just told a dead male, no name.'

'We've identified him,' Atherton said. 'It's the owner of the flat – Edward, otherwise Ed, Stonax. Lovely Viking sort of name, that: stone axe. It's got a swish to it.'

Slider frowned. 'I know the name. Why do I know the name?'

'You've seen him on the telly,' Atherton suggested. 'He was a BBC correspondent.' He paused on a landing, assumed the posture and the voice, and intoned to camera, 'This is Ed Stonax. For the BBC. In Basra.'

'Oh, is that what it was?' Slider digested this, and then asked, 'Wasn't he in some kind of trouble a while back? Some kind of scandal?'

'You're improving,' said Atherton. Crowded though life was, he could never understand a grown man who didn't keep abreast of the news. Slider said he didn't have time to read newspapers, and the television was all propaganda anyway, and relied on Atherton to keep him up to speed. But then, he had a woman to keep him warm at night. Atherton was currently without a female attachment, something unusual enough to keep him awake at night – whereas in the past it had been the female attachments, plural, which had – etcetera, etcetera.

'Stonax left broadcasting a couple of years back and joined

the civil service. Unusual to do it that way round – poacher turned gamekeeper kind of thing. Became one of the new army of "special advisers" at the Department of Trade and Industry. Had to walk the plank in December last year after a sex scandal. Headlines in all the tabloids, *Minister's Three-In-A-Bed High Jinks* – that sort of thing. Stonax and Sid Andrew, the Trade and Industry Secretary, were caught sharing a nubile junior press officer from Andrew's department after some drinky-do at Industry House. Stonax and the girl got sacked, Andrew got kicked upstairs.'

'Oh,' said Slider blankly.

'How can you not remember that?' Atherton said affectionately.

'Three-in-a-bed high jinks tend to slip under my radar,' Slider admitted. 'Give me credit that I remembered he was in trouble.'

'Well, he's not in trouble any more,' Atherton said.

They paused in the corridor outside the flat while Gallon, the PC on duty, put them in the book.

'Who called it in?' Slider asked him.

'His daughter, sir, apparently. Emily Stonax. Asher took her back to the station.'

The neighbours on one side, an elderly couple, were standing outside their door being helpful to Tony Hart, one of Slider's DCs, who was looking extremely cute this morning in a grey trouser suit, her hair subdued, for once, in a reverse plait. She flung him a welcoming grin, and the neighbours looked to see who she was looking at. Out of the corner of his eye he saw them yearn towards him, surmising he was the greater authority, wanting their moment of glory to go to the best audience. He stepped hastily inside.

The flat was a scene of orderly forensic activity. The front door opened on to a vestibule with a large open archway into the drawing-room and Slider stood there and looked. On the far side of the room – as Bob Bailey, the local SOCO manager came across and explained – another door gave on to a branching passageway that led to the kitchen and dining-room one way and the three bedrooms and bathroom the other.

'Three beds? The man must have been raking it in,' Slider commented. 'Is it all as tidy as this?'

'Looks that way,' said Bailey. 'We haven't done much yet. Didn't get here much before you.'

'Has the doctor been? Prawalha only lives round the corner, doesn't he?'

'He's on holiday,' said Bailey. 'It'll be Wasim from Ealing.'

'He'll be hours, then,' said Atherton. 'The traffic's murder coming in that way.'

'I know,' said Slider, who had just done it himself.

'It looks like robbery from the person, anyway,' said Bailey helpfully. 'Pockets emptied, and his watch is missing. You can see the mark where he wore it.'

The drawing-room was of the brown furniture and agreeable paintings order: tasteful, comfortable, unremarkable – and, Slider felt instinctively, a bachelor's place. It had the air of a gentleman's club, antiques and leather, dim old Turkish carpet, a couple of bronzes, a few bits of jade and ivory and ancient figurines that might have been Roman – *objets* that were evidently more valuable and interesting than decorative. There were no pot plants or scatter cushions, no half-read books or other signs of human occupation. It was the room of a person whose important life was led in a different place, either physical or mental, who needed of his dwelling only that it did not offend the senses. Women, however busy they were in their public lives, were never so indifferent to their domestic surroundings. They nested.

'Was he married?' he asked of no-one in particular.

It was Atherton who answered. He always seemed to know the background of any figure in the political arena. 'Divorced, a good long time ago. And his wife was killed about a year back, if I remember rightly.'

'Killed?'

'Helicopter crash, trying to land at the multimillion pound mansion belonging to the new husband. She married Feyderman, the commodities millionaire – he was killed too.'

'So Stonax lived here alone?'

'Dunno,' Atherton was forced to admit. 'I can't remember if he was connected with any other woman.'

'You don't *know*?' Slider bated him. 'You know so much

about him I thought you were going to give me the brand of his underpants.'

'I knew about the wife being killed because I knew about Feyderman. But if you're really interested in his Ys—'

'Thank you, I'll pass. It doesn't *look* as though there's a female resident,' Slider said.

'Only one of the bedrooms seems to be occupied,' Bailey supplied. 'One's made up like a spare room and the other's a study.'

Slider nodded, and looked at last at the body. He had remembered Stonax in context now, a tall, lanky figure often to be seen wearing a flak jacket against a background of baked earth and battered cement houses in some Middle-Eastern hot spot. Or in a suit before the White House; a view so familiar it always looked two-dimensional, like a movie flat.

Though his accent had been neutrally English, he'd had the thick, unruly black hair and very white skin of a certain kind of Scot. He'd had brown eyes, it turned out: Slider couldn't have said from seeing him on television. They were staring now, fixed and expressionless, like those of a very superior stuffed toy. Some people in death continue to look like real people, but Stonax, perhaps because he had been famous, looked like a model of himself, a waxwork. In the white expressionless face the lines of humour and character seemed oddly irrelevant, as though they had been marked in the wax with an orange stick after death. His skull had been smashed at the left temple by a tremendous blow, but because he was lying supine the blood had run backwards into his hair, leaving his face unsullied, but gluing the back of his head to the carpet.

He was fully dressed in business suit, shirt, tie, socks and shiny shoes, as if he'd just got back from work.

'Robbery?' Slider said thoughtfully.

They were joined in the doorway by Jerry Fathom, who had just arrived. He was a new DC sent to them to replace Tony Anderson – away on secondment so long he had been seconded right out of their world and up to the SO firma-ment. Fathom was young and keen, a tall, meaty lad with fidgety eyes and a rather petulant mouth. He was so new

Slider hadn't yet found out what he was good for. This was the first murder since he'd joined the firm, and as he stood at Slider's shoulder, Slider could hear his breathing. He hoped he wasn't going to throw up, or Slider would get it right down the ear.

But it seemed it was excitement rather than nausea that was making Fathom's heart pound. 'Looks straightforward to me,' he said in the sort of voice that's meant to impress someone. Slider could imagine him in a pub telling girls about his job. 'Some crackhead doing the place over, looking for cash or something to flog. Householder comes home and surprises him. Bosh.'

'Felonius interruptus?' said Atherton.

'Wallop,' Fathom agreed importantly.

'Very tidy crackhead,' Atherton pointed out. 'Nothing seems to have been disturbed.'

'Well, maybe he'd only just started,' Fathom offered generously.

Slider turned his head, though not his eyes, to the new boy. 'Look at the door,' he said. 'No sign of forced entry.'

Fathom was not put off. 'Chummy could've stolen the keys. Or the vic could've lost 'em.'

Slider winced at the abbreviation 'vic' which the younger officers all picked up from American cop shows. They so desperately longed to be cool, but it was hard without a gun at your hip.

'Or maybe he picked the lock,' Fathom concluded.

'A very tidy crazed crackhead with unusual skills, then?' Atherton suggested.

'Well, it didn't have to be a crackhead,' Fathom conceded at last. 'Could have been any sort of burglar. Do we know what's missing?'

Atherton winced at the 'we'. 'There's plenty of door-to-door to be getting on with. Every flat in the block will have to be canvassed, for starters. Hart will tell you where to go.' Fathom removed himself reluctantly and by inches.

'He's right, of course,' Slider said when he'd gone. 'The lack of door-forcing doesn't rule out burglary. There's any number of possibilities. Chummy could have followed Stonax into the building and caught up with him before he'd closed the door. Or he could have rung the doorbell and pushed his way in.'

'No sign of a struggle,' Atherton said.

'Quite. I think he was let in,' said Slider.

'You think Stonax knew him?'

'Or had a reason to let him in – meter reader or something. But there's more to it than that.'

'How so?'

'The way he's lying, supine. He was struck from the front. If he'd let the man in it would be natural for him to be walking away and be struck from behind.'

'Perhaps he was struck as soon as he opened the door,' said Atherton, though the answer to that presented itself to him as soon as he said it.

'But then he'd be lying closer to the door. No, he walked away, and then turned back. Why? And why was nothing taken but what was in his pockets? If it was straightforward robbery, why not take more?'

Atherton looked round the room and shrugged. 'Your basic thief doesn't want to be burdened with objay dee. And we don't know yet that nothing else *was* taken.'

'True,' said Slider.

'One thing,' said Atherton, 'the place is so tidy it ought to be easy to spot any gaps.'

'Yes,' said Slider. There was something about the economy of despatch that made him feel uneasily that it was a professional hit. It would have been extremely lucky for an opportunist amateur to have found the precise spot on the skull where a single blow would kill. And if it was professional, what was he after? A stolen-to-order painting or other artefact? Or was it something like bonds or valuable documents? 'Do we know if he had a safe?' he asked.

By the time Slider had inspected the rest of the building, to get the lay of the land and to look for access, exits, security cameras etc, the doctor had arrived and was on his knees beside the body. It was not Wasim, however, but his old friend Freddie Cameron, the original Dapper Doctor. Cameron was the forensic pathologist, but was not averse to a bit of police surgeon work, especially when it was a case that was going to come to him anyway. He liked to see the body in situ and to get to it before anyone else fouled the pitch.

'Ah,' he said, looking up with satisfaction as Slider appeared in the doorway, 'the old firm, back at the usual stand.'

'Hello, Freddie. How's tricks?'

'All serene, old boy. How's Joanna? Are you a father yet?'

'No, seven weeks to go yet. And she's fine, or as fine as you can be in those circumstances.' It seemed odd to Slider to be discussing cheerful life in this place of death, with Stonax still lying where he had fallen, still dead. 'She says it's like being a ventriloquist's dummy, only you've got the whole ventriloquist inside, not just his hand.'

'I'm still waiting to be invited to the wedding,' Freddie said sternly. 'I hope you're not going to be adding to the statistics.'

'I've been *trying* to get married,' Slider said, wounded. 'Arranging a wedding between a policeman and a musician is like trying to push a balloon into a milk bottle.'

'Well, stop trying to arrange it and just do it,' Freddie suggested helpfully. 'You know who *this* is, don't you?'

'Ed Stonax, the TV bloke.'

'Bingo. Strange how different a body looks when you've seen it on the telly in life.'

'I was thinking the same thing. Anything to tell me? I assume it was the blow that killed him?'

'It certainly looks that way. The bones of the skull are crushed here. It was a very violent blow, with something small but heavy, and rounded in profile, like a nice old-fashioned lead cosh. With a good right arm behind it, it could have been something small enough to conceal in a pocket.'

'And given that it's to the left temple, it looks like a right-handed blow?'

'Unless the murderer's a tennis ace,' said Freddie. 'Possible, but unlikely. Professionals don't generally swipe their victims backhand.'

'You think it's professional, then?'

'Either that, or a lucky guess.' He stood up. 'I've bagged the hands, but I don't think they'll yield anything. There's no sign of a struggle or any defensive wounds. Eyes open. I think he was taken by surprise and felled before he even knew it was coming. The why of it, I leave to you.'

'Time of death?' Slider asked.

Freddie glanced automatically at his watch. 'I'd say it was four to six hours, so that would put it between five and seven this morning.'

Slider's eyebrows went up. 'This morning? We were assuming it was last night. He's fully dressed, as if he came home from work and it happened then.'

'Well, these times are not precise as you very well know, but I'm pretty sure it wasn't that long ago. He must have been on his way to work,' said Freddie.

'You're just giving me problems,' Slider said. 'Burglars, as a race, are not early risers.'

'There's always the exception,' said Freddie. He looked at Bob Bailey. 'Right, if it's OK with you, I'll take him away.'

'Yes, OK. We've got everything,' said Bailey.

Freddie's assistants laid the bag down and with trained knack lifted the body easily, despite its size, across and on to it. Something moved on the carpet.

'What's that?' said Slider.

Bailey picked it up and held it out for Slider to see. It was a biro, an ordinary, amorphous, cheap biro, white with a black top and no cap, the sort that charities send you in begging envelopes in the hope that you'll use it to write them a cheque. The body had been lying on it.

'I'll dust it for prints,' Bailey said. 'You never know.'

'If there are any, they'll only be Stonax's,' Slider said. 'Although I wouldn't have put him down as a cheap biro man. I'd have thought he'd have a gold Mont Blanc.'

'Maybe it's chummy's?' said Bailey.

Maybe – and how lovely it would be, Slider thought, to get a clear and perfect lift of the murderer from it. But life was never than easy. 'Send it off anyway, Bob,' he said. 'There may be something else on it that will help.'

Porson, their Detective Superintendent, arrived as Slider was preparing to leave.

'Chuffing Nora, it's bloody madness out there,' he

complained, stamping into the vestibule, his vast ancient coat swirling about him like a cloak. As he came to rest, Slider noticed that one of his shirt collar points was curling upwards, there was a shiny grey stain of what looked like porridge on his tie, and a ghostly line of dried shaving-soap along his jaw. When his wife was alive she would never have allowed him to leave the house in a less than perfect state of hygiene. Slider wondered if he was having difficulty coping.

'Bloody press are going bezique,' Porson rumbled on. 'Just because it's one of their own. Always the same when a journo gets hit. You'd think the world revolved around 'em.'

'He wasn't a journo any more, sir,' Slider pointed out.

'What does that lot care? *And* he was telly, as well – that makes him a god. Telly *and* BBC. They're going to be all over us like a cheap rash. I've had a word with that Forster woman at Hammersmith and she's going to co-ordinate the TV coverage.' Mo Forster was the new Press Officer for the area.

'Does that mean one of us will have to go down to the publicity suite and do an interview?' Slider asked, feeling depressed. Porson hated doing it as much as he did, but Porson had the rank to get out of it.

Porson's face didn't soften – it was built like a bagful of spanners and softening wasn't an option – but there was a sympathetic gleam in his eye as he answered. 'No, laddie. Mr Palfreyman's doing all the fronting. Too important to be left to the likes of us to mess up. In fact – ' he almost smiled – 'I've been given a pacific injuncture to pass on, that we're to avoid talking to the press at all costs.'

'Thank God for that,' Slider said.

Palfreyman, head of the Homicide Advice Team, had been busily empire-building ever since he came to Hammersmith, and the chance to be the face on the screen in a big case like this must have set him drooling.

'Thank Him all you like,' Porson said shortly, scowling. 'But don't forget that what Mr Palfreyman wants to be remembered for is solving the case. He doesn't want to be up there looking like a prat, being questioned about a cock-up. So if anything goes wrong it'll be my gonads in the cross-hairs. And when I say mine, I mean yours.'

'Of course, sir.'

'Right. As long as you know.' The massive eyebrows resumed normal position. 'You know me, laddie. Threats are water off a duck's bridge to me. But this case is going to have a searchlight on it all the way. What's the story so far?'

'There isn't much yet. No forcible entry, no ransacking. Deceased killed with a single blow to the head, pockets emptied and watch removed. I think it's meant to look like robbery from the person.'

'Only it's not?'

'Of course, it could be. We haven't had a chance yet to see if there's anything else missing.'

'But this bloke moved in high places, probably pissed off some arsey people, and it could be a hit?'

'Yes, sir. There are things about it that don't sit right with me.'

Porson looked thoughtful. He knew Slider's instincts by now and trusted him. 'We'll go with motiveless robbery for the time being. Keep anything else out of the news as long as we can. I'll tell Mr Palfreyman. The last thing we want is a rabid pack of journos peculating about conspiracies.'

Peculating was a good word for it, considering Porson's view of the honesty of the press. 'It'll make life easier if we can keep it at that, sir,' Slider said.

'Oh, I think Mr Palfreyman will see it our way,' said Porson. 'Going back to the factory?'

'If I can run the gauntlet out there.'

'Just ignore them. Don't say anything. That's an order. And tell your firm not to speak to anyone. No comment all the way, if anyone asks.'

'Yes, sir.'

'Meanwhile, you'd better get digging, see what dirt you can turn up. There should be plenty. This Stonax bloke wasn't exactly a parody of virtue.'

It was Porson's way, in his energetic passage through life, to take a wild swing at vocabulary, hit or miss, to get his meaning across. Like the famed chemist of old, he dispensed with accuracy.

Two

No Folk Without Mire

Outside, Slider put his head down and scuttled for his car, blocking out the shouted questions, ignoring the eyes and open mouths massed around the barrier tape, keeping his head turned away from the rattlesnake clicking of cameras. As he reached his car and opened the door, something he saw across its roof caught his attention, but in such a subliminal way that when he looked properly, he could not see what it was. But it reminded him of the black Ford Focus again, and he made a mental note to get one of the firm to run the number plate he had taken down.

He drove off, was let out of the roadblock, and turned on to King Street. A few minutes later his mobile rang.

He flipped it open. 'Slider,' he said.

'Don't you know it's illegal to answer the phone while you're driving?' said a voice. A male voice, vaguely familiar, precise, accentless. The words were spoken not as a pleasantry but with – as far as one sentence could reveal this – a kind of menace.

'Who is that?' Slider said.

'Oh, you know who it is. You haven't forgotten me, surely, Inspector Plod? The last time we met I told you you'd regret meddling in my business.'

He knew it now. 'Bates,' he said.

'*Mr* Bates to you. Don't forget you're a public servant and I pay your wages.'

Trevor Bates, alias The Needle. Wealthy businessman, property dealer, electronics expert, murderer of a prostitute called Susie Mabbot. He had stuck her full of acupuncture needles (his fetish), broken her neck and thrown her in the Thames.

Slider suspected him of commissioning, if not actually committing with his own hands, other murders, and who knew what else besides? Slider had been in on the capture of The Needle, helping to trap him in his hotel room at a conference, for which Bates had vowed revenge. Slider had heeded it as little as the idle wind at the time; but Bates had not remained long in custody. He had never even gone to trial. While he was being moved to the maximum security remand facility at Woodhill, the security van was held up and he was sprung. He had been missing for over a month now, not seen or heard of by anyone in authority. Until now.

'How did you get this number?' Slider asked.

Bates laughed. 'Oh, come, Mr Plod. A man of my stature? I can find out anything I want to know. I know all about you. I know where you live.'

'What do you want?' Slider asked, striving to sound untroubled, though he was thinking of Joanna. He had been threatened before, many times, and he knew most threats were simply made to aggrandise the threatener. They were never carried out. But Bates was not quite in that class. He was intellectual, cold-blooded, and pathologically vain. He might just mean it.

'You know what I want,' Bates said. 'To make you regret messing with me. And you will, I promise you.'

'You're talking like a bad movie,' Slider said, taking furtive looks around him in his rear-view and wing mirrors. If the man knew he was answering while driving, he might be somewhere near, following him. There seemed to be a lot of background noise to the call but he couldn't identify it as anything in particular. It could have been a call made from a car. Slider thought at once of the black Focus. He couldn't see one anywhere, but it might have dropped back too far to spot. Or Bates might have changed to another car. He had been fabulously rich in more than one country, so it was possible that not all his assets had been seized, and he certainly had the know-how to mount secret-service type surveillance. 'Every policeman in the country is looking for you,' Slider said. 'You'll be back inside any time now.'

'Don't you know I have friends in high places? Very high places, Mr Plod. You'll be wanting to try to trace this call, so I shall ring off now, but we'll talk again soon. Or I may pop in and visit you. How would you like that?'

He was gone before Slider could say anything more. He knows, of course, Slider thought, how long it takes to do a trace. All that kind of thing was nursery stuff to Bates – electronics was his field; he had provided listening services to the CIA in London. But wait a minute, if Bates knew he was talking to Slider's mobile, he must know that calls to and from a mobile are all logged automatically, so why had he said that?

Just to sow confusion and fear, he answered himself. Blast the man, popping up at a time like this, when he was going to have his hands full with Stonax. An unwelcome distraction, to say the least. And there was Joanna . . . He was glad she was not at home today – though of course she'd be coming back. Was the threat serious? He thought of Susie Mabbot and shuddered. No, The Needle wasn't as mad as that, surely? It was out of all proportion to Slider's puny role in capturing him. There had been a dozen people there, and the operation had been run by Chief Superintendent Ormerod of the Serious Organised Crime Liaison Group. Ormerod was Bates's nemesis, surely? He was the one who ought to be being threatened. Unless it was simply Slider's lowliness that offended him: all right to be pursued by top-ranking brass, but not to be toppled by a dog-eared inspector.

He'd report it to Porson, of course, when he got in, and Porson would hand it further up the line. Probably Bates was the responsibility of the Serious Organised Crime mob now – SOCA – and Ormerod, who had moved on and up to be head of another group of initials under the same umbrella, would no doubt be itching to nail the sod who'd slipped his grasp.

Anyway, it was not his problem. And he had his own work to do. He shoved the whole mess firmly to the back of his mind, with the final thought that his old instincts had – probably – been right. He had – probably – been being followed.

Back at the factory, he met Atherton on the stairs. 'Where's the daughter?' he asked briskly.

'In the soft room,' Atherton said. That was what he called

the 'interview suite', refusing to use the official title because, he said, a suite had to have more than one room to it. The others frequently mocked Atherton's pickiness, but often, as in this case, his verbal amendments stuck. Everyone now called it the soft room. It was, in fact, simply an interview room, but unlike the ones downstairs it was meant to be reassuring for witnesses in a delicate mental state. It had carpet, sofa and chairs, and pictures on the walls so bland they could have been used to dilute water. Also it didn't smell of feet and imperfectly expunged vomit, which was a great plus all round.

'Good. Has anyone had a go at her?'

'Asher brought her in, and Swilley's been holding her hand, but they only took the basic statement of how she found him.'

'Right. We'll go and do her now, then,' Slider said. Atherton followed him after a tiny but noticeable pause. 'What's the matter with you?'

'Nothing,' Atherton said. There was an odd blankness in his expression, which he shook away instantly. As they turned on to the corridor he said in his normal, conversational tone, 'Have you heard of a *coup de foudre*?'

'New car?' Slider said, not really listening. 'Is that the next thing you're after?'

'Oh, no, I've already got it,' Atherton said, opening the door to the soft room.

Slider beckoned Swilley out, and they had a brief chat, sotto voce, in the corridor as she brought him up to date. Kathleen 'Norma' Swilley was tall, blonde and gorgeous in a curiously unmemorable way, like a Miss World contestant. She was also one of Slider's best officers, and highly trained in unarmed combat. It was said she could kick the nuts off a fly at five paces, so sexist comments about her were not generally aired in her presence – though what was said behind her back would curl the hair of anyone but a policeman. Canteen culture was more than just a mould found on the sandwiches.

Slider passed over to her the registration number of the Focus and asked her to get someone to check it.

'And I was called on my mobile ten minutes ago. Can you find out who it was that called me and where they were?'

'Yes, boss.' She jotted down the number.

'When Hart comes in, you and she can start sorting the statements. Get Fathom on it too, so he can learn from you. Oh, and let me know when Mr Porson gets back.'

'Right, boss.'

In the soft room, Emily Stonax was sitting on the sofa with WPC 'For God's Sake Stop Calling Me Jane' Asher beside her. Asher stood and Miss Stonax looked up as Slider and Atherton came in. So far, Slider noted with relief, there seemed to be no tears. Emily Stonax was dry-eyed, though white with shock, but evidently doing her best to hold it together. She was twenty-eight, according to Swilley, though she looked younger – but then, he thought, most people did these days, probably because they dressed younger. Slider noted the suitcase, carry-on bag and duty-free carrier in the corner, with a donkey jacket dumped over them, and took in the dry, weary look of the recently flight-arrived.

'I'm Detective Inspector Slider,' he said. 'I'm very sorry for your loss, Miss Stonax. I know it must be hard for you, but would you mind if I asked you a few questions?'

She was sitting a little hunched, with her hands clasped between her knees, screwing a paper handkerchief about between her fingers: a slim but nicely made young woman in cargo pants and soft ankle boots, a white shirt – understandably a little crumpled – and a brown suede jerkin. Her only jewellery was a large, oval gold locket on a chain round her neck, which hung like a slightly flattened pullet's egg in the V of her shirt neck. Her hair, as abundant, black and coarse as her father's, was cut short and spiky, and stood out round her head, but pointing backwards like the quills of a hedgehog. It was, he saw, meant to look cute rather than challenging. No Goth, this: she had no make-up on and no piercings, her nails were short and unpolished, and there was about her face a look of intelligence, and of sense – not always the same thing. Her full mouth, brown eyes and thick eyelashes gave warmth to a face otherwise notable for character, with its straight nose, strongly marked brows and firm chin. She met Slider's eyes directly, and he felt the attractiveness of her, even as he was admiring her determination not to give in to wailing and gnashing while there was something that had to be done.

'Ask me anything,' she said. 'I want to help.'

Slider took the chair opposite her, on the other side of the lamentable coffee table. It reminded him to ask, 'Has someone offered you coffee?'

'Yes, thanks,' she said, nodding towards Asher. 'I didn't want any, but I'd love a glass of water.'

Atherton beat Asher off the mark and brought it. The soft room had a water-cooler, but was also provided with proper glasses so he was spared the shame of bringing her a plastic cup. She took it from him with a smile that did things to his spine, and he took himself off to one side, out of her line of sight to Slider, so that he would not distract her, but also so that he could study her face without her looking at him. There was something about her that he could not take his eyes from. Slider, a normal but almost-married man, had merely felt her attractiveness, but it had pierced Atherton like a skewer to the vitals. She took his breath away.

'Would you begin by telling me what happened this morning?' Slider opened. He knew it, of course, from Swilley, but he found it helped to get people talking, to repeat something they'd already said. Safe ground, easy to get across. 'You've just flown in from America, I believe?'

'Yes. I live in New York now. I'm a journalist – freelance, but I do a lot of work for the *New York Herald*.' Her lips gave a quirk that would have been a smile in other circumstances. 'It's not quite challenging the *New York Times* yet, but it's getting there. There's a good team, dedicated to serious news, and it already had a lot more international coverage than most other American papers. Dad's such a help there – was such a help,' she corrected herself faintly, her eyes lowering for a moment. Slider saw her swallow hard and then brace her shoulders, sitting up straighter.

'I'm sorry,' he said again. She made a little 'carry on' gesture with her hand, and went back to tormenting the tissue. 'So why did you make the trip to London today?'

'I come home three or four times a year to visit Dad. I was due a break, and he said he wanted to see me, so I packed a bag and hopped on a plane. I rang Dad on my mobile from Heathrow but he didn't answer. I thought it was a bit odd because he knew what time I was getting in, but then I thought he must have had to go out suddenly.' She frowned. 'Though if he'd gone out he'd have put the answer-machine on. I ought to have thought of that.'

'People can forget,' Slider said, helping her out.

'Not Dad,' she said. 'He was a journalist. Communication is everything. Anyway, I took a taxi home and let myself in. And I saw—' She couldn't quite, for all her determination, say it aloud. She took a breath and said, 'You know what I saw. So I rang the police.'

'You didn't touch anything or move anything?'

'I know that much. I went across to Dad just in case—' She shook her head. 'I could see it was no good.' She met Slider's eyes. 'I've never seen anyone dead before. Of course, Dad's seen dozens, maybe hundreds of bodies. I suppose if I want to call myself a proper journalist I ought to be able to face up to things like that. But it's hard when it's your own father. It must be harder, surely, than with a stranger?'

He saw that she wanted him to answer. She was deferring to his knowledge, given his job, of looking at dead bodies. He was touched, and impressed that her intellect was still functioning independently. She was not one who would enjoy the histrionics of grief, and he had seen plenty of those over a long career and admired her for it. 'I think it's always hard, whether it's a stranger or not,' he said. 'If you care about people. Something has been taken away that can't be replaced.'

He felt Atherton stir at that, and supposed it a rebuke for getting too personal. But this woman was going to have to help them a lot, and he wanted to treat her as an equal by taking her questions seriously.

'You don't get used to it?' she followed up his answer.

'Not really,' he said. 'You cope.' She nodded thoughtfully, and he got back on line. 'You say you let yourself in?'

'I have my own key,' she said.

'You have your own room there?'

'Not that, exactly. I don't keep any stuff with him any more – that's all in New York. But somehow, wherever Dad lives is still "home" to me.'

'Does anyone else have a key that you know of?'

She shook her head, but a faint colour touched her pale

face. 'I don't know for sure, but he might have given one to Candida.'

'Candida?'

'You don't know about her? She's his . . . girlfriend? Mistress? I don't know what the proper term is. I'm not being censorious,' she added with a frank look. 'I don't mind about her, honestly. Why should I? Mummy's dead, and anyway *she* left *him* long before that. He's entitled to a life of his own. I just don't know how you would classify her. Candida Scott-Chatton. I expect you know who she is?'

Atherton anticipated Slider's ignorance. 'She's the head of the Countryside Protection Trust and a spokesman on ecological matters.'

Emily Stonax looked at him. 'And a journalist.'

'Yes, I've heard of her,' Slider said, who actually had – *and* had seen her on television, round about the time of the Countryside March. Tall, blonde, aristocratic, gorgeous. And hard as nails – as he supposed she'd have to be with such a thankless brief. 'Do you have an address for her?'

'Ten, Hyde Park Terrace,' she said promptly. 'It's just off Queen's Gate, near the Albert Hall. I think she and Dad were quite close. I mean, she stuck by him after that business last year?' The sentence ended on an upward note as she looked to see if Slider understood the reference. He nodded. 'I suppose someone will have to tell her,' she added, faltering.

'We'll do that. Unless you'd rather . . .?'

'No. God no. I don't want to have to tell anyone – is that normal?'

'It's normal not to want to put it into words.'

'That's what it is,' she said eagerly. 'If I say it, it will make it real. Luckily there's no family to speak of. Since Mummy died, it's just the two of us.'

'So, no other keys that you know of?'

'No. He wouldn't have handed them out. I don't even know that Candida had one, really. Dad was quite safety-conscious. I mean, there were locks on all the windows and a deadlock on the door.' She looked at him thoughtfully. 'The door was closed when I got there and there was no damage to it. I mean, someone didn't jemmy their way in. Is that why you're asking about keys? That policewoman I spoke to said it was a burglary. Is that what you think it was?'

'His wallet and watch seem to be missing. His pockets were empty, and they haven't been found anywhere else in the house.'

'Someone killed him and went through his pockets?' Tears jumped into her eyes for the first time. 'They killed him for *that*?'

'We don't know if anything else is missing. The flat is very tidy and there's no sign of any disturbance.'

'Yes, Dad was always very tidy.' She wiped the wetness from below her eyes. 'He gave me a hard time in my teenage rebel years. But it was a good lesson to learn.'

'Do you know if he kept anything valuable about the house?'

'Well, the paintings and bronzes were quite valuable, and those little Etruscan figures on the mantelpiece.'

'They're still there.'

'I don't think he ever had much cash about him – he preferred cards, like I do. He wasn't the sort to have envelopes full of tenners in a shoe box in the wardrobe, if that's what you mean.'

'Did he have a safe on the premises?'

'I don't think so. He's never had one to my knowledge. But I suppose he might have had one put in recently and not told me about it. It wasn't something that would ever come up in conversation.'

'Later, when the forensic teams have finished, I'd like you to come back to the flat, if you will, and look around, see if you can tell if anything's missing.'

'Yes, of course,' she said. She studied his face. 'You don't think it was a burglar, do you? You don't think he was killed for what was in his pockets?'

'I'm not at the stage of thinking anything yet. I have to consider all possibilities.'

She was thinking. 'If it wasn't burglary, I know the next question: did he have any enemies?'

'Something like that,' Slider said with a small smile, admiring her spirit. She reminded him a little of Joanna, in the way her mind worked doggedly through the logic. (Joanna! He must phone her before she left Eastbourne.)

Emily Stonax blew her nose, reached into the massive handbag by her feet to exchange the soggy tissue for a fresh one, and said, shaking her head, 'He was a well-known figure. Thousands of people knew him from television, millions probably recognised him, and there are so many nutcases about these days who will attack anyone famous. Look at Jill Dando. But if that's what it was, it's no use looking for reasons, is it? As to specific enemies, it's hard to think anyone could hate him enough to kill him. He was such a *good* man. He was honest, and he was an idealist. He *believed* in goodness.'

Atherton spoke. 'He was a career journalist, and then he worked for the government, but we haven't heard anything of him since that trouble last year. Do you know what he's been doing since he left the DTI?'

A spot of colour appeared in her cheeks. 'He didn't leave. It was character assassination. He hasn't had another job since. How could he, after that? No-one would touch him. As far as I know he's been living on his capital.'

Atherton said, 'But a man like him wouldn't do *nothing.*'

'No, I'm sure he kept up his interests – his charity work and so on – but he was terribly shocked and low for a while after the photograph thing. Although just lately I've suspected there *was* something he was working on.'

'Only suspected?' Slider said.

'Well, he usually talked to me about his work, but if it was something investigative and serious he would keep it to himself until it was all worked out. Not that he didn't trust me, he just wouldn't tell anyone. That way no-one could be put in a difficult position. And just lately when I've phoned it's been quite hard to talk to him, as if his mind was elsewhere. He gets like that when he's writing sometimes. You talk to him but nothing much comes back. It's like blowing out of a window.'

She obviously thought of something, and Slider said encouragingly, 'Yes?'

'Well, I had been meaning to come over for a visit next month, but when I rang Dad to thank him for my birthday present, he asked me if I could make it sooner. As it happened I didn't have anything urgent on, so I said I'd see if I could get a last-minute ticket, and I did.'

'Did he say why he wanted you to come?'

'I asked, of course, and he said he had something he wanted to talk to me about, but he wouldn't tell me what. I said couldn't it wait until next month, and he said it *was* rather urgent, but that it was nothing to worry about, and not to be anxious.'

'So what did you *think* it might be about?' Atherton asked, intrigued.

'Well, my first thought was that he'd got some bad news about his health. Then I thought – well, I thought maybe he and Candida were getting married or something. Although there was no reason not to tell me that on the phone. So I assumed it must be something work-related, that maybe he had a really hot story lead for me.'

'Couldn't he have told you about that on the phone?' said Atherton.

'Phones aren't secure, you know. Suppose it was something to do with the government? The US government, I mean. You never know who might be listening. And there'd be documentary evidence to show me. Papers, photos. But that was just a guess. He was being tight-lipped, and when he's like that you can't shift him.'

There was a knock at the door and Swilley looked in to say that Porson was back. Slider decided to take a break. Miss Stonax was looking drained.

'I still have some more questions I'd like to ask you,' he said, 'and I'd like you to look at the flat later, but I can see you're tired and you must be hungry by now.'

She considered a moment. 'I'm starving,' she discovered.

'Then may I suggest that Constable Asher here takes you up to the canteen, and you can get some lunch, and we'll talk again afterwards. How would that be?'

She shrugged. 'I've nowhere else to go,' she said bleakly.

That was so true, it gave Slider a pang of pity. 'Is there anything else we can do for you?' he asked gently.

'I'd love a shower and a change of clothes. I've been in these things since yesterday.'

Slider nodded. 'Asher will show you where. You've got things in your bag to change into, I imagine?'

'Obviously,' she said, and then remembered her manners. 'I mean, thank you. You're very kind.'

Outside, in the corridor, Atherton said, 'Poor kid.'

'Kid? That's a bit rich, coming from you.'

'Manner of speaking,' Atherton said. 'So, what do you think?'

'It could be that he was investigating something after all—'

'And it turned round and bit him?' Atherton finished.

'Yes, but what could it be that was worth his death? Let's not get carried away by conspiracy theories. It could still have been simple robbery.'

Atherton rolled his eyes. 'Must you always see both sides of everything?'

'And it could have been accidental,' Slider went on reasonably. 'Maybe the intruder only wanted to knock him out, and just hit him too hard. And then panicked and ran away.'

Three

So Long Succour

Porson was standing by the window, reading. He hardly ever sat down unless he really had to. He looked up at Slider appeared in the doorway and raised his eyebrows.

'Got something already?'

'Not yet, sir. There's something else I need to talk to you about.' He closed the door and told him about the telephone call from The Needle.

Porson frowned, fiddling with a paper clip. 'He knew you were in the car?'

'It may have been a lucky guess. Or he may have been able to hear the engine noise in the background.'

'Or he may have been following you,' Porson concluded. He thought a moment. 'If he knew you were on your mobile, he must have known we could trace the call.'

'I've put Swilley on it already.'

'Then as soon as he rings again we can pinpoint him?'

'Yes, and he must know that as well as we do,' Slider said.

'Hmm. What's he up to?' Porson said.

'Playing us for fools, if I know anything about him,' Slider said. 'It won't be that easy to catch him.'

The eyebrows levelled out. 'Well, it's out of our hands now, anyway. He's a big player and he's wanted in high places. I'll pass it on to Mr Wetherspoon and he'll pass it to SOCA, or whichever SO is handling him. It'll take it off our budget and manpower, at least.'

'That's a blessing, sir,' said Slider.

Porson gave him a scowl for the irony. 'Don't you think of going after him on your own!' he barked. 'I'm not interested in mock heroics!'

'How do you feel about the real kind?' Slider murmured, though he knew he shouldn't.

Porson looked more kindly at him. 'You know and I know these slags just want to put the frighteners on us. Nine times out of ten they don't mean it. But Bates – well, I'm not saying be worried, but keep your wits about you. I don't want one of my officers walking into a trap, and there's something queer about this. Doesn't smell right.' He rapped the end of the paper clip on the desk in an irritated rhythm. Slider was interested that Porson's nasal radar was making him uneasy, too. 'Why'd he have to surface now, of all times?' Porson burst out at last. 'Just when we've got our hands full.'

'I presume I should leave my mobile switched on, so that the tracing unit can do the necessary?'

'Yes, yes,' said Porson, miles away.

'You'll let me know what's being done?'

The attention snapped back to the present. 'Of course, laddie. I'll keep you in the loop. Anything they tell me, I'll tell you.'

Which wasn't the same thing, of course.

'But meanwhile, you concentrate on the Stonax business. That's sacrospect. We want answers on that and we want 'em quick.'

When Slider got back to the CID room it was quieter than a Trappist library. The troops that were back were eating sandwiches at their desks. 'Hey,' he said.

'We got you one, guv,' Mackay reassured him crumbily. 'It's on your desk.'

'I got you a jumbo sausage baguette,' Norma Swilley added informatively.

McLaren leered at her automatically. 'Jumbo sausage? Oy-oy!'

'The king of single entendre,' Norma said witheringly. 'I've got the report on that car, boss.'

'Come through,' he said, heading for his office. 'McLaren, get me a cup of tea.'

'What did I do?' McLaren protested.

'It's your turn,' said Slider.

'Since when?'

'Since the sausage remark.'

The sausage was still warm, and they had remembered the mustard. What it was to have a highly trained team at your fingertips! He took a huge bite. He was ravenous. Swilley perched on his windowsill – it seemed to be everyone's preferred place for making reports to him – and looked at her notes. The weather was still warm enough for her not to have gone into trousers, for which the man in him was grateful. He was happily spoken-for, but there was no harm in admiring the scenery, even if you were on a non-stopping train.

'Right, boss, that reg number you gave me belonged to a Renault Clio that was scrapped last month. Registered owner was a Brian Delaney, address in Rodney Road, Lambeth, got it for his eighteenth birthday and totalled it on the Old Kent Road the day after. I spoke to his dad. He sounded genuine. Want me to chase up where the wreck went?'

Slider shook his head. 'It's easy enough for someone to get the information and use the reg number without involving the wrecking yard. The important thing is that the number doesn't match the car, which means there *was* something going on.'

She didn't know why he was asking about the car, of course, and looked at him receptively. When he didn't immediately go on, she said, 'I also checked on black Focuses stolen in the last three months. There were six in the Met area, and one, stolen from an address in Isleworth, had tinted windows. But it didn't have any damage on the rear quarter. D'you want the details?' She gestured to the papers in her hand.

He shook his head again, but it was in thought rather than negation. He said, 'You'd better let the stolen cars unit know that it might be operating under that reg number. And put out an all-units – if it's spotted anywhere, they can bring it in. But I don't think it's going to be that easy. He may well have more numbers. Have you got the mobile phone dump yet?'

'They've not come back on it yet. I'll chase them up,' Norma said. 'Can I know what it is, boss?'

'I'll tell everyone,' Slider said. 'Give me ten minutes and I'll be out for a rundown on what we've got so far.'

When he was alone, he took another mouthful of sandwich and dialled Joanna's number. 'Hello, Inspector,' she answered him before he spoke. She had number recognition, of course.

The sound of her voice gave him a frisson, as always, and

he reflected how lucky he was to have found his soulmate against all the odds. He had been married fairly joylessly to Irene for fourteen years but, being the sort of person he was, he hadn't been looking for anyone else. A promise was a promise in his book, and he had meant to stick by her and do his best to be a good husband. It wasn't her fault they had grown apart. But then he had met Joanna and everything became instantly different. It had plunged him into a tornado of troubles, doubts and self-loathing as he tried to square his sense of duty towards Irene and the children with the visceral conviction that his life lay with Joanna. Well, they had been through some difficult places on the rocky road to divorce, Irene's remarriage, and the present blissful state of Joanna's expecting their first child, but in all the turbulence the one thing that had never wavered was his conviction that he and Joanna were meant to be together and would get through it somehow.

'Where are you?' he asked, hearing sounds of conversation in the background.

'The Spotted Dog,' she said. 'I've taken Mum and Dad out for a pub lunch. Madly gay, isn't it? I love the way they've branched out since Dad retired. Eating out was completely unthought of when I was a kid.'

'Everything all right?' he asked.

'They're still agitating about the wedding,' she said. 'I keep telling them that it's a matter of finding the time to do it, but they narrow their eyes and look sceptical. They think you're trying to wriggle out of your responsibilities.'

'If only they knew, I'm desperately trying to wriggle in,' Slider said sadly.

'I know. I tell them that. They'll understand one day,' she said. 'They want us to call the baby Derek after Dad's father.'

'Oh my God.'

'I thought that would prove a nice counter-irritant,' she chuckled.

'What if it's a girl?' he asked flinchingly. Did he have a vague memory that the paternal grandmother had been named Gladys?

'Rebecca,' said Joanna.

'Oh. How come?'

'Heroine in a book Mum's reading. She thought it was a pretty name. They can't understand why we don't want to know which sex it is, given that we can.'

'Very modern of them. Look, I can't really chat, I haven't got long.'

'I know, you must be busy.' The shout had come in before she left. 'Is it awful?'

'I'll tell you about it when I see you. But, listen, something else has come up.' And he told her briefly about Trevor Bates ringing him.

When he had finished she said, 'Is it serious? I mean, is he really likely to do anything?' Slider hesitated before answering, only so as to assemble his words carefully, but she misunderstood and said, 'Please don't just tell me not to worry. I want to know the truth. We're in this together, you know – all three of us.'

'I wasn't going to hide anything from you,' he said quickly. 'It's just that I really don't know how serious it is. He wants to frighten me, that's plain enough. Whether he'd go any further I simply don't know. But I *don't* want you to worry, and I *do* want you to be careful.'

'Careful how?' she said. She sounded a bit bleak. It was not a nice thing to have dumped on you – and she had the baby to worry about as well. The world had become hostile and comfortless, and who was to help them now?

'When you come back today, come to the station first, and we'll go home together.'

'Oh. It's that bad, is it?'

'I don't *know*,' he said, frustrated. 'I wish I did.'

She heard the strain in his voice and hastened to take up the slack. 'All right, I'll see you later. Don't worry about me – you've got enough to be going on with.'

Out in the main office, DS Hollis was back and was marking up the whiteboard. He was a laconical Mancunian with a scrawny moustache and pale green eyes like bottled gooseberries, but despite his odd appearance – or perhaps because of it – he had a wonderful way of getting witnesses to trust him and tell him All. He was always office manager by default, because he didn't mind doing it and everyone else did, but Slider sometimes thought it was a bit of a waste of his talents.

Swilley and Atherton had their heads together in a serious and sotto-voce conversation, and from their glances upwards when he came in he guessed they were talking about him. But he was so glad to see them getting on together after the tensions in the past that he didn't mind being the cause. Hart had brought in the first heap of statements and Mackay, the office swot, was stolidly working his way through them; while McLaren, the face that lunched on a thousand chips, was stolidly working his way through a Ginsters Mexican Chicken Wrap, which he was eating cold straight from the packet, the shiny sauce smearing his mouth like gloss lipstick.

'Right,' Slider said. 'Ed Stonax.' They all looked up. 'First of all I have to tell you that there is a complete embargo on speaking to the press. That means any form of news media, and it means all of you. They're going to be all over you—'

'They've been ringing up already, guv,' Hart said.

'I'm not surprised. But you do not give them anything, repeat *anything*.' He looked round the room and noted Fathom's expression of insouciance along with his slight pinkness of complexion.

Fathom, meeting the boss's eyes reluctantly, said, 'What are we supposed to say if they ask us stuff?'

'You say no comment. Can you repeat that? Two words, *no comment*. Say it.'

Fathom, realising he meant it, muttered sheepishly, 'No comment.'

'Good. Now, anything to report?'

Hart said, 'I had a long chat with the next door neighbours, guv. Mr and Mrs Arbuthnot.'

'Yes, I saw that.'

'They never heard nothing.'

'That's a surprise,' said Swilley.

'Ooh, irony! You could put someone's eye out with that,' said Atherton.

'They have their wireless on a lot,' said Hart said imperturbably. 'That's what they call it, love 'em. But they did say that when they didn't have it on, they could hear him typing through the walls.'

'Wouldn't that be normal? He was a journalist,' Hollis said.

'Yeah, but he's been doing an awful lot of it lately. They always could hear him when he was working, because his desk is against the party wall, but they said for about the last week or ten days he was always at it. Whenever they turned off the radio they could hear him, and in the night, too. Like a death-watch beetle, Mr A said – whatever that is.'

'A parasitical beetle that chews wood and destroys churches and makes a clicking noise,' Atherton said. 'How can you not know that?'

Hart shrugged. 'Education's failed me.'

'How would you know?'

'Can we get on?' Swilley said in a pained voice.

Hart resumed. 'Well, they didn't have anything else to tell me except that they liked him and reckoned he was dead straight and dead public spirited. They said he was a real help with the tenants' meetings, jollying people along and getting round the awkward customers and that. They wanted him to take over as chairman only he said he didn't have the time. So he seems to have been a stand-up bloke.'

'Nice to know,' said Slider, 'but it would have been nicer if they'd heard something.'

'No-one we've interviewed so far heard anything,' Fathom said.

'But, guv, the front door's broken,' Hart said. 'That could be something?'

'Yes, I heard. In what way broken?'

'It's one of them where you buzz people in, but the buzzer wasn't working and the door wouldn't latch. Anyone could have just pushed the door open. It was supposed to have been mended yesterday, but the Arbuthnots said it was broken again today.'

'Who was supposed to have repaired it?' Slider asked.

'There's a sort of handyman, caretaker kind of person. He lives in the basement. Name of—' she inspected her notes '—Borthwick, David Keith. He's supposed to do repairs, or get people in if he can't do them himself. I haven't had a chance to talk to him yet.'

Slider nodded. 'That's something to follow up, anyway.

What about the lift? That was out of order as well. Did the Arbuthnots say anything about it?'

'No, guv,' said Hart, 'but I didn't ask. I didn't notice any sign. I just used the stairs anyway. Lifts give me the creeps.'

'Something else to check on with the caretaker. Anything else?'

There was a general shaking of heads. 'But we haven't spoken to all the residents yet,' Atherton said. 'There was no answer from numbers five and nine.'

'Right, follow up on them – Mackay, Fathom. Uniform's still doing the street canvass. Interview the caretaker, Hart. See what you can get out of him. Someone has to go and see Candida Scott-Chatton. Swilley, you can do that. I have to take the daughter back to the flat this afternoon to see if anything's missing. Hollis, records.'

'Yeah, guv. Local slags, anyone doing householders, same MO, all that stuff.'

'That should keep you busy. All right,' Slider concluded. 'Before we scatter, I have something else to tell you, not connected with the case.' And he told them about Trevor Bates. There was some growled comment. No-one had been pleased when Bates had escaped. They had all put hard work into the case.

'It will be handed over to SOCA, I imagine, though Mr Porson has promised to keep me informed,' Slider concluded.

'But, guv,' McLaren objected, 'we can't just sit on our arses and do nothing.'

'We've got a very important murder case on our hands,' Slider reminded him.

'Yeah, but Bates was our collar, by rights. And you're our guv'nor.' He looked round and saw agreement in every face.

'We can't get officially involved. However,' he added to stem the protest, 'there's no reason we shouldn't do what we can unofficially. At the very least I'd like everyone to keep his or her eyes open for any sightings of this man. I'd be grateful to have my back watched.'

'We'll do that all right,' Hollis said, 'but can't we try and nail the sod? This was his old ground, and if he's come back here, it gives us a chance, doesn't it? We know the place as well as he does, and if anyone's going to catch him, it ought to be us, not SOCA.'

Slider was pleased, but didn't allow it to show. 'We can't let the Stonax case fail because we've got our minds elsewhere.'

Atherton spoke up. 'We've all got enough brain cells to work both at once. Well, all of us except Maurice.'

'Don't be such a snot,' Swilley rebuked him automatically.

'Don't mind me,' said McLaren. 'I never know what he's talking about anyway.'

Slider ignored the exchange. 'You could all get into trouble for working on it unofficially.'

'We're all grown-ups here,' Atherton said. 'We can stand a few rapped knuckles.'

Everyone nodded.

'All right,' Slider said, warmed by the response. He was not facing Bates alone after all. The posse was riding for the gulch hard on his heels. 'Thank you for that. We'll do what we can. But listen – this has to be kept among ourselves. No-one outside our firm must know. And I'm afraid we have to keep Mr Porson out of the loop, for his own sake. Hollis, you'll office manage the Stonax case; Atherton, you'll be c-in-c on Bates. Everyone, report anything you get on Bates either to Atherton or me direct.'

'Had we better have a code name?' Mackay asked. 'In case anyone overhears us talking about him?'

'Yeah, let's call him The Needle,' McLaren suggested.

'Duh!' said Hart. 'That's his nickname anyway, dumbo. Everyone knows it.'

'Maurice, you have to stop pushing the Q-tip when you feel resistance,' Atherton advised kindly.

'Let's call him Roberts,' Mackay intervened. 'After Roberts radios, because he's an electronics whiz.'

'This is not Bletchley Park,' Slider said. 'Forget code names. Just don't let anyone overhear you talking about him.'

Swilley had missed the last few exchanges because her phone had rung. She was writing rapid notes as she listened. When she replaced the receiver, she said, 'Boss, that was the mobile dump. The call you got from Bates was made from a mobile. It was a pay as you go, and the location was King Street, Hammersmith.'

'So he *was* following me,' Slider said. 'Who's it registered to?'

Swilley made a face. 'Paid for by cash. That's the trouble with those things.'

'Still, we've got the number, and we can trace the signal, can't we?' Fathom said.

'If he turns it on. It's off at the moment,' said Swilley.

'But SOCA will do the same thing, won't they?' Atherton said. 'The mobile trace unit will report to them. How do we get them to give us the information without SOCA knowing?'

Swilley looked at Slider. 'There's this guy at the unit – Mick Hutton – he's a sort of friend of mine.' She almost blushed. An ex-lover, everyone thought. 'From way back,' she added as though she'd heard the thought.

'Would he do it for you without telling anyone?'

'Yeah, he'd do that for me, if I asked him.'

Slider thought for a moment. Maybe nothing would come of it anyway, but he'd feel better about trusting the Bates inquiry to his own people than waiting for a lofty SO department to get itself moving. If his own firm did nail Bates and there were questions about how they found him – so be it. He'd face that when and if it happened.

'Do it,' he said.

A couple of phone calls located Candida Scott-Chatton at her office, the headquarters of the Countryside Protection Trust in Queen's Gate Place – handily round the corner from her house, Swilley thought. She spoke to the woman's secretary, who said her name was Shawna Weedon, and who told her that Scott-Chatton knew about Stonax's death. 'It's on all the newscasts. It's terrible. He was such a nice man. He used to come in a lot and he was always so friendly and polite. I really liked him.'

'I'll come round straight away and talk to her,' Swilley said.

The office was on the ground floor of one of those splendid white-stuccoed Kensington houses, so the inside spaces were lofty and grand, with plenty of what was known to viewers of house makeover programmes as 'original feachers'. There were two rooms, and the rear one was labelled Reception and Enquiries. It had the massive marble fireplace with an oil painting over it of a man with a funny hat and a red coat holding a horse, and was furnished with dark blue carpet, a visitor's sofa, and a coffee table on which were spread various appropriate magazines, such as *Country Life*, *The Lady*, *Horse and Hound*, and the Trust's own glossy quarterly, cutely entitled *Countryside Matters*.

It also contained the desk of the secretary. Shawna Weedon greeted Swilley with a sort of self-conscious fluttering, and at once buzzed the intercom to her boss, invited Swilley to take a seat, and then got on ostentatiously with typing something on to the computer. Swilley stood, to make the point that her time was valuable, but she was not kept waiting more than a couple of minutes before the communicating door to the front room was opened and Candida Scott-Chatton invited her in with a, 'Do come through, won't you?' as though it were a social visit.

The front room was even more splendid and spacious than the waiting-room, with a more elaborate fireplace, a lot more paintings on the walls, antique furniture, and a blue and white Chinese carpet over the same dark-blue wall-to-wall as the other room. There was a highly polished antique partners' desk on which the computer looked the only out-of-place thing in the room, and there were huge flower arrangements in probably priceless vases, on a side table, on the hearth in front of the fireplace, and on a torchère stand in a corner. It was, Swilley thought with loathing, like something out of a National Trust stately home. She liked everything modern and minimalist; and besides, she had an old-fashioned chippiness about people with double-barrelled names.

Candida Scott-Chatton was tall, blonde and classically beautiful, exquisitely dressed in what Swilley would have liked to bet was a Chanel or Prada suit – something expensive and exclusive, anyway – with pearls at neck and ears. No hair of her smooth bob was out of place, and her make-up was so perfect that it gave her a kind of expressionless immobility, as if, having got herself to this state of perfection, she didn't want to do anything else with her face for fear of spoiling it.

Swilley shook her hand (thin, extremely cold, with long fingers made longer by polished nails so perfect Swilley guessed they were false) and looked into her eyes. The blue eyes that looked back were as cold as a highland spring.

'I'm sorry to disturb you at a time like this,' Swilley said. 'I gather you've heard what happened to Mr Stonax. You must be very upset.'

'I'm devastated,' said Candida Scott-Chatton. She didn't meet Swilley's eyes and her voice was rather high and strained, but it seemed to Swilley more like nervousness than grief. 'Of course, we live in dangerous times and we all know something like that could happen to any of us, any time. But somehow you never expect it to happen to you, or to someone you know.'

She doesn't care a jot, Swilley thought.

Perhaps something of the thought showed in her face, because Scott-Chatton turned away abruptly, went behind her desk, and with her back turned took out a handkerchief and seemed to attend to her nose and eyes with it. 'I'm sorry,' she said in a muffled sort of voice. 'Will you give me a moment?'

'Take your time,' said Swilley, unmoving and unmoved.

When Scott-Chatton turned back her eyes did seem a little moist, but Swilley, determined to yield nothing, told herself that *that* was easy enough to fake.

'Won't you sit down?' Scott-Chatton gestured to a leather upholstered upright chair by the desk, and Swilley sat. 'I'm not sure that there's anything much I can tell you, though I'm willing to help in any way I can. On the news they seemed to be saying it was a burglary that went wrong. Is that true?'

'That's what it looks like,' Swilley said. 'How well did you know Mr Stonax?'

'We've been friends for some years. He was always interested in environmental and countryside issues, and of course he was environment correspondent at the BBC at one time, so we tended to meet in a professional way quite often.'

'But you were more than friends, weren't you?'

She seemed taken aback. She paused too long for the answer, whatever it was going to be, to look unstudied. 'I don't know what you mean,' she said faintly, uncertainly.

'I think you do,' Swilley said, interested that she should want to deny the connection. She wasn't married – Swilley had checked that in *Who's Who*. 'I should mention that we've spoken to his daughter.'

Was it relief that flickered through her eyes? She said now, in a calm voice, as if she had never prevaricated, 'We've been lovers for about two years, if that's what you mean.'

What else? Swilley thought. There was something here she didn't understand. 'When did you last see him?'

'Oh – it would be last week. We went out to dinner. Wednesday evening, I think? Or Tuesday? No, Wednesday, the twenty-third. We both have busy lives, so we don't – didn't – get to see each other as often as we'd like.'

'And how did he seem on that occasion?'

'Just as usual.'

'Was he worried about anything? Preoccupied?'

'No, why should he be?'

'What did you talk about?'

There was a hint of impatience in the reply. 'Goodness, I can't remember. Nothing in particular. Just what we always talked about. Why on earth are you asking me these questions? What relevance can our dinner conversation a week ago have to his being attacked by a burglar?'

'It's just routine,' Swilley said soothingly. 'We have to cover all possible angles. Someone might have overheard you saying something that helped them decide on the break-in.'

'Well, we didn't talk about his flat being full of valuables,' she said with grim humour. 'I think he talked about his daughter – he was looking forward to her visiting sometime soon – but otherwise I can't think of anything specific.'

Swilley nodded and changed tack. 'You say you both had busy lives. Do you know what Mr Stonax was doing that kept him so busy? As far as we know he didn't have a job.'

Scott-Chatton would have frowned if she were a frowner. The eyes glittered frostily. 'He was involved with several charities, and he always took an interest in our campaigns and wrote letters and went to see people. I can tell you he never sat around idly feeling sorry for himself. Ed wasn't that kind of man. He's a great, great loss, to the country, as well as to me personally. It's awful to think of him being cut down in his prime for nothing more than the contents of his wallet. I hope you put every effort into catching this young thug, and putting him away for a long, long time.'

'We will,' Swilley said. 'We are. Do you have a key to his flat?'

She threw the question in out of the blue and was gratified to see the faintest hesitation before Scott-Chatton replied, 'I used to have one, but in fact I gave it back to Ed. We didn't meet at his flat any more. Why do you ask?'

'It's just a routine question,' Swilley said, her eyes unmovingly on Scott-Chatton's alabaster face. 'Something we have to ask people.' There seemed to be no more forthcoming and Swilley stood up. 'Well, thank you for your time. If there's anything else we need to know I'm sure you won't mind if I contact you again.'

'No, not at all,' Scott-Chatton said, seeming – to Swilley's quiet pleasure – a little put out. She rose too and they walked towards the door.

'I'm afraid the press will be hounding you soon, if they aren't already,' Swilley said with a sympathetic smile.

'No, they haven't troubled me yet,' Scott-Chatton said absently. Then her gaze sharpened. 'I hope nothing the police say or do will expose me to unwelcome press attention.'

'We don't talk to the press unless we absolutely have to,' Swilley said, 'and then we make a point of not telling them anything they don't already know. Goodbye, and thank you again.'

In the outer room the secretary had flung Swilley a fleeting but searing look before going back to her typing, so she made a business of putting her notebook away and fiddling in her handbag until Candida Scott-Chatton had closed the door to her own room behind her. Swilley turned to Shawna Weedon, but before she could speak the girl flung a silencing finger against her lips, shoved a folded piece of paper across the table, and continued with her typing, having missed only a beat or two.

Swilley took the paper, winked, said aloud, 'Well, goodbye, then,' and took her departure.

At a safe distance from the building she opened the note. 'Ciggie break, 10 min, down mews.'

An assignation, Swilley thought, amused. Now what could young Shawna have to say that her tartar of a boss would object to?

Four

Widow of Opportunity

'So tell me – if you don't mind talking about it – about your father's bit of trouble last year,' said Slider.

Emily Stonax was sitting beside him in the car, hands between her knees for comfort. The low afternoon light striking her face through the windscreen emphasised how tired she was. She looked grey.

She sighed, as if talking was an effort, but she answered freely enough. 'It was very strange. I mean, that sort of thing just isn't *like* Dad. He's the straightest person I know. And as for sharing *anything* with Sid Andrew – he'd as soon lick the pavements. He had a very low opinion of him.'

'Why do you say that?'

'Oh, he told me more than once that Sid was a waste of space, a complete liability in the department. He's the sort of man Dad always despised – a time-serving career politician, who got on by being lobby fodder and a cabinet lickspittle. He was punching well above his weight at the DTI – the Permanent Secretary practically had to guide his hand when he signed things. But then, look what happened when the scandal broke: Sid Andrew does a couple of months in purdah and then he's *Lord* Andrew of Leuchars. Now he's sitting pretty – directorships, quangos, committees, you name it.'

'So what do you think really happened?' Slider asked.

'I don't *know*,' she said in frustration. 'Dad would never talk about it. I was out of the country at the time, of course, but I read all the British papers and I watch the BBC so of course I saw everything that was in the news. It was taken up by one or two of the American papers, because Dad had been Washington correspondent for a while, but they didn't run with it past one issue. We have our own sex scandals over there, much fruitier ones, and no-one had ever heard of Sid Andrew so it wasn't interesting enough. But I phoned Dad straight away, of course, and asked what was going on. I said I *know* it isn't true, and all he said is, "It's pointless for me to deny it. You've seen the photos." I said to him, "Dad, I know you wouldn't do something like that." And he said, "The evidence is irrefutable." And then he changed the subject and wouldn't talk about it any more. And when I next came over, it was a forbidden subject between us.'

'So what's your theory?' Slider asked. She looked at him, and he gave a faint smile. 'I'm sure you must have a theory, a thinking woman like you.'

She shrugged off the compliment. 'I suppose he must have been tricked into it somehow. But I can't think how. What was he doing with that girl in the first place, when he and Candida were so close? Maybe he was drunk,' she added, as though anticipating that he would say it, 'but being drunk doesn't excuse bad behaviour.'

'Was it so very bad? I mean, these days, don't men have these little flings now and then?'

She looked disappointed in him. 'Other people, maybe, but not Dad. And not like that. Anyway, the government thought it was serious enough to sack him and Andrew.'

'Why do you think your father wouldn't talk about it to you?'

She looked down at her hands. 'Maybe because he was ashamed,' she said quietly. 'That's what I'm afraid of. I could bear it if he did it and was defiant and said, "Mind your own business," to everyone. But I couldn't stand it if he did something he was ashamed of. Not Dad.'

It was quite a pedestal, Slider thought. Was Stonax really that virtuous? They were silent until they turned into Riverene Road, and then she said, 'You don't think that old stuff has anything to do with . . . with this?'

'I don't know,' Slider said. 'Probably not, but I like to know everything I can in cases like this. And I was born curious.'

'I thought you said it was just a robbery?'

'It looks that way,' Slider said. 'I'm just being thorough.'

'Well, I suppose I should be glad about that,' she said bleakly.

Swilley walked down Queen's Gate a little way and came back into the mews from the other end, and then stationed herself in the shadow of a fire escape to wait. Soon enough Shawna Weedon came scuttling across the road from the office. Swilley made herself visible and the girl almost flung herself into the hiding place as if the Feds were after her.

'I can't stay long,' she said, fumbling in her handbag for a cigarette. She offered them to Swilley, who took one in the interests of the case, though she hardly ever smoked any more. Shawna lit them both and savaged the weed as though it was her last. '*She* doesn't like me smoking,' she said, 'and of course I can't do it in the office, but it's in my contract, two ten minute breaks as well as lunch-hour, and she can't stop me taking them. But I daren't be a minute late.'

'All right, what did you want to tell me?' Swilley asked calmly.

'Only to set the record straight, that's all, because it's so shocking about poor Ed Stonax. He was such a lovely man. He often used to come into the office, and always so polite and friendly. Not like *some* people, who think they're better than everyone else. But he was a complete gentleman.'

'Well, up to a point,' Swilley said. 'There was that three-in-a-bed stuff last year.'

'Oh, that!' Shawna said with robust scorn. 'Well, if you want my opinion, there was something fishy about that. I said so at the time. He just wouldn't *do* a thing like that. If you want to know what *I* think, I think he was drugged to make him do it. Because there was no way he would have if he was in his right mind.'

'But then why didn't he complain about it afterwards?'

She shrugged. 'Oh, well, you know how these things go. Once something's been in the papers no-one ever believes you again. He'd have just looked like a fool to argue. And according to what I heard they gave him a big settlement, so unless he wanted his job back he was better to leave sleeping dogs lie. And he wouldn't have wanted it back after that, would he? Besides, they'd never have given it him anyway because I believe that's what they did it for, the whole photo thing – to get rid of him. But that wasn't good enough for *madam*.' She jerked her head back towards the office. 'Dropped him like a hot potato as soon as he was in trouble.'

'I heard that she stood by him,' Swilley said.

'The moment she realised there was bad publicity in it, she gave him the elbow. She's mad about publicity – lives for it – but it's got to be the right kind. Got to reflect well on Miss Snooty Pants and the old school, doncha know.' She put on a ludicrous 'posh' accent.

'When you say she gave him the elbow . . .?'

'There was this time, just after it all broke, when she phoned him and I picked up the line by mistake. Well, I couldn't put it down again because it would have made a click and then she'd have thought I was listening.'

'So you listened?'

She had no shame about it. The end had justified the means for her. 'I heard him say they needed to talk about it, and she said no they didn't, there was nothing to say. So then he said could he come round and see her and she said he could, but it wouldn't make any difference, he wouldn't be able to change her mind. So then he rang off and about half an hour later he came in through the door and she took him into her office and shut the door. I couldn't hear what they were saying – they must have been keeping their voices down – but then she buzzed me and when I went in they were standing on opposite sides of the room, and she was quite red in the face and he was looking really fed up. So she says, all polite and chilly, "Will you have a cup of coffee?" And he says, "No, thank you. I'd better go." Might just as well have said, "No thanks, it'd choke me," because it was obvious he'd been pleading with her and she'd been giving him the old heave-ho. So he just up and leaves, and she turns to me and says, "I think you should know that Mr Stonax and I are no longer going out together." I felt like saying, surprise, surprise!'

'I wonder why she would tell you that,' Swilley said, almost to herself.

'Well, we all knew how things were between them before that, so I suppose she was making sure we knew she wanted nothing more to do with him. Too good for him, the stuck-up cow.'

'But he *had* two-timed her in a pretty nasty way.'

'I told you, I never believed in that. He was set up. Anyway, what about "stand by your man"? She should have forgiven him and taken him back,' Shawna said sententiously, straight from the pages of whatever magazine she had most recently been reading. It wasn't *Country Life*, that was for sure. 'Anyway, before you can turn round, she's started going out with someone else.'

'Who is that?'

'Freddie Bell,' Shawn said, with a certain ripe, significant look.

'The casino mogul?'

'That's him. And a real rough diamond he is. When he comes in the office to see her it's "What are you lot staring at? Haven't you got any work to do?" Never stopping for a chat like poor Mr Stonax did.'

Swilley was fascinated. 'Are you sure about that – Candida Scott-Chatton going out with Freddie Bell? I wouldn't have thought he was her type at all.'

'Well, if you want my opinion, she likes a bit of rough. And of course he's mega-rich. It got her into the papers all right – didn't you see?' Swilley shook her head. 'They were photographed together all over the place. Rubbing Mr Stonax's nose in it, I thought.'

'So she wasn't still seeing Ed Stonax?'

'You kidding? He was history. Besides, Freddie Bell's not the sharing type, and he's got a temper on him. He broke that bloke's arm just for looking at his girlfriend funny – didn't you read about that? It was in *What She Wants* and *Chat* magazines.'

'I don't get those.'

'I couldn't live without them! It's the only way you find out what's really going on in this world. Anyway, that was years ago, but it shows what kind of man he is. I suppose that's what she likes. So all I'm saying, if she comes over all holier-than-thou and pretends to be the grieving widow, don't you believe her.' She looked at her watch. 'Christ, I must go.' She dashed the cigarette to the ground and stamped it out.

Swilley said, 'Thanks, you've been a great help. Just one last thing – did she see Mr Stonax at all after that time?'

'Oh, yes, now and then, because they were interested in the same campaigns. But it was just official stuff. Freddie Bell would never have stood for anything else.'

The rest of Stonax's flat seemed as immaculate as the drawing-room, except for the obvious signs of forensic activity. There were taped 'safe lines', and Slider conducted Emily Stonax through them to look around the flat. She seemed pale but in control, and said that she couldn't see anything out of place or missing. 'It all looks just the same,' she said. There was a bad moment when they looked into the spare room. She said, 'He made the bed up for me,' and pressed her fingers to the inner corners of her eyes, to keep the tears back. When they came to his bedroom, she couldn't speak at all.

Bob Bailey came up to say to Slider in a low tone, 'We didn't find any money, credit cards or wallet, but there are a couple of watches in one of the drawers. If you could ask her . . .?'

Slider offered her his handkerchief and she shook her head, dragged out another tissue, blew her nose briskly and said in a reasonably controlled way, 'They'll have been his old watches. Dad had a gold Oyster Perpetual he wore all the time. He loved it. He was always mad about watches and of course he needed a good, reliable one in his work, but the Oyster was his great treasure. Candida bought it for him last Christmas, and I don't think he ever took it off, except in the shower.'

Seeing she was back in charge, Bailey asked, 'We didn't find a mobile phone . . .?'

She turned to him. 'He had the latest Nikoti Cyber-box, the F283. It's a 3G Smartphone that does everything – VGA camera, camcorder, mobile, broadband, video calling, the lot, plus the electronic notebook facility. You can write or dictate notes into it and download them to your computer through a wireless link. He took it everywhere. It would have been in his pocket.'

Slider nodded. Even he had heard of the Cyber-box. There had been queues round the block in New York when it came out, gadget aficionados wanting to be the first to own one. It made robbery from the person look a better bet.

'We'll put a trace on it. And on his credit cards, once we have the numbers. I suppose all that sort of thing will be in his office.' There was something at the back of his mind which wouldn't come forward, but it prompted him to ask, without really knowing why, 'Did your dad have a fountain pen or a fancy ballpoint? A Mont Blanc or anything like that, that he carried in his pocket?'

'No,' she said. 'He just used ordinary biros. He wasn't interested in pens. Why?'

'Oh, just wondering what else might have been in his pocket.'

'Well, it wouldn't have been a biro. He hated people who had them sticking out of their pockets. Like men who wore signet rings. He had a lot of those little prejudices.'

'We all do,' Slider said, to comfort her.

They moved on to the third bedroom, which was furnished as an office, with a desk, computer, filing cabinets and so on. Again, everything looked orderly, and Emily Stonax said she couldn't see anything missing.

Bob Bailey eased Slider aside and said quietly, 'There's something interesting about one of those filing cabinets. Fingermarks on the top and on this drawer. Don't get excited – they're gloved prints, so we won't get a match, but it's an indication?'

'Yes,' said Slider. *What normal person puts gloves on to do their filing? Someone had been in.* 'You'd better have a look for footprints as well. That's quite a new carpet with a good pile.'

'Already on it. And here's something else – a quick analysis of one of the smears suggests oil of some kind, probably petroleum based.'

'I didn't know you had a field test kit for oil,' said Slider.

Bailey gave him a withering look. 'It's called smell and taste.'

'Well, get me a sample and I'll shove it off to the lab,' Slider said, his interest quickening. If the oil came from the perpetrator's car, it might be possible to get a match: the oil in each car had a unique combination of impurities – dirt, soot, pollen etc. Of course, there was no register of car-prints, but it was good evidence once they had a suspect. 'Have you opened any of the drawers yet?'

'Not yet. Still doing externals.'

'Well, I'd like Miss Stonax to have a look into the one with the fingermarks.'

It hardly needed the eye of a relative, when it came to it, because as soon as the drawer was opened it could be seen that one of the hanging folders was empty. The plastic name tag from it had been taken, too – pulled out so roughly that the slots that had held it had been torn.

'I suppose you can't tell us what was in it?' Slider asked without much hope.

She shook her head slowly, obviously trying to help. 'I've never really looked through his files. All I can say is that he was very tidy-minded and kept everything in a logical order, either alphabetical or by category.' She looked at Slider. 'So what does this mean? If someone took a file out of his office, doesn't it change things?'

'Let's not get ahead of ourselves,' Slider said. 'The two things might not be related at all. This folder might have been empty to begin with, or the file might have been removed at some other time. Your father might have lent it to someone, or just refiled it somewhere else.'

Emily was looking at the tags on the rest of the files. 'This is all environmental stuff. I recognise some of the names – campaigns and enquiries he's mentioned to me in the past.'

Slider sighed inwardly at the thought of having to go through everything. There were three cabinets of four drawers each, enough paper-chasing to keep them up nights for months, unless a good lead turned up. 'I'd just like to find his credit card numbers so we can get a fix on those,' he said.

'This drawer's labelled "Financial",' said Bob Bailey, from another stack. There were folders inside with credit-card state-ments neatly filed in date order, each entry on each statement with a small precise tick against it where, presumably, it had been checked against the counterfoils in the officially approved manner. Stonax's tidy, logical methods certainly made it easier to find things. Unfortunately – if the 'missing' folder were indeed missing, and significant – it also made it easier for an intruder to find what he wanted.

'That's all I want for now,' Slider said, noting how Emily Stonax was drooping with weariness as the brief, spurious excitement wore off. 'Would you like to make your way back to the door and I'll see about getting you some transport.'

She retraced her steps, while Bailey bagged the credit-card folders. 'I'll take his chequebook and bank statements, and that big diary, too,' Slider said. 'And the pile of papers on the corner of the desk – that might be recent correspond-ence. I suppose we'll have to get into his computer, too.'

'You may be too late for that,' Bailey said. 'If the villain was after something documentary, now he's got the Cyber-box he can get in there and take what he wants.'

'He can?'

'It uploads as well as downloads.'

'Oh, bloody Nora, don't tell me that!'

'If he knows or can figure out the password, that is,' Bailey said hastily, in an effort to comfort him.

Slider met his eyes. 'I was hoping the stolen Cyber-box meant it *was* a simple robbery from the person. But combine it with a missing file, and it starts to look more complicated. And complicated I can do without at the moment.'

'We don't *know* the file's missing,' said Bailey encour-agingly. 'And Stonax might have made those fingermarks himself – on his way out with his gloves on, say, and he suddenly remembers he needs the file for something. Dashes back in . . .'

'Thanks for reminding me,' Slider said, though not with overwhelming gratitude. 'Now we've got to look through his clothes for gloves as well.'

At the door to the flat Slider found Atherton, standing outside in the corridor and talking to Emily Stonax. Hart was also there, looking on with an expressionless face, her arms folded across her chest in what in other circumstances might have been a defensive posture. Slider took Atherton to one side and handed him the bag of papers. 'You can take these back and start going through them. The credit-card numbers are in there.'

'Do you want them stopped?'

'Not immediately,' said Slider. 'Put an alert on them. It's possible one of them might be used and then we'll get a fix on the user.'

'Right. Oh, and Mackay was just here. He's managed to get the old lady next door to answer at last. Number five, the other side. A Mrs Koontz. Apparently she was out walking her dog this morning at about half past seven and she saw someone coming out of the main door downstairs.'

'Half past seven? That could be all right,' said Slider.

'It's not much help to us, though,' said Atherton. 'Apparently it was one of those motorbike couriers, in leathers, with the smoked-glass visor on the helmet.'

Slider almost clicked his fingers. 'That was it!'

'What was what?'

'I saw something this morning, when I was leaving here. It caught my attention, but just out of the corner of my mind, and I didn't really take in what it was. But now you remind me, it was a man in a motorbike helmet. He was standing in the crowd.'

Atherton cocked his head slightly. 'Is that it?'

'I just thought it was odd that someone standing watching like that shouldn't have taken off his helmet.'

Atherton shrugged. 'If he'd just paused for an instant to look . . .?'

'I know. It's probably nothing.'

'What's probably nothing?' Hart asked, joining them.

'Neighbour saw a motorbike courier leaving this morning at an interesting time, and the guv'nor saw a man in a bike helmet in the crowd,' Atherton explained. 'Naturally in a city of twenty million people they'd have to be one and the same.'

'You think you're kidding.' Hart looked serious. 'I was waiting to tell you about the caretaker, guv, Borthwick, but now I think there's something you ought to see for yourself.'

Slider was aware that Emily Stonax was standing un-attended since Hart had left her. 'I'll come,' he said. 'Atherton,

Miss Stonax needs a lift. Can you look after her? Drop that stuff at the station on your way if that fits in.'

'Certainly,' Atherton said, and almost leapt to her side with an alacrity that had Hart muttering, 'Boy scout!' under her breath, but rather sourly.

In the car, Atherton said, 'I have to take these things back to the station, but of course your bags are still there, aren't they? So we can pick them up at the same time. Is that all right?'

'Yes,' she said, staring listlessly out of the window.

'And where would you like me to take you afterwards?'

She roused herself. 'I don't know. I was going to stay with my dad, wasn't I? I suppose that's out of the question now.'

'Well, for a day or two, until all the forensic tests are done. Is there anyone else you can stay with in London? Friends? Family?'

'I don't have any other family, I've already told you that.' Weariness and shock was making her a little irritable. 'And I don't have friends in London any more – not anyone I'd want to stay with, anyway.'

'Well, we do need you to stay nearby for a little while,' he said gently.

'Oh, I'm staying,' she said, suddenly forceful. 'I'm staying until you find who did this, and catch him, and lock him up.' The little burst of energy dissipated. 'I suppose I'll have to go to an hotel. I don't know any round here. Can you recommend anywhere?'

The thought of her shacked up in some horrible hotel was unthinkable – soulless modern chain or tacky local cheap, either way it hurt him. He paused a moment to frame his words carefully. 'Don't be afraid to say no right away if you don't like the idea, but I've got a spare room. You can stay there if you like.' He dared to look at her, and she met his eyes doubtfully, wondering what was implied. He lifted one hand off the steering wheel in an open-handed gesture to indicate innocence. 'No funny business. I mean it purely in a friendly way. You can have your own key and come and go as you please. I won't bother you. And you can stay as long as you like. It isn't grand, but it's adequate, and it's near a tube station.'

'Are you serious?' she asked slowly.

He felt a certain heat in his face. Ridiculous, at his age! 'Yes, of course I am. But as I said, don't be shy about saying no if you think it's inappropriate.'

'Inappropriate,' she mused. 'That's a really American expression. No, I don't think it's inappropriate. I think it's very kind, and I think it would be brilliant because you'd be able to keep me up to date on what's being done and what you've found out. I was dreading going off to some hotel and being forgotten and left out. But do you really mean it? Won't I be in the way?'

His heart lifted. 'Not the slightest. I'd be glad to have you stay. As long as you like cats.'

'I love them. Why?'

'I've got two Siameses.'

'My favourite sort.'

'They're mad as snakes, but very clean.'

'Siameses are always clean.'

He turned into the yard and pulled into his parking slot, and only then dared to turn and look at her. He saw that in the weariness and pain of her face there had come a small measure of comfort, and he felt thrilled and humbled to have been able to do that.

As if she heard his thought she said, 'It will be so much nicer to stay in someone's home rather than an hotel. Thank you for offering.'

He tried not to grin like an ape in his pleasure. 'The only thing is I won't be able to take you back there right away. A lot of stuff to do. Do you mind waiting? I mean, you can go off and do things, of course, and come back later. You don't have to hang around the station.'

'Don't worry, I'll fit in with whatever you have to do. I don't want to get in the way of the investigation.' They both got out of the car, and she faced him across the roof. 'Right now I'd really love a cup of tea, though.'

'Nothing easier. You can use the canteen. And if you want to crash out for a bit, you can use the soft room – the inter-view room where you went this morning. The sofa there's not too bad.'

They walked in together and up the stairs to the office,

where her things had been stacked in a corner to wait for her. The first person Atherton saw as he entered was Joanna, sitting on the edge of a desk looking anxious. She jumped up as soon as she saw him. Until yesterday, it had given him a sharp pang to see her like that, all taut and curved down the front with Slider's baby. Today, since meeting Emily, he was filled only with friendly affection. They kissed cheeks.

'Where is he?' she asked.

'Still at the site. Don't worry,' he said, and introduced Emily Stonax before she could say anything inappropriate.

Joanna's face immediately registered concern and vicarious distress. It was one of the things Slider liked about her, that every feeling – and often every thought – was visible in her expression. As a policeman he was so accustomed to being lied to it was refreshing to know a person without guile.

She held out her hand to Emily. 'I'm *so* sorry,' she said. 'I can't begin to imagine how awful you must feel.'

Emily shook the hand. 'At the moment I think I'm cushioned a bit by jetlag. I only got in from New York this morning.'

Atherton said, 'Emily's pining for a cup of tea. Could you show her the way to the canteen?'

'It's all right, I can find it,' Emily said.

But Joanna said, 'I'm dying for one myself. Do you mind if I come with you?'

'No, I'd be glad of the company.'

'Will you tell me when he gets back?' Joanna asked Atherton, and they went off together.

'So you're Inspector Slider's . . . partner?' Emily said, a little hesitantly, as they walked up the stairs.

'Soon to be wife,' Joanna said. 'It's just that it's so hard to find a time when we're both free. Whenever we do tentatively fix a date for the wedding, something always comes up.'

'Like my father.'

'I'm so sorry. I hope you didn't think I meant—'

'No, no. Look, if we're going to sit and have tea together, you'll have to not tiptoe round me. The whole thing's too

awful for me to know what I feel about anything yet. I'm
pretty numb, if you want the truth.'

'Probably just as well,' said Joanna.

The canteen was almost empty. They got tea and Joanna,
feeling they needed a sugar hit, picked up a packet of two
giant chocolate chip cookies, and they made their way to a
table by the window.

'It must be strange for you,' Emily said when they were
seated. 'What's it like to be with a man who investigates
murders for a living?'

'I used to mind it terribly at first,' Joanna said, tearing the
end off the cookie packet. 'I've had to switch off from it a
bit, they way they do. They can't get emotional or it inter-
feres with their judgement.' She handed one of the cookies
to Emily, who took it absently. 'All the same, he minds dread-
fully. He's always very depressed at the end of a case, when
the adrenaline lets him down and he's able to let his feelings
loose.' She smiled faintly. 'That's where I come in – general
hand-holding, head-cradling and so on.'

Emily nodded seriously. 'That must be tough. How did
you meet him?'

'He investigated the murder of a violinist I shared a desk
with. I was about her only friend, but even I didn't know
her well. It was so sad and awful.'

'It must have been.'

'He was married to someone else at the time, but I don't
think she'd ever really understood what he felt about these
things. He did tend to keep his feelings very much to himself.
You know what men of his generation are like. So it all built
up and he had a kind of nervous breakdown. And out of the
mess, he and I got together and we've been together ever since.'

'So, good coming out of evil. I wish I could think anything
good would come out of this.' She broke off a small piece
of cookie and watched her fingers turning it into crumbs. 'Is
he good?' she asked abruptly.

'Bill? He's the best. And he never gives up. Best of all,
you can talk to him, and he really listens.'

'And the other one? Sergeant Atherton?'

'Jim is Bill's friend as well as his bagman, so he's my
friend too. He's brilliant in his way.'

'Is he seeing anyone?'

Joanna thought it an odd question, but took jetlag into account. 'He was going out with a friend of mine, another violinist, but they split up a while back.' She didn't say, 'Why do you ask?' but her tone asked the question clearly enough.

Emily said, 'He offered me his spare room. I didn't want to be treading on anyone's toes.'

'You won't be.' Speculation was so rife it was lucky Emily was not looking at her just then.

'Why d'you think he did it?' Now she looked up. 'Offered?'

'Just kindness,' Joanna said firmly. 'He's a kind person underneath.'

Emily nodded wearily. 'That's what I thought. I'm glad I was right.'

Five

To Err is Divine . . .

The basement of Valancy House ran under the whole building so it was very spacious. The caretaker's flat occupied only part of it: sitting-room, bedroom, bathroom and kitchen, reasonably sized, according to Hart, but dark and depressing, with bars at all the windows, which looked out on to the small yard at the back where the dustbins lived. 'Still, to get a flat that size in this area, you'd put up with a lot worse,' she concluded. 'I reckon Dave Borthwick knows he's lucky, 'cos to my mind he'd never earn enough if the flat didn't come with the job.'

'Not very bright?'

'Not very anything,' Hart said, 'except muscle-bound and ugly. Though I reckon we'll find he's well tasty. If he's not got a record, my arse is an apricot. Sorry, boss.'

'Think nothing of it,' Slider said graciously. 'We'll put Hollis on it when we get back. Borthwick's record, I mean, not . . .'

'Gotcha.'

The rest of the basement was windowless, stone-floored, the walls clad to shoulder height with those glazed brown tiles beloved of Edwardians, the bare bricks painted above with pale green distemper, lit by naked forty-watt bulbs hanging from flexes that were probably the originals. Footsteps echoed down there, and there were distant mysterious groans, thumps and gurgles of pipes, and a monotonous dripping as if an unseen tap somewhere had a faulty washer.

'I could feel right at home here,' Hart said chirpily. 'My school was just like this.'

Part of the space was taken up with the pit of the lift-shaft and the bottom of the stairs. There was an open area around them, a door in the adjacent wall into the flat (battered metal with a massive keyhole) and then various rooms around the perimeter, linked by corridors. Presumably at one time the caretaker had had a lot more to do for the residents than in modern days. One room was evidently the coal-store, for there was a chute leading up to a circular bronze hatch in the pavement above, and a lingering, ghostly smell of coal, though it was swept clean. Next door was an ancient boiler squatting on a concrete dais, though all its pipes had been removed.

'Must've used to run the central heating. They've all got individual gas boilers in the flats now,' Hart said.

In another room was an array of grey metal cupboards housing the fuses and access to the circuits for the whole building. One cupboard, Slider noticed, had a sticker on the front, a white plastic circle with a telephone logo in the centre and the words RING 4 SECURITY around the perimeter.

'That, presumably, is the security door,' said Slider.

He tried the door but it was locked. The sticker looked newly applied and did not quite cover an elderly paper sticker underneath, which was triangular rather than round, so its faded, frayed corners just showed.

'This is what I wanted to show you, guv,' Hart said, leading him to another room, the one nearest the door to Borthwick's flat.

There was a massive metal sink in the corner with a single cold tap above it – the source of the dripping sound – and the marks on the walls of various machines and pipes long removed. It looked as though it had once been a laundry, either self-service or for the caretaker or his wife to perform service washes. Or perhaps people had kept servants in the old days. It was an interesting speculation to Slider, who always wanted to know how people had lived in times past, but not nearly as interesting as the object which occupied the centre of the room: a large Triumph motorbike, propped on its foot stand, an oil-stain underneath it, and a tool-kit spread out on a filthy square of canvas beside it.

'Borthwick's?' Slider asked.

'Yeah. I thought you'd like it,' said Hart with pleasure.

'How does he get it out? Not through his flat?'

'Nah. There's a door into the yard under the stairs over there. For taking the rubbish out.'

'Locked?'

'One of them push-bar jobs. It looks in good nick. But it doesn't matter, does it?' She went to the reason for the question. 'The stairs down to here are open, anyone could come down, and we know the security door wasn't working.' She thought a bit more. 'But why d'you think the murderer might come down here?'

'Just covering the bases,' Slider said. 'You always need to know where the access points are. So, Borthwick's got a bike, has he?'

'Yeah,' said Hart. 'I wonder if he's got leathers, an' all.'

Emily and Joanna had gone to a second cup of tea and a pack of three custard creams. They were still talking (Emily was intelligent about music and interesting about journalism, so the conversation generated itself spontaneously) when April behind the counter, telephone in hand, called across, 'Mr Slider's back, love.'

'Do you mind?' Joanna said, rising. 'I want to talk to him.'

'So do I,' said Emily.

They got down to the CID room to find new events already in train. Slider hadn't even got as far as his room. He put his arm round Joanna and kissed her cheek but his attention was on Norma Swilley, at her desk and on the phone.

Atherton, coming up beside Emily, explained. 'It's not about your dad, it's another case.' And to Joanna, 'Someone's using the mobile that Bates called on this morning.'

'Really? Then if you can get a trace on it, you might catch him?'

Slider glanced at her. 'In theory. But in practice—' He broke off as Swilley looked up.

'Boss,' she said, with a shadow of puzzlement in her eyes, 'Mick Hutton says he hasn't had an official request yet to monitor that number. Not from any of the SOs. No-one has.'

That was strange. Wouldn't they be eager to follow up the only lead they had on a wanted, dangerous, jailbreak master criminal? But there was no time to wonder about it.

'It's their loss and our opportunity. Let's get after him. Mackay, McLaren – who's next door from uniform?'

'Renker and Gallon.'

'Good.' They were both big, hefty lads. 'Get 'em. Norma, stay on the line with Hutton and liaise with us through Atherton.'

'You're going?' Atherton asked, seeing Joanna's eyes widen. Slider gave him a silencing look. Of *course* he was going!

Fathom spoke up excitedly. 'Guv, let me come.'

Atherton, still holding Slider's eyes, said, 'He might not be alone.'

Slider nodded. 'Come on, then,' he said to Fathom, heading for the door through which the other two had already disappeared. 'But do exactly as you're told.'

'Yes, guv,' Fathom said, grinning in triumph as he followed.

Into the small silence that followed, Norma said, 'He's still on the line.'

'What *is* all this?' Emily asked.

Atherton had gone to his phone to establish the link with Slider, so Joanna answered.

'Come over here, out of the way, and I'll tell you about it,' she said.

She found her hands were shaking a little. She so badly wanted Bates caught; but Slider had gone himself, and a cornered fox was unpredictable.

The time seemed to drag by horribly, but in fact they were not away very long. When Slider came back into the room Joanna's heart clenched with relief; only afterwards did she realise with sickening disappointment that his rapid return meant it had been a false alarm.

'You didn't get him?'

'Oh, we got him all right,' he said grimly. ' "Him" being a fourteen-year-old boy.' He held up the evidence bag with the mobile in it. 'Jason Clifton. Found it lying on the front garden wall of a house, partly hidden by the privet hedge. He'd just come out of school, couldn't believe his luck. Pocketed it, then as soon as he'd put a bit of distance between himself and the site, he rang up a mate to boast about it, and was still having a long, luxurious chat when we turned up.'

'You believe him?' Joanna asked.

'Oh, yes,' Slider said wearily. 'I think it was Bates's idea of a joke. I think he bought the mobile for the single purpose of making fools of us. The only possible help it might be is that he might have hung around to see the fun, so we're bringing the boy in for questioning as soon as we've got hold of his appropriate adult. But I doubt if he can tell us anything. We know what Bates looks like. What we don't know is where to find him.'

'I suppose,' Joanna said hesitantly, 'he wouldn't be at home? Is that a silly question?'

'The house was sealed up when he was arrested, and they've been watching it ever since he was sprung from the security van,' Atherton answered.

'*They* being?'

'SOCA – the Serious Organised Crime Agency.'

'And is that the same SOCA that didn't get the mobile phone monitored?' Joanna asked.

'Good point,' Atherton said. He looked at Slider. 'Should we maybe check that it *is* being done?'

'If you can think of a way to do it discreetly,' Slider said.

'I'm on it, guv,' Hart said. 'Phil Warzynski at Notting Hill's an old mate of mine.'

In the car on the way home, Joanna asked for more detail on the Bates business, but there wasn't much more Slider could tell her.

'I'm glad the others are going to help you try and find him,' she said.

'So am I. Though they're putting themselves on the line – could be disciplinary action if they're found out.'

'Don't sound so surprised. They love you, stupid.'

'You look tired.'

'It's been a long day. Did you know Jim's taking Emily Stonax home?'

'I heard.'

'You don't mind?'

'It won't hurt. She's not a suspect. She wasn't even in the country.'

'I was in the country,' she reminded him.

'Well, we got away with it,' he said, putting a hand on her knee. 'Do you mind?'

'About us or about Jim?'

'He and Sue are really all over?'

'They weren't really suited. It's a shame, but . . .' She shrugged. 'I think he's just being kind – about Emily, I mean. I hope so, anyway. I wouldn't like to think he'd take advantage of someone in her position.'

'He wouldn't. He's a nice lad.'

'Lad!' She snorted. 'You're getting soft in your old age, you know,' she added as he backed in to the last parking space in Turnham Green, which was fortuitously only fifty yards up the road from home.

Slider got out, and was just closing the car door when there was a tremendous roar. His instinct reacted before his mind had even worked out what the sound was, and he sprang like a springbok into the space between his car and the one in front as the motorbike howled past so close that the wind of it buffeted him. There was a crack, crash and tinkle as the wing-mirror of the car in front ripped off, hit the road and the glass shattered.

Joanna, on the pavement on her side of the car, gripped the edge of the roof with whitened fingers. He met her shocked eyes. 'What the hell was that?' she said through stiff lips.

'Did you see it? Anything?' he asked. Adrenaline was dashing about in his body like a headless chicken.

'Nuh,' she managed to bleat. Then she shook her head and said, in a more normal voice, 'It was too quick. I wasn't really looking. Just a blur.'

He went round the car and took her in his arms. 'Are you all right?'

'That's my line,' she said, and he knew she was. After a minute he released her, and she looked up into his face and said, 'Was that *him*. Bates?'

'I don't know,' he said. 'It could have been.'

'He knows where we live? Or has he been following us?'

He took her by the elbows. 'It might have been him, or it might have been nothing to do with him. But the point is this: if he wanted to kill me or hurt me he could have done so. If that was him, what he wants to do is frighten me, and by extension, you.'

'Tell him he's succeeded,' Joanna said with grim humour.

They walked up the road and went indoors, Slider leading, eyes everywhere, senses on the stretch. But his instincts told him that there was no-one watching him, and there seemed nothing amiss in the house. They changed, washed, prepared a meal, and sat down with it. They didn't talk until the food was gone.

Then Joanna said, 'It's not just us we have to think of.'

'I know.'

'There's the baby.'

'I know.'

'I have to ask you again: do you think we're in danger?'

He thought for an intense moment, but he could only say again, 'I don't know.' He studied her face. 'Are you afraid?'

She thought. 'A bit. Not a lot, but a bit. Mostly I'm angry. No-one has the right to do this to us. It's blackmail and I *hate* blackmail.'

'Nice, normal, healthy reactions.' He smiled, a trifle wearily. 'I'm wondering if it might be better if you went away. Just for a little while.'

'Until you catch him? But you don't know how long that might be.'

'I don't want you to be here alone,' he said. 'Just in case.'

'Well, I've got Leeds tomorrow and Huddersfield the day after. My last two dates. I could stay up there overnight, if it helps.'

'You weren't going to drive back and then back again?' he discovered.

'Of course.'

'In your condition?'

'I'd sooner my condition slept in its own bed, thank you. But if it would stop you worrying . . .'

'I think it would, a bit.' Forty-eight hours wasn't much time to catch him, but it was better than nothing. After that, they would have to talk again.

In bed, later, they held each other closely, and each pretended for the other's sake to be asleep. After an hour or so they made love, carefully, because of the baby, and then they really did fall asleep.

In Atherton's bijou artisan cottage, the teenage Siameses did their usual wall-of-death act, racing round the house without ever touching the ground, so fast they were just a blur. Sredni Vashtar and Tiglath Pileser – known as Vash and Tig for ease – were the legacy of his last attempt to get it together with Sue. She had persuaded him into getting them, but then when they finally broke up said she couldn't have them because with her job she was away from home too much. There was truth in that; also, as she further pointed out, that he had had a cat before and she never had. So the kits stayed and mutated into mobile shredders. Once he had learned to put every piece of paper away and wedge the books into the bookcase, they worked out how to open the loo door and thereafter all his loo rolls became elegant white lace.

But they were a great ice-breaker and got Emily over any awkwardness there might have been in finding herself alone with Atherton in his house. Chatting about the cats, he took her bags up to the spare room and dumped them, showed her where the bathroom was, and then mixed them both a gin and tonic large enough to wash in. He left her playing with the cats while he went to the kitchen to start supper, and called over his shoulder that she should put some music on. He thought sorting through his CDs and then figuring out how to work the player would make her feel at home, and her choice of music might tell him something about her. He was eager to learn everything about her he could, but he didn't know where to start. In the end it didn't take her long either to select or to make the machine work. He was still chopping onion when she appeared in the kitchen doorway, glass in hand, with the opening chords of the *Symphonie Fantastique* behind her.

He glanced up. His heart looped the loop again. 'Nice and noisy,' he commented.

'I started with the Bs,' she admitted. 'And it couldn't be Brahms, Beethoven or Bach.'

'No, I can see that,' he said. 'Too emotional.'

Her face cleared. 'You understand. You know a lot about
– well, stuff, don't you?'

'I did stuff at A Level.'

She watched him chop for a moment. 'Can I help?'

'Thanks, but there's not really room in here for two.'

'You like to cook?'

'I like to eat, so there's no alternative. Yes, I like to cook.
I hope you like pasta. It's just the quickest thing I've got
ingredients for.'

'I love pasta,' she said. The cats had oozed past her into
the kitchen and were winding themselves sinuously round his
ankles, making suggestive remarks. 'If you've got something
to twiddle I'll keep them out of your way. If you're sure I
can't help.'

'You can lay the table when the time comes. Thanks. There's
a catnip mouse on a string somewhere – probably under the
sofa. Most things end up there.'

'I see what you mean,' she said a moment later, and brought
out a sock and the inside bit of a toilet roll as well as the
mouse. She was a good twiddler and the cats were soon
absorbed in one of their monotonously ferocious games. 'Your
boss seems nice,' she called out.

'He is,' Atherton replied. 'He's the best.'

'That's what Joanna said. She's nice too.'

'He's the only man I can think of who deserves her.'

'We had a good long talk in the canteen. She's very sympathetic.' She whipped the mouse across the room again and it
disappeared under a writhe of cream fur. 'She told me about
this Bates person. Is he really dangerous?'

'It's hard to say. Usually these threats are only meant to
frighten, but Bates was a pretty hard case.' The chopping
sounds stopped and he appeared in the doorway. 'I don't want
you to think that anything will come in the way of your
father's investigation.'

'I know,' she said, looking up from her position, crouched
on the floor. 'But it occurred to me that I could help you.
With two things going on you must be stretched, and I'm
sure you never have enough staff. You read about it in the
papers all the time, about the police being short-staffed.
Obviously,' she forestalled him, 'I couldn't do police things,

I know that. But I could do research for you.' He still looked
at her doubtfully, and she urged, 'I'm really good at that. It's
my job – a large part of it, anyway.'

'Oh, I'm sure you are. I mean – yes, obviously you
must be. You couldn't use the police computer system, of
course—'

'I know that, but there must be lots of information in the
public domain that might be useful to you. And then there's
all Dad's paperwork to sort through. That'll take a lot of time,
if you don't have enough people.'

'I'll have to ask Bill,' Atherton said, 'but, if you really want
to get involved, I'm sure there's something you could do.'
He smelled his onions catching and hurried back to the stove.

The pasta didn't take long, and soon they were sitting down
at the table with their bowls and a bottle of wine. He had a
block of fresh Parmesan and leaned over to grate some for
her.

'This is really nice of you,' she said. 'To go to all this
trouble.'

'I told you, I like to eat.'

'I didn't mean only the food, but everything. It would have
been hideous going to an hotel.'

'That's what I thought. Wine?'

'Yes, please. I don't want any risk of not sleeping tonight.'
She watched him pour, idly caressing the gold locket, something he guessed she did all the time and wasn't aware of.

'Nice locket,' he said, sitting down. 'Unusual. Is it old?'

'Not to me – Dad sent it to me for my birthday last week.
But it is antique, I think.'

'It looks heavy.'

'It is. Dad said it's very valuable and warned me not to
lose it, so I wear it all the time. It has his picture in it.' Her
eyes filled suddenly and dangerously with tears. 'I can't get
used to the idea—'

'I know,' he said, getting up again, meaning to go round
the table to her, but she shook her head, putting her hand up
in a defensive gesture to stop him. He paused, awkwardly
half up and half down, and she got out another tissue from
her sleeve and blew her nose.

'I'm all right,' she said. 'Please, sit down.' He sat, watching her anxiously, and she said, 'Will you tell me about you? I don't want to talk about me because it will make me think about things, and I don't want to think just now.'

'Well, if you like,' he said, feeling oddly shy about it. He had talked about himself often enough to women, but it was usually a seduction ploy – and they usually knew it as well as he did, so no-one was actually listening. But to tell her, really tell her, about himself would be – well, at the very least a novel sensation. 'If you're sure you want to know. It isn't that interesting.'

'I bet it is,' she said.

It occurred to him that he had never seen anyone look more tired in his entire life. So he talked.

When they had finished eating, it was obvious that she was finished. 'Would you like a bath?' he offered.

'I had a shower at the police station. I don't think I've got the strength for any more washing.' The wine and the gin had done their work – her eyes were closing as she spoke.

'OK. You go in the bathroom and clean your teeth while I make the bed up, and then you can just fall in.'

It didn't take him a minute to whip on a sheet and a duvet cover. She came back from the bathroom as he was doing the second pillow. He switched on the bedside lamp and said, 'I hope you sleep all right. If you need anything in the night, I'm just across there. Call out and I'll hear you.'

She nodded, seeming not to have the strength even to say goodnight. He backed out and closed the door, and went back downstairs.

In the middle of the night he woke with a start to the realisation that someone was in the room with him, and was half out of bed before he remembered that Emily was in the house; then she advanced to his bedside and he could see her dimly in the light filtering through the curtains from the street lamp outside. She was wearing an outsize tee shirt which presumably did service instead of nightclothes, and he could see the gleam of the locket hanging against her chest. So she really did wear it all the time.

'Are you all right?' he asked.

'I can't stop shivering,' she said in a low tone. Her arms

were wrapped round herself and she was hunched as if in pain.

'Can I get you another blanket? An aspirin? A hot drink?'

'No. Thanks. Can – can I get in with you for a bit? Just for the company? I can't—'

That sentence didn't seem to have anywhere to go. Silently he opened the bed to her and she climbed in, and he lay down and took her in his arms. She felt icy cold and was quivering and rigid with it. He held her quietly and gradually she warmed up and the quivering grew less. And then she started to cry.

It was like a summer storm, short and violent. He held her, cradling her head against his shoulder while she wept as if it were being torn out of her, and the hot tears soaked his neck. At last the tears eased and the sobbing died down, like thunder retreating. When she was quiet, breathing steadily, he thought she had fallen asleep.

Very gently, he kissed the crown of her head, and felt things stirring in him that he had never felt before, emotions he had never thought to feel.

After a while she moved against him, almost languorously, and turned her face up to him. He moved his head back to look down at her and see what she wanted. He saw the gleam of her half-open eyes. She reached and took his hand from her back, brought it round and placed it on her breast, at the same time craning upwards and placing her lips against his. He resisted, afraid on so many levels it was bewildering. But she murmured, 'Please. Please,' against his mouth, holding his hand to her. He kissed her, tentatively, feeling his body getting away from his control. But her response was urgent, and she was pressing her body against him, kissing him as though it might save her life.

Well, who knew but that it might?

So he made love to her, half his mind splitting away with guilt and anxiety while the other half was faint with love and joy. Afterwards she fell asleep suddenly, instantly, as the kittens would sometimes do in the middle of play, without warning.

Early in the morning he woke and found her caressing him, and they did it again, with great tenderness, and this time, with all his mind.

Six

Voi Che Sapete

In the morning, Atherton got up quietly while Emily was still asleep, showered and dressed and went downstairs to feed the cats and let them out, and make coffee. He had no idea how she was going to feel, when she woke, about the events of the night. Would she regret them, blame him for 'taking advantage of her'? At best there might be embarrassment, at worst blazing resentment. For himself, he wanted only to be with her all the time, a sensation he had not previously known. Even with Sue, to whom he had once proposed marriage, he had not envisaged spending every moment of the rest of his life in her company. The very idea would have made him nuts. Now, though he knew she must be exhausted, he longed for her to wake up so he could talk to her again.

Fortunately, or unfortunately depending on how you looked at it, the kits, not being used to having visitors in the house, thundered upstairs in their usual manner. As soon as he came downstairs in the morning they liked to race to the top full speed and fling themselves from the bedroom door on to the bed in one splendid Baryshnikov leap. They were gone before he could stop them and he distinctly heard Vash say 'Wah!' in astonishment, before the pair of them thundered back down with their tails in bloom and disappeared into the garden and under the ceanothus.

Atherton hastened upstairs. Emily was sitting up in bed, clutching the duvet to her chest, looking bleary. 'What the hell was that?' she asked thickly.

'The cats. I'm sorry, they dashed off before I could stop them. I'll keep them shut in downstairs now and you can go back to sleep.'

She rubbed her eyes. 'You're dressed,' she said.

'I have to go to work. But you can go back to sleep. You must need it.'

'No, no,' she said, beginning to wriggle to the edge of the bed. 'I want to come in with you. I want to know what's happening. When do you have to leave?'

'About fifteen minutes. I was just making some coffee.'

'Me for that,' she said. 'I'm a really quick dresser. I'll be downstairs in five minutes. Don't go without me.'

Well, at least she didn't seem either embarrassed or angry, he thought, going downstairs again. It seemed like an excellent start – unless she'd completely forgotten the events of the night before? Oh, there was a depressing thought!

But when she appeared, really only five minutes later, she gave him a shy look as she took the mug of coffee from him and said, 'About last night – I want you to know it wasn't just, you know, Dad and everything. I hope you didn't feel, well, forced into it.'

'God, no!' he said fervently, handing her a mug of coffee. 'I was just hoping you didn't feel I'd taken advantage of you.'

'If I remember rightly, I was the one who made the advances. And it would have been hard for you to push me away, in the circumstances.'

'Pushing you away was the last thing I wanted.'

'I'm glad about that,' she said. 'Can we . . .? I don't know how to put this . . .'

'Carry on where we left off?' he suggested.

'Something like that.' There was colour in her cheeks and she was looking down into the mug as if the coffee was a crystal ball.

'I said you could stay here as long as you liked, and that still goes. Even more so.'

'Thanks,' she said. At that moment, fortunately, the kits came back, tiptoeing to the back door, boggling at her, and she put her mug down and hunkered, holding out her fingers to them. 'Come on, you two, I'm not a monster. Isn't it amazing how something as dainty as a cat can make so much noise? They sounded like a cattle stampede coming upstairs.'

So it seemed that everything was all right.

*   *   *

Slider woke feeling unrested, and guessed from the heaviness of Joanna's movements that she felt the same. When she came back from the bathroom she put her arms round him and said, 'I half wish I didn't have these dates. I don't want to be away from you. I hate that man.'

'I feel the same way.'

He cooked breakfast while she packed an overnight bag, which he took out to the car, looking carefully in all directions before each movement. But all seemed quiet and he did not feel the sensation of being watched. He supposed even crazed psychopaths had to sleep, and they were deliberately starting off early, before anything that would be normal time for either of them. Even so he watched the rear view all the time, and scrutinised every car that came in sight for unusual behaviour. In the station yard he transferred her things to her own car.

'Be careful,' he said, hugging her. 'Change speeds and lanes every now and then and watch for anyone following you. I don't think anyone will, but it's best to keep an eye out. If you're worried about anything, phone me.'

She held him close for a moment, and he felt the baby kick him through both their sets of clothes. Then she pulled away, releasing him to the work he had to do. 'Be brilliant, Inspector.'

'I will. Be talented, beautiful and desirable.'

'How can I help it?'

There were two telephone messages for him on his desk and he sat down and returned the calls while it was quiet. The first was from Freddie Cameron.

'No surprises, old bean,' he said. 'Death was caused by the blow to the head. Would have been virtually instantaneous. We're talking about something rounded, possibly padded, very heavy, and wielded with great force. Cease looking for frail women, old-age pensioners or children.'

'Isn't it always the last person you suspect?'

'Not in this life. One other thing – there were traces of oil on the pockets, where chummy went through them, and a large mark on the sleeve of the jacket, where I suppose it was pulled back to expose the watch. From first tests it looks like motor oil of some kind. Do you want it tested further?'

'Might as well. I don't think there'll be any budgetary restraints on this one. Send off the best sample to Les Patterson, will you?'

'Ah, the alien-substances chappie. Will do. Anything else?'

'I don't think so, at the moment, thanks, Freddie.'

The second message was from Bob Bailey. Slider tried his office, and was told he was at the site already, and rang him there on his mobile.

'I thought you'd like to know that we came up with more oil traces,' Bailey said. 'On the files in that filing cabinet and on the front door. I think we can get a good enough sample to analyse, possibly get a match when you get a suspect. D'you want to go ahead?'

'Yes, please. Bung it off to Les Patterson, will you? Freddie Cameron says he's found oil on the clothes, too.'

'Careless buggers, criminals,' said Bailey.

'Anything else?'

'Footprints by the filing cabinet. Two, where he stood still, probably while he was looking through the drawer. They're really only impressions in the pile of the carpet, so I can't get much for you – no nice whorls and lugs – but it looks to be some kind of heavy boot, not the leather-soled city shoes the victim was wearing. And smaller. Victim wore a size eleven, and these are a nine at the most – I'd say possibly even an eight, given that with a boot the outside profile tends to be bigger than with a shoe. Any good?'

'I don't know yet. Were the boot marks oily too?'

'No, we didn't find any particular traces connected with them. I suppose he will have walked off anything coming up the stairs and along the corridor. Do you want me to try and trace them back? The carpet outside the flat doesn't have much pile on it,' he said doubtfully.

'Well, you can have a look, but don't knock yourself out. There've been too many people in and out.'

'OK. Well, good luck. There's a stack of press people here already. I got in early to avoid them but there's a lot of media interest in this one.'

'Don't I know it,' said Slider.

*　　*　　*

In the car on the way to the station, Atherton asked, 'Why did your father leave the BBC? It seemed such an odd thing to do. I would have thought he was at the top of the tree there.'

'It seemed odd to me, too,' she said. 'Until I took into account the change in the BBC culture. Dad had been there for ever, and he couldn't stand the new regime. He felt – we both feel – that the news ought to be taken seriously. The Beeb kept dumbing it down until the Six was little more than a magazine programme and the Ten not much better. And he didn't like the editorial control. He felt a journalist ought to be allowed to tell it the way it seemed to him. Well, of course, being Dad he didn't keep his feelings to himself. He spoke out a little too frankly for the bosses, made himself unpopular, and was invited to leave.'

'Sacked?' Atherton asked.

She made a comical face. 'Nobody's sacked from the BBC. But they have ways of punishing you if you don't go when you're invited. He was ready to go, anyway. He was fed up with it, and wanted a change. He was at the top of his game and he didn't think he'd have any difficulty in getting another job. And he didn't. He started with the DTI the moment his notice at the Beeb ended.'

'But why there?'

'Oh, it was one of the government's periodical recruitment drives of outsiders. Every now and then they have a spasm of thinking they need media savvy types with outside experience. And of course everyone had heard of Dad. The news that he and the Beeb weren't on speaking terms any more filtered through and they were thrilled with the idea of having someone who knew the organisation from the inside but didn't like it.' She gave him a frank look. 'They're pretty paranoid about Auntie, you know.'

'And did he like it there?'

'He did at first. He said it was interesting seeing government from the inside, and quite exciting to be close to the seat of power. But he never thought much of Sid Andrew, and he got frustrated at the way things were done.'

'Specifically?'

'Oh, I don't know really. He didn't go into detail with me.

I think he just felt too many things were happening behind closed doors. He was never a great one for conspiracy,' she said with a wry smile.

'Why did he choose the DTI?'

'He didn't – they chose him. He'd had a lot of experience covering industrial relations and disputes before he became a foreign correspondent, so I suppose they thought he'd speak their language. But mostly I think they just wanted to have the kudos of getting Ed Stonax of the BBC on to their books. I think he felt he was pretty under-used.'

She lapsed into silence and as he had to concentrate just then on the traffic there was a silence between them. When he could look again, he saw her staring at her hands, her head bowed. It was not a happy posture.

'I'm sorry,' he said, 'do you mind talking about him?'

She roused herself from her reverie. 'No,' she said. 'Talking about him helps me stop thinking about what's happened. I can't take it in, except in tiny flashes, and then it hurts too much. I just want to see him and talk to him about it, because he always had the best ideas about everything. Is that stupid? To want to talk to someone about who murdered them?'

'Who would know better?' said Atherton.

She screwed up her eyes in pain. 'I hate that word. Murdered. I can't take it. Not Dad! Not him!'

He reached across and touched her hand and hers folded quickly round his and hung on, as though for salvation. 'We'll be there soon. It's the next turning. Do you want to go off and do other things? You've got a key for the house so you can come and go as you like.'

She squeezed his hand and then drew hers back. 'I haven't got anything else to do,' she said. 'And I want to help. I want to come in with you.'

'All right, then,' Atherton said, turning into Stanlake Road.

Slider looked surprised. 'What's come over you?'

'I think you ought to know the answer to that, seeing you started with Joanna when she was a witness in the Austin case.'

'And as I remember you thoroughly disapproved.'

'And you said she wasn't a material witness, which she

wasn't, only happened to know the deceased. Emily wasn't even in the country. She's just the victim's daughter.'

'All the same, at a moment when she's in emotional turmoil—'

'This is a moral objection, then, not a police procedural one?' Atherton asked with his head up.

'It's not like you,' Slider said.

'No, it isn't. And for the record, she came on to me. And I've no intention of letting her down. I'm extremely serious about her.'

Slider surveyed his friend's face and was baffled. Atherton was a serial womaniser and he was so attractive to the opposite sex he had to fight them off with a plank. But to be bedding a woman when she'd only found out that day that her father had been murdered . . . When Emily Stonax was back in her right mind, she might well bring a complaint, and though Atherton hadn't broken any specific rule it could be viewed as misconduct. As to including her in the investigation – would it make her more or less likely to want to sue if she saw the way the department operated? On the other hand, she might have useful insights to share. Joanna had been extremely helpful during the Austin case.

'She can't sit in on our meetings,' he said at last. 'But you can pass things on to her unless I specifically say you can't. You'll have to use your judgement about how much you want to tell her.'

'She wants to help. She wants to be useful.'

'Well, I expect she will be,' Slider said.

'Can't we give her something to do? She says she's very good at research. She must be, given her job.' Slider began shaking his head halfway through this, and Atherton added, 'I brought in my own laptop, so she wouldn't have to use one of ours.'

'If anything comes up that's suitable, we'll talk about it then,' Slider said, standing up. 'For now, I have a meeting to conduct.'

When everyone was assembled and more or less quiet, Slider began with the summary.

'In the case of Edward Philip Stonax, BSc, PhD, DBA—'

McLaren looked up from his fried egg sandwich. 'It's not spelt like it sounds, then?'

Slider continued, but louder. 'Ed Stonax was killed yesterday morning by a single blow to the head with something like a cosh. His pockets were emptied and his watch was removed – an expensive Rolex. We believe his wallet, credit cards and mobile phone were also taken.'

'I've asked Mick Hutton to put a trace on the mobile,' Swilley said.

'Thanks. OK, so far it looks like simple robbery from the person. However, Bob Bailey found oily fingermarks – gloved – on a filing cabinet in Stonax's office in the flat, and a file seems to have been removed from it – at least, there's an empty hanging folder. So there may be another motive. One of the neighbours, Mrs Koontz, saw a motorbike courier leaving the flats at half past seven when she was walking her dog.'

'Guv,' said Hart, 'how did she know he was a courier and not just any old bloke in leathers?'

'Good question. Mackay?'

Mackay looked at his notes of the interview with Mrs Koontz. 'She didn't say he was, she just said he was a man in leathers and a dark helmet. He was carrying a large envelope, and he got on to a motorbike which had a white box on the back, and put the envelope in it. The box had a logo on it. So I assumed from that he was a courier of some sort.'

'Fair enough. Now, Freddie Cameron says there were traces of oil on the victim's pockets and sleeve, and the security door to the building wasn't working, so anyone could have come in off the street. Conclusions?'

'It looks,' said Hollis, 'as though either someone posed as a courier to rob Stonax—'

'Or someone wants to make us think that's what happened,' said Atherton.

'The courier might have been legitimate. Did anyone in the building receive a visit from a courier that morning?' Slider asked.

'No-one said they did,' Hart reported.

'Better check that point.'

'Guv, there was that biro found underneath the body,' she

went on. 'Say the murderer *was* pretending to be a courier, he could've asked Stonax to sign something and given him the biro. That could've been where it came from.'

'Good point. Now, further to this courier theory, as far as it *is* one, the caretaker, Dave Borthwick, has a bike in his basement, a Triumph. However the bike does *not* have a box on the back. Hollis, have you looked into Borthwick yet?'

'Yes, guv, and he's got some previous. No burglary or robbery, but he's done some thieving. Started with nicking cars for joyriding when he was fourteen. Nicking hubcaps and wire wheels to order when he was fifteen. Then as an adult, got done for stealing tools from B and Q – cautioned. Stealing a motorbike – got community service for that. Couple of drunk and disorderlies. And he was involved in that car-ringing gang four years ago, but there wasn't enough evidence against him and there were no charges brought. Nothing against him since then, and he got the caretaker's job at Valancy House just over two years ago.'

'How come they took him on with a record like that?' Fathom asked.

'I don't suppose anyone asked,' Hollis said. 'The land-lord's a property company, JK Holdings, owns all three of those identical blocks in Riverene Road. Previous caretaker left suddenly, and they'd be in a hurry to get someone in, not wanting to leave the place empty. Caretaker gets the flat plus a small salary to do general maintenance and a bit of light cleaning of the public areas – hall and stairs. I gave 'em a ring and they said there'd been no complaints against him, so we have to reckon he was discharging his duties all right.'

'Yeah,' said Hart. 'The average age in that building must be about ninety-five, and them old trouts really love complaining.'

'But if it was Borthwick who did it,' Fathom said, 'why would he dress himself up as a courier to do the robbery? I mean, he must have had plenty of opportunities to do the place over while people were out.'

'Yeah, that would look good, him being the caretaker!' Hart said derisively. 'Of course he had to cover himself up, because any of the old biddies would've recognised him.

And he had to make it look like an outsider, didn't he, to take the heat off himself? That's why he broke the security door.'

'Hmm,' said Slider. 'But he'd not done anything like that before. Why Stonax, why robbery from the person, and why now?'

'Maybe he'd seen the F283,' Hart said. 'People'd kill for that Cyber-box. He wouldn't have any trouble shifting it afterwards. Say he'd seen Stonax come in using it? He might not've meant to kill him – just hit him a bit too hard.'

'But what about the oil smears on the filing cabinet?' Slider said. 'If the Cyber-box was his object, what was he doing in the office?'

Hart shrugged. 'Maybe once he'd slugged Stonax he reckoned he might as well look round. Hoping to find some cash or something portable.'

'He didn't take anything,' Atherton said.

'Maybe he was disturbed,' Mackay said. 'Thought he heard something. If it wasn't his usual style, he would have been well nervous.'

'All right,' said Slider, 'we'd better turn him over. Bring him in for questioning, and search his flat while he's here. Get some samples of oil from various parts of the motorbike and send them off to Les Patterson. If we can get a match on that we'll know something, at least. What else?'

Swilley spoke up. 'Boss, there's something about Candida Scott-Chatton that doesn't make sense.'

'Her name for a start,' McLaren muttered.

'She seemed as if she was hiding something. And she didn't seem upset enough. Then, Stonax's daughter says she stuck by her father after his bit of trouble last year, but Candida's secretary says she dropped him like a hot potato and started to go out with Freddie Bell.'

Slider frowned. 'But the daughter says she gave Stonax an expensive watch for Christmas.'

'A *really* expensive watch,' Atherton said. 'Depending on the model, a Rolex Oyster Perpetual knocks out at five thousand upwards. Not the sort of thing you give to someone you aren't seeing any more.'

'Maybe it was Freddie Bell give it her,' Hart said. 'He blows his nose on fifty-pound notes.'

'Worth another go,' Slider nodded to Swilley. 'Especially with the Freddie Bell connection. I can't see the head of the Countryside Protection Trust lamming Stonax on the head, but Freddie Bell's a different matter.'

'He's got no form, guv,' Hollis reminded him. 'Clean as a whistle.'

'A whistle might be shiny on the outside, but on the inside it's full of germs and old spit. Have another word with Scott-Chatton, Norma, and see where it leads. And Hollis, see if there's anything *un*official against Bell. I've got an idea in the back of my head there was some sort of story about him a while back.'

'So you don't think it was robbery from the person, then?' Fathom said.

'I'm not at the stage of thinking anything yet,' Slider said, his old formula. 'I'm just looking for anomalies and asking questions. Mackay, go back to Mrs Koontz and find out more about this courier she saw. What kind and size of envelope? What did the logo look like? Where did he go? McLaren, did anyone in the building have a courier call that morning. Everyone else, start going through the papers. Questions?' No-one spoke. He looked at Hart. 'Regarding Bates's house being watched?'

She started blankly, then jerked. 'Oh! Yeah – I forgot for a minute. Phil Warzynski says the house was sealed off when the forensic mob had done their number. They keep a man on all the time, who keeps a note of who goes in and out.'

'So there have been people going in and out?' Slider asked.

'Various SO people, but they all have to have proper ID. And everything they take out is logged. Phil says they took out a load of electronics gear a couple of weeks ago, but it was all signed for.'

'So he couldn't be living there,' Mackay said.

'But he must have a place to hang out,' Hart went on, 'and if he was following you, guv, it must be fairly local.'

'We need to look into his local contacts,' Slider said. 'Anyone he might bunk up with, any other properties he's got an interest in.'

'And what about his sidekicks?' Atherton said. 'His driver, Thomas Mark, and that bodyguard of his, what was his name? Norman something?'

'Norman Grant. But he's still inside,' Slider said. 'He was nicked for carrying a firearm at the same time that we took his boss. But there was that butler-type he employed – what was his name?'

'Archie Gordon,' Hollis supplied. 'He and Mark disappeared when Bates was taken, and we don't know where they are. They might be helping him.'

Atherton looked significantly at Slider. 'It seems we could do with someone to do some research, but who have we got to spare?'

'Oh, all right,' Slider said. 'Give her the biographical bits of the file and the names, and see what she can come up with.'

'Her who?' Hart demanded.

Atherton wasn't going to answer so Slider did. 'Emily Stonax. She wants to help, and she needs something to do to keep her mind off things.'

'Makes sense,' Norma said. 'We're not officially on Bates, and she's not officially here.'

Seven

Into the Valley of Debt
Flowed the 500

S lider let Borthwick sweat, once they'd booked him in, while Atherton and Fathom searched the flat. Atherton phoned straight away with the most urgent piece of information Slider had requested, and once he had that, Slider went up to see Porson.

He found the old man pacing about his office while he watched the news on television.

'They've got your arrest on already,' he said as Slider entered. They stood in silence watching on the rolling newscast as Borthwick came out between two uniformed policemen and was helped into the marked car with the usual hand-on-the-head, while the news ribbon underneath read 'Arrest made in Stonax case'.

'I thought they'd jump on it, but that's even quicker than I expected,' Slider said.

Porson looked at him, oddly still for a moment. 'I've had a call from Mr Wetherspoon, congratulating us on our quick work,' he said neutrally. 'D'you want to tell me what's going on?'

'There was a footmark, just an impression in the carpet pile, by the filing cabinet where we think a file was taken. Bob Bailey says it was no more than a size nine. Victim's feet are an eleven, and Atherton's just rung through to say Borthwick's various bits of footwear in the flat – ' disgusting trainers, was what Atherton had said – 'are size twelve.'

'Easy enough to fake a footprint larger than your own,' Porson said, 'but you can't make your feet smaller.'

'Exactly. I think Borthwick's being set up to take the fall.

That's why I told them to take Borthwick out of the front door, make sure the press got a good look at him.'

'Stupid old Mr Plod's taken the bait, eh?' Porson was on the move again.

'I don't like being led by the nose,' Slider said grimly. 'So now I need to know if Borthwick was a willing accomplice, and who he'll roll over for if I lean on him.'

'So if it's not robbery from the person, what is it?'

Slider shrugged unhappily. 'It's got to be something to do with Stonax's past life.'

'The missing file?'

'Possibly. But that could be another red herring. His ex-lady friend was going out with Freddie Bell—'

That caught his attention. 'Tasty!'

'But we think she was still seeing Stonax.'

Porson got the point at once. 'Oh, Freddie Bell would love that.'

'Question is, would he be devoted to her enough to hit his rival?'

'Well, I'll leave you to find out. We'll let them think we've bought the story, anyway, hold on to Borthwick as long as we can. I want to give you time to look into every asset of Stonax's life.'

'Yes, sir.'

Slider was at the door when Porson said quietly, 'What about the other business?'

'Sir?'

'You had a little outing yesterday.' Slider turned back reluctantly. The old man always knew everything. 'Any luck?'

'No, sir.'

Porson seemed to sigh. 'I can't expect you to take it lying down, like a sitting duck. You're a tethered goat, and Headquarters've got no right to make you a sacrificial lamb, in my book. But bigger things are at stake here than either you or I know about. We've been pacifically told not to investigate, and if you pee on some SO's carpet, they'll be down on you like a ton of bricks. I won't be flavour of the month either,' he added, almost as an afterthought. Like a good general, he thought about his troops first.

'Whatever I did, it was without your permission, sir, and behind your back. You didn't know anything about it.'

'Didn't know anything about what?' Porson barked.

'Yes, sir.' He paused to see if anything else was coming, and headed for the door again.

This time, Porson said very quietly, but with feeling, 'For God's sake be careful. This bastard's dangerous. You're not in the Job to get your head blown off.'

To which no reply was needed.

Dave Borthwick looked as though he hadn't slept. His face was both puffy and drawn. His hair, too long, thinning on the top, hung down in limp and greasy strands, and he smelled of sweat both old and new, as though he hadn't changed his clothes in a couple of days. He had a full beard and a gold earring in the right earlobe, but neither feature managed to give him a buccaneer air. He was a big man, heavily built, both in the manner of muscles gone to seed and too much indulgence in fast food, pub snacks and beer. His sheer size and weight would give him the edge in a fight, but he didn't look like a man who had much to do with edges in any aspect of his life. There was about him, to the experienced copper's eye, the look of a whiner, the kind of small-time crook who thought the world owed him a living, and that it wasn't coming up to scratch.

Slider felt that whoever had chosen Borthwick as accomplice had got the wrong man. This was not a hero ready to throw himself on the grenade. Atherton described him as thixotropic: turns to jelly when agitated. But Slider supposed they hadn't had any choice.

He went in to the interview almost with relish. 'Well, Dave – d'you mind if I call you Dave?' He didn't give Borthwick a chance to answer. 'This is a bit of a turn up, isn't it? You're in a lot of trouble, you know. A lot of trouble.'

Borthwick's eyes flitted about like moths round a table lamp. 'I never done nothing. You got nothing on me.'

'Don't be silly,' Slider said dismissively. 'We've got everything on you. In case you hadn't noticed, one of your tenants got murdered yesterday.'

Panic and self-righteousness competed for control of

Borthwick's features. 'Bloody 'ell, what's goin' on?' he cried in what sounded like genuine pain. 'Just because some geezer gets offed! Whajjer come down on me for? I never even knew the bloke. All the people 'at live in that house, and just because I got a bit o' form . . . You lot are all the same. I been clean for four soddin' years, but you lot can't ever give a bloke a fuckin' break. I never done *nothing*! What . . . what . . .?'

Slider intervened before he exploded. 'Shut up, Dave,' he said, not unkindly. 'To save you wasting your breath, I feel I should tell you that a man in motorbike leathers and a helmet with a dark visor was seen leaving the house just about the time of the murder, and we've found leathers and helmet in your place that match the description. Also there were marks and smears of oil on the victim's clothing where his pockets were searched. Now, in case you don't know it, the oil in a motor quickly picks up impurities – dirt, soot, tiny specks of swarf – and the pattern of those impurities is unique to that machine. It's like DNA for motorbikes, if you like. You know what DNA is, don't you? It stands for Do Not Argue, because there's no getting away from it. It's the ultimate proof. And would it surprise you very much to learn that the oil from the victim's clothing matches the oil from your bike?' He hadn't had the report back yet, of course, so he couldn't say that it *did* match, but linguistic subtlety would be lost on Borthwick anyway.

Borthwick had lost his voice at last. He simply stared, appalled, his mouth open. Slider almost wished he would put up more of a fight. This was like taking sweeties from babies.

Slider went on, 'Not only that, Dave, but while we were looking round your flat we found the money. Five hundred pounds in used notes under your mattress, and another thousand in a drawer in your kitchen. The drawer also contains,' he added in deep pity, 'the victims' watch.'

It took time for this to filter through Borthwick's mental rigidity. 'The victim's—?' he said. 'That watch was—?' Slider nodded. 'Bastards!' Borthwick yelled suddenly. He heaved in his chair, and Atherton, standing behind Slider, took a step and said menacingly, 'Sit down!'

Borthwick subsided but he had found his tongue. 'I never did it, I swear on my mum's grave! I never knew the bloke!

Never even been *in* his flat. Some of 'em – that old Koontz bitch next door – there's always something wrong. Mend this, fix that. Like I'm a bloody 'eaven slave. Called me up there to change a light bulb last week. I mean, what am I? I don't get paid to run up and down after the likes of 'er!' He recollected the specific from the general complaint that was threatening to carry him away. 'But that Stonax bloke, he's never once asked for anything, so I've never been up there, never. Never set foot in there.'

'Funny you should say that,' Slider said. 'About the foot. It's the one thing in your favour.'

'What the *fuck* are you talking about?' Borthwick cried in desperate bewilderment.

'You've been set up, Dave, is what I'm talking about.' He watched this sink in. 'They want you to take the rap for them. And it's not just any old rap, it's murder in the course of a robbery, which is life, automatic. Am I getting through to you, Dave old pal? Even with remission you'll be an old, old man by the time you get out. If you get out at all. You might die in there. Not nice places, gaols, you know.'

Borthwick was trying to think now, which was painful to watch, like a dog walking on its hind legs. 'But – you *can't*,' he stumbled, 'prove – I mean, I never done it so you can't—'

Slider counted on his fingers. 'Eye witness, oil matching your bike, money, victim's watch. Plus you're the man in charge of the security door, which was so conveniently not working that day.'

'But that's the 'ole point, that's the thing. He—' Borthwick stopped himself, but the protest had begun eagerly, even passionately.

Slider felt the thrill of knowing he had been right. He nodded sympathetically. 'Yes, it didn't look like much, did it? But, come on, Dave, did you never think it was a lot of money for what they wanted you to do?'

'It was business,' he protested. 'He said it was worth a lot to his business.'

'It's worth a lot for them to get you to do life for their murder. But is it enough for you?' Borthwick stared, calculating. 'Come on, Dave. Use your loaf. Tell me all about it.

Why should you go down for them? They've set you up, and you're not going to let them get away with it, are you?'

'If I tell you,' Borthwick said slowly, 'and they find out . . . He looked like a right tasty bloke. I dunno . . .'

'Twenty years inside,' Slider said. 'Minimum. And for what?'

'All right,' he said, and seemed to deflate, as if his sigh was letting more than air out of him. He didn't seem to know where to begin, so Slider helped him along.

'Where did you meet the man?'

'In the pub,' he answered easily. 'I go down there most nights.'

'Which one's that?'

'The Sally.' This was what locals called the Salutation, an old-fashioned Fullers' pub on King Street, practically opposite the end of Riverene Road.

'That's a bit posh for you, isn't it?'

Borthwick shrugged. 'It's nearest. Anyway, I like a proper pint, not that pissy lager,' he added, and went up a tiny notch in Slider's estimation.

'So how did you know this bloke?'

'I never. He come up to me when I was sitting at the bar, and he says wasn't I the caretaker at Valancy House.'

'How did he know that?' Atherton put in.

'I asked him that,' Borthwick said as if answering an accusation of stupidity. 'He said he'd seen me go in and out. Anyway, he bought me a pint, and asked if I was interested in a business proposition.'

'And you said yes, because you're in a bit of financial trouble, aren't you?' Atherton put in. 'All the paperwork in your flat seems to consist of betting slips and unpaid bills.'

Borthwick shrugged resentfully.

'So what was this business, then?' Slider asked.

'This bloke said he worked for a security firm – Ring 4 – and he wanted to get the maintenance contracts for places like mine. He said it was worth a lot of money to his firm if he could get in, because there's 'undreds of security doors around the area. And then there's other stuff – CCTV an' that – what people are putting in all the time. He said he just needed a foot 'old to get started.'

'And that's where you came in?'

'I told him it was Wellings what put our doors in, and they still do the maintenance. So he said all I had to do was put the doors out of order, wait for someone to complain, and then call him to come in and fix 'em. Tell the tenants Wellings said they couldn't come out for two days, but his firm guaranteed a one-hour call-out. Well,' he added, 'the residents couldn't give a monkey's who does the maintenance, it's the company, JK Holdings, and they won't care as long as it costs the same. So the bloke says he'd start off doing it cheaper than Wellings just to get 'em hooked, and there'd be something for me if he got the contract.'

'And what exactly did he tell you to do?'

'I was to pull the fuse so the doors didn't work. When there's a power cut or anything the locking system shuts off and they just open and close like ordinary doors – so people could still get in and out in an emergency.'

'I understand. Then what?'

'Well, I was to ring him on this number he give me, and he'd come round and fix it, sweet as you like. He'd give me a thou before, and the same after.'

Atherton intervened. 'Two thousand? But there was only five hundred under the mattress.'

Borthwick looked sulky. 'I put a bit on a horse. Bloke I know give me a tip. Pretty Polly, two thirty at Newmarket.'

Evidently it hadn't won. 'Did he say when all this was to happen, or leave it up to you?' Slider asked.

'Nah, he said it had to be when he was in the area so he could get there quick. So he said I should do it Tuesday. Said he'd be waiting somewhere near for me call. Anyway, I done my bit, and he comes all right Tuesday and his bloke fixes the door—'

'His bloke?'

'Well, he was like the manager or sales rep or summink, wasn't he? He don't do the work himself. He had his technical bloke in the van, waiting. Anyway, he fixes it, but Tuesday night when I get back from the pub it's out again, and when I ring 'is number – nothing.'

'There was no answer?'

'It was turned off. It was a mobile. I keep ringing it, but nothing. And the bloody door's still not fixed.'

'What about the lift?' Atherton asked.

'It's on the same system. One goes out the other goes out. The wiring's shit in these old places, anyway.' Borthwick looked bitter. 'I'll have them old bitches nagging me blue about it. I dunno what the bloke did to it, but it was definitely working all right after he left. Could have been just an accident, I s'pose?' he said hopefully, looking from one to the other.

'I don't think so, Dave,' Slider said kindly. 'I don't think the nice man gave you two thousand quid to get the maintenance contract. I think he fixed the door on a timer so it would go out when he wanted it to go out, so he could slip in and murder Mr Stonax when he wanted. And, of course,' he added, as Borthwick paled at the reminder of the shit he was in, 'so as to make it look even more as if you did it.'

'Overkill, really,' Atherton said, 'seeing you had the victim's watch. When did you take that?'

'I never!' Borthwick protested fiercely. 'It was the bloke, in the pub, just when he was going, he said was I interested in nice watches, he had a mate brought 'em in from Switzerland, proper Rolexes real cheap. I said I might be. I mean, stuff like that, you can usually knock 'em out to your mates if they're cheap enough. Well, I didn't reckon they'd be genuine ones, but if they was *good* fakes . . . Anyway, he said he'd let me have one as a sample, and if I didn't want any more, I could still keep it for meself, part of the fee for the job. So when he gives me the other grand, I says what about the watch, and he says he's forgotten it, he'll bring it me another time, next time he calls. Well, I thought that was that, y'know? And I wasn't that bothered, tell you the trufe, but this morning I found he'd pushed it under the door, in an omberlope. Well, it looked a bit nice, like it *was* genuine, so I stuck it in the drawer. I was going to take it to my mate Timmy, see what he thought about it. I mean, the bloke said he could do 'em for thirty quid each, and I bet I could knock a lot of 'em out at fifty, maybe more,' he concluded excitedly.

'Dave, it wasn't a genuine offer,' Slider reminded him. 'This man doesn't really have a friend who imports Rolexes.

It was the victim's watch and it was taken off his dead wrist to help incriminate you.'

'Oh. Yeah.' Borthwick slumped, looking sullen.

'When did you find it?' Atherton asked.

'I dunno,' Borthwick said sulkily. 'This morning, when I went out to see what all the fuss was about. When you lot arrived.'

'It wasn't there last night when you got back from the pub?'

'I dunno. I don't go in and out that way unless I'm on me bike. I got a door into the yard I use, and I walked to the pub.' He seemed suddenly to tire. 'What's going to happen to me?' he asked, almost indifferently. All the excitement had taken it out of him.

'We're going to keep you here for a while, while you help us with our inquiries. And if you are completely co-operative, there will probably be no charges against you. What they'll think of you at Valancy House I can't tell.'

'Wasn't my fault,' he said. 'I never done nothing.'

Slider waved that aside. 'Tell me what this man looked like.'

Borthwick made an effort, rubbing his hand back and forth across his beard to aid memory. 'He was tall – about six foot. Buff – like he worked out a lot. Wore a nice leather jacket – expensive. Nice clothes. He looked the business all right.'

'Name? Age?'

'He said his name was Patrick Steel. I dunno his age. Not old. Not young. Mid-thirties, maybe. I'm not good at ages. Dark hair, real poof's-parlour cut like yours,' he nodded at Atherton, 'not a five quid back an' sides job like yours.' This to Slider. 'You could see he was well-off. But he was a hard man, not some soft office job wanker. You wouldn't want to cross him.'

'What about the other man, the man who did the repair?'

'I never seen him. This Steel, he comes to the door, gives me the money, says he'll get his man in, what's waiting in the van, and he kinda like waits for me to go. So I go in me flat and shut the door, because you don't piss off a bloke like him, know't I mean?'

'All right, I'm going to ask you to look at some photographs later, see if you can spot Patrick Steel, and maybe ask you to help create a photofit. Meanwhile you can give me the telephone number.'

'I got the number here.' He handed over a dirty scrap of paper.

'Is that his writing?'

'No, he like told me it an' I wrote it down.'

A careful villain, Slider thought. He stood up. 'That's all for now. We'll probably talk again later. Do you want anything? Cup of tea?'

'Two sugars,' Borthwick said eagerly. 'And can I have summink to eat? I ain't had nothing since last night.'

Outside, Slider said to the constable, 'Get him some tea, two sugars, and a couple of rounds of bacon sarnies. Make him feel loved.'

'Be the first time in his life,' Atherton said as they walked upstairs together. 'Are you sure you want to bother? Subtlety's wasted on him.'

'Oxygen's wasted on him,' Slider said.

'What a dipstick,' Atherton said. 'If they gave Air Miles for stupidity, he'd be the first man on Mars. Are you going to run that number?'

'Have to go through the motions,' Slider said, 'but Fort Knox to a Frisbee it'll be at the bottom of a sewer by now. And he won't find a photograph. Whoever did the fronting, he won't have a record, Patrick Steel won't be his name, and he won't have worked for Ring 4. I wonder how he fixed the doors to fail again.'

'Something on a timer that blew the fuse,' Atherton said. 'Shouldn't be hard to rig. Want to get someone in to look at it?'

'Yes, we'd better do that. It might have a signature method about it, like a bomb-maker's. But I'm not sure it's going to be that easy. This is starting to look horribly professional. I think we're going to have to trawl Stonax's life to find out why someone wanted to go to so much trouble to kill him.'

They climbed a few steps in silence and then Slider looked at Atherton, and Atherton anticipated his thought. 'You're glad now I took the trouble to befriend his daughter, aren't you?'

'Oh, is that what you call it nowadays – befriending?'

'I'm not sure how much help she'll be, given that she lives

in New York, and it seems that he kept a lot of secrets from her,' Atherton said, 'but I know she'll want to help, and she'll do everything she can.'

'Yes,' said Slider. 'And we'll need all the help we can get, going through his papers. Maybe I'd better ask Porson's permission to bring her in on the case. Now we know it isn't Borthwick, he'll see the point.'

'I wish you hadn't mentioned bacon sandwiches,' Atherton complained as they reached the corridor. 'It's made me hungry.'

'We'll send someone for tea and sticky buns,' Slider said, turning into the office.

McLaren was there, at his desk, and Atherton said, 'Oy, Maurice, you know all about the ponies: heard of a horse called Pretty Polly?'

McLaren looked up. 'You don't half pick 'em. It was in the two thirty at Newbury yesterday. Came in so late it had to tiptoe into the stables. How much d'you lose?'

'Not me, another bloke. Put a monkey on it.'

'Barmy,' McLaren shook his head sadly.

Slider was heading on to his office. Atherton said to McLaren, 'You're not hungry, are you?'

'Kidding? I could eat a nun's arse through a convent gate.'

'Excellent. Then while you're in the canteen, can you get something for the guv'nor and me? One tea, one coffee, and two sticky buns. Pay you when you get back.'

McLaren grumbled, but he got up. Never let it be said he shirked a trip to the canteen, even for a friend.

Eight
Outrageous Fortune

S willey traced Candida Scott-Chatton to her home this time, and found a very different person from the poised, controlling woman of the previous day. It was as if the reality of Stonax's death has suddenly sunk in. She didn't quite look unkempt – probably she could have emerged from an earthquake with no hair out of place – but there was something ragged in her expression and demeanour, and when she moved it was both sluggish and curiously jerky, as though she had taken some drug and it hadn't quite worked off.

An elderly, uniformed maid had let Swilley in, and she was shown into a drawing-room which was like the office all over again, only more so – high ceilings, antiques, oil paintings, bronzes; that expensive silence only the houses of the very wealthy seem to have, the stillness of air that no unruly passions would ever stir; the absence of smell, except for a breath of clean carpets and the faintest ghost of potpourri.

When Scott-Chatton entered she was preceded by two elegant whippets, one black with a white mark on its breast, the other brindle-grey. They looked at Swilley from a distance, twitching their tucked-down tails ingratiatingly but not venturing close. Swilley noted that they were both wearing diamond collars. It struck her as not what she would have expected from Scott-Chatton – too vulgarly ostentatious. It also looked, to her admittedly inexpert eye, as if they were real diamonds.

'Eos and Aurora,' Scott-Chatton said, as if Swilley had asked. 'Do you like dogs?'

'I can take 'em or leave 'em,' Swilley said.

Scott-Chatton did not ask her to sit, nor sat herself, but

remained standing where she had halted, a little way into the
room, looking at Swilley with eyes that were no longer chips
of ice, rubbing her fingers very slowly as if they were cold,
or aching. Swilley had seen old people do that, and it was not
a gesture she would have associated with this woman. 'I have
a few questions I want to put to you, if that's all right.'

Scott-Chatton searched her face. 'It wasn't robbery, was it?'

'We don't know yet, but it may have had something to do
with Mr Stonax's life, so we need to find out as much about
him as possible. I'm afraid we're a bit confused about what
your relationship was with him. His daughter seems to think
you and he were still going out together, which is what you
suggested to me, but someone else says you dropped him
when he got the sack from the DTI.'

'I can guess who that was,' she said. 'You mustn't take
everything Shawna says literally. She has a grudge against
me.'

'Oh?' said Swilley receptively.

'She came in to work one day quite unsuitably dressed and
I asked her to go home and change. Naturally she took that
as a mortal insult, and she's been waging a war of attrition
on me ever since.'

'Why don't you sack her, then?'

Scott-Chatton only raised her eyebrows. 'You can't dismiss
a person these days except for stealing. Surely you know that?'

'She says Mr Stonax tried to persuade you to keep seeing
him and you refused. She overheard him saying he wanted to
talk to you and you saying it wouldn't make any difference.'
A blush of anger coloured Scott-Chatton's face and Swilley
reckoned she might yet find a way of sacking young Shawna,
employment laws or no employment laws. 'Also the gossip
papers say you're going out with Mr Freddie Bell of the Three
Bells gaming company.'

Now Scott-Chatton sat. She did it gracefully, but there was
a look of involuntariness about it. The dogs came close to her,
shivering in that disconcerting way whippets have.

'I'll tell you everything,' she said, 'because I can see otherwise you will take away all the wrong impressions. But I don't
think it will help you, because I don't understand any of it
myself.'

Swilley seated herself, uninvited, in the chair opposite, and got out her notebook. 'Go on.'

'I want you to know that I loved Ed,' she began, looking at her hands. 'He was a wonderful man – a truly *good* man. He was tireless in his pursuit of truth. He was honourable in his profession. And more than that, he was so warm – he lit up a room when he came into it. I was still married when I first met him, though Hugo and I had already separated. When my divorce came through, Ed and I were going to marry, but then his ex-wife died, and he said for decency's sake we ought to wait a few months. I honoured him for that. How many men would have so much delicacy?' She looked up as she said this, as if she wanted an answer.

Swilley was interested in the choice of the word delicacy, and wondered what, really, it meant. She declined to answer, saying merely, 'Go on.'

Scott-Chatton made a little, unhappy movement of her shoulders. 'I wish to God, now, he had not been so sensitive. At least we would have been married. We would have had that. As it was, that awful trouble came along.'

'The three-in-a-bed high jinks?'

She flinched at the words. 'Please, don't say it like that. And don't think for a moment there was anything in it. I *know* he was innocent.'

'How do you know?'

'Because he told me.' She met Swilley's eyes. 'I know what you're thinking, but you're wrong. He would never lie to me. And he wasn't the sort of man who would ever do something like that, anyway. The whole thing was a fraud, to blackmail him into leaving the department.'

'If you knew he was innocent, why did you dump him?'

'I *didn't*,' she cried, with sufficient anguish to make the little dogs stare up at her in what looked like shock. Voices were never raised in these hallowed spaces. 'I would have stood by him publicly, but Ed persuaded me to *seem* to part company with him, for the sake of our various causes. I was very much against it, but he said I had to think of the greater good. The scandal was quite dreadful at the time, and he said it would rub off on to me, and on to the Trust and the other various charities that we had both worked so hard for. Donors would have pulled out. The press would have revived it every time the Trust was mentioned. He said I would be throwing away all we had worked for. We argued about it very much – that must be what Shawna overheard, and she got it quite the wrong way around, you see. But I knew there was truth in what he said and I allowed myself to be persuaded. But I wish – you don't know *how* I wish – I had resisted him.'

Swilley wasn't interested in her remorse. 'If the thing was a fraud, why didn't he make a fuss? Challenge it? Take it to court?'

'They had the photographs. Oh, *I* knew they were faked, *he* knew they were faked – well, of course *he* did,' she corrected herself with a little shake of the head. 'But there they were, and at the first hint of resistance on his part they went to the papers. You know the rest. They were splashed everywhere, and once the genie is out of the bottle you can't put it back. It's no use protesting your innocence, because no-one will believe you. As it was, if he had gone quietly when they showed the photographs to him privately, it would have saved two other people from disgrace – Sid Andrew and that poor girl. I've forgotten her name, now. Isn't that dreadful? But they were both ruined. And if he'd challenged them publicly, who knows what would have happened next?' She looked up and met Swilley's sceptical gaze, and said with a touch of heat, 'Ed said they would target me next, or his daughter. Probably both of us. He said it was better for him to say nothing and go. Photographs are easy to fake – my God, they proved that all right! – and other documents too. Imagine what they could have done to his daughter's life. I'd have been willing to risk it, for myself, but Ed wanted me to distance myself from him as soon as possible, and so – and so that's what I did.'

'So why did they want him out? And why not just sack him?' Swilley asked.

'He wouldn't tell me anything about it. He said it was better if I didn't know. But from what I can gather he had found something out that they didn't want known. They couldn't just dismiss him – they had to do it in a way that would discredit him, so that he couldn't go public with what he knew. But as to what it was – I truly don't know.' She looked at Swilley unhappily. 'You don't believe me. You think I'm exaggerating the whole affair.'

Swilley shook the comment away. 'It's not for me to say. I just have to ask questions and write down the answers. Why didn't you tell me all this the first time?'

'I was shocked. Bewildered. I didn't know what to think. I wasn't sure – what I *ought* to say. What Ed would have wanted me to say. I didn't know where it might lead, you see, if I told you all this.'

'And you're not worried now?'

She almost shrugged. 'They've killed him. How can it get any worse?' she said quietly.

There was a silence while Swilley made up her notes. Then she looked up and asked, 'How does Mr Bell come into all this?'

Candida blushed. 'It isn't what you may think.'

'What *do* I think?' Swilley invited.

'People misunderstand Freddie. He is a very kind, gentle man underneath.'

Yeah, underneath the brutal uncaring exterior, Swilley thought. 'How did you meet him?'

'At a fundraiser. He's very generous in giving to charity, and he's particularly interested in green issues.'

The only green issue Swilley would have expected him to be interested in was dollar bills but she let it pass. 'How did you start going out with him?'

She blushed deeper. 'It was after Ed – when he said I should distance myself from him. Freddie had been pursuing me for years. I'd made it clear I wasn't interested in him but he persisted, and he was very kind and thoughtful in so many ways. So – after – Ed's trouble – when he asked again – I said yes.' Her eyes filled with tears of justification. 'He's been so kind and thoughtful – and he's very good company.'

'I've seen pictures of you together at functions,' Swilley said. She had looked them up after Shawna's hint. 'It's good publicity for him.'

'And for me. For the Trust, I mean. I don't see that there's any harm in serving the greater good at the same time as . . .'

She tailed off, looking down at her dogs. She stroked their heads with a slow, almost sad movement, and Swilley suddenly guessed that Bell had given her the diamond collars for them, and that, yes, they were real diamonds. It made sense, she thought, for Freddie Bell to want to hitch himself to the respectability of Candida Scott-Chatton, the daughter of a marquess and ex-wife of an earl; and for her . . . well, he probably made generous donations to her charities.

'Did he know you were still seeing Mr Stonax?'

She looked up, startled. 'I – I don't think so. He's never said anything about it. Ed and I were very discreet. No, I'm sure he didn't know.'

'Are you sleeping with him? Mr Bell, I mean,' Swilley asked brutally.

Scott-Chatton mottled and her eyes flashed as she was shaken equally by anger and embarrassment. 'I don't think that's any of your business.'

'I'm afraid everything becomes our business in a case of murder.'

She stared. 'You surely aren't thinking that Freddie had anything to do with it?'

'We have to consider all possibilities.'

'Well, I can tell you at once,' she said with determination, 'that your suggestion is as wrong as it is offensive. Freddie is much misunderstood and the media are unkind to him, but I know him well enough to be able to tell you categorically that he would never dream of such a thing. And now I think I must ask you to leave.'

She stood up, and Swilley did likewise. 'One last thing,' she said. 'When you spoke about Mr Stonax being forced to resign, and the photographs being faked, you kept saying "they". 'As in "they had to make him leave", and so on. Can you tell me who "they" are?'

She looked faintly puzzled for an instant, and then her face grew both hard and expressionless. 'I really cannot tell you. Ed told me as little about the business as possible, for my own safety. I have no idea who was behind it all.'

Swilley went away, thinking what a bleedin' liar she is, Mrs Fancypants Scottwotsit.

Swilley was reporting back to Slider when his telephone rang, and he signalled to her to wait while he answered it.

It was Bates.

'Did you find the mobile I left for you?' he asked.

'Yes, I did,' Slider said, and he made the signal to Norma that means 'get a trace on this call' and mouthed 'Bates' to her. Her eyes widened and she dashed from the room.

'I knew you'd follow it up as soon as it was used,' Bates said. 'Where was it?'

'A schoolboy found it and was using it to chat to a friend,' Slider said. He had to keep Bates talking. 'Where did you hope it would be?'

'I thought it would be fun to let you chase your tail for a while. I didn't mind where it went, as long as it was found and used. I left it near a school. I was sure no kid could resist a free phone call or two, and it seems I was right. Again. Sometimes perfection is almost wearying.'

'I'm sure it must be,' said Slider. 'Every time you brush shoulders with the law, the law comes off worse. Wouldn't you like to try getting caught, just for variety?'

Bates laughed. 'Are you trying to make friends with me, Mr Plod? I don't recommend it. Remember that I have a large grudge against you, and I intend to pay it back. I'm in the process of setting up a few little surprises for you. Do you like surprises?'

'Not especially,' Slider said, watching the door for Norma. She was using the telephone at her own desk which was just out of sight round the corner. 'But tell me, why in particular do you have a grudge against me? I wasn't the only person involved in your capture – temporary capture, I should say. In fact, I was quite a minor player. Why are you singling me out?'

'How do you know I'm singling you out?'

'I can't imagine even *you* have the resources to mount a campaign against the whole squad. What makes me special?'

'I think you will find that out sooner or later, so I don't mind telling you that you have enemies in high places – quite a distinction for such a lowly bungler, wouldn't you say? Yes, you've made enemies along the way, and those enemies have resources that make even mine look puny. They are encouraging me to put you at the top of the list. Are you pleased? Don't you think that's an honour?'

'Not really. I rather like being obscure. So, who are these mighty enemies – or are they figments of your imagination? I expect being on the run is rather stressful, and stress can bring on delusions.'

Bates laughed again, but there was an edge to it that had not been there before. 'You'll find out how delusional all this is. I shall make sure of that. And now, since you have had ample time to trace this call, I shall say goodbye and let you get on with amusing yourself. Say hello to Mick Hutton for me, by the way. I won't say I taught him all I know, but we've had some interesting conversations in our time.'

And he was gone.

Slider slammed down the receiver and went through to the CID room. Swilley was talking on the phone. She looked at him and said, 'Wait, he's here. D'you want to tell him yourself?'

Slider took the phone from her. 'Any luck?'

'No, sir,' Hutton said. 'It was a landline, but it's been routed via several satellites round the globe. We were on the third when he hung up, but even if you'd kept him talking I doubt we'd have been able to pin him down. He'll have gone in through a computer, radioed another remote computer and that will have initiated the call. Then the satellites bounce it back and forth across the world. If we could find the remote computer, we could probably trace the home computer, but it could be anywhere – New York, Tokyo, anywhere.'

'Clever stuff,' Slider said.

'Well, if you've got the equipment and the know-how, it isn't technically that difficult. Communications satellites are easy enough to get into – that's their purpose in life. And he's certainly got the know-how. Whether he's now got the equipment I can't say.'

'He seemed to know you. Sent you his regards.'

Hutton made a disgusted sound. 'I met him a few times at trade fairs and so on. I didn't know then he was anything but honest. He put up a good front – and he was working for the American trade delegation. Well, you know what that means.'

'Yes,' said Slider. It was the accepted cover for the intelligence agencies.

'It occurs to me,' Hutton said, 'that he'd have had plenty

of opportunities to set up remotes in America during his trips over there. He'd have had access to the satellites and as much kit as he could ever want. I wouldn't be surprised if he had a little place or two tucked away over there, an office in Washington, New York, maybe Seattle for the west coast. It wouldn't need to be big – a single room with a computer and a telephone and a good lock on the door. He could have rented any number of them. If you could find them, or any one of them . . .'

'Yes,' said Slider. 'Probably easier to find him.'

Swilley was sitting on Slider's windowsill with her notes. He told her the rest of what Hutton had said, and she frowned. 'But, boss, why would he mullock about with that mobile when he'd set up the safe landline?'

'Just to amuse himself,' Slider said. 'He said he wanted us to chase our own tails for a bit.'

'Do you think he could be back in his house? He'd got the kit in there, and those massive aerials. He could do all that stuff from there, easy.'

'It's sealed and guarded.'

'But suppose he had a way to sneak in—'

'A secret passage, you mean?' said Atherton from the door. 'Gosh, little Anne, fancy you thinking of something as clever as that. You're nearly as brainy as Uncle Quentin.'

Swilley defended herself. 'It'd be the last place we'd look for him, wouldn't it?'

'With reason,' Atherton said. 'Anyway, his kit was taken out, according to Notting Hill. So he'd have nothing to Famous Five himself back in there for.'

Norma gave him a look and flounced out.

'This Bates business is making everyone scratchy,' Slider said. 'You'd better go and do some paid work to put you in a better mood. You can interview Freddie Bell.'

'You know how I like hanging out with the rich and shameless,' Atherton said.

When Slider was alone again, the phone rang, and it was Joanna. At the sound of her calm voice, something in him unknotted. At least she had got there safely.

'I did what you said,' she reported, 'changed lanes and

watched the rear view, but I didn't see anything suspicious – not that I'm entirely sure what something suspicious looks like, but nobody obviously followed me. I even,' she added with pride, 'went up an exit ramp and straight back down the other side on to the motorway.'

'Very inventive of you.'

'That's what I thought. Anyway, nobody who followed me off followed me back on. So I think I'm clean.'

'I think you are too,' he said. 'But still be careful.'

'Always. But you be careful too. I hate to put it this way, but on the evidence it's you he's after.'

'On the evidence, he wants to frighten me. If he wanted to kill me he could have done it by now.'

'Doesn't mean he won't try to kill you *after* he's frightened you,' she said, sounding deadly serious. 'Is everybody doing everything they can to catch him?'

'All my people are. And the SOCA must want him very badly indeed. Try not to worry, darling—'

'I know. Bad for baby Derek.'

'You've decided it's a boy, then?'

'I just don't like the name Rebecca. I sat next to a Rebecca at school and she used to pick her nose and eat the bogies.'

'Lifelong prejudices are born that way. Let's call it Gladys if it's a girl.'

'Deal. Anything new?'

So to give her something to think about, he told her about Atherton and Emily Stonax. She was not as surprised as he expected her to be. 'I could see she was interested in him.'

'But on the very day she finds her father's been murdered?'

'That's the very day you most need comfort. I hope for his sake that's not all it is. But I had a long chat with her and she's got the intellect he needs, and the same sort of interests.'

'Funny, I've never heard him say, "Phwoah, look at the brain on that!" or "I wouldn't half like to give *her* a game of chess."'

'Scoff away, my lad. But don't forget you're talking about the man who once dated *two* solicitors.' Someone spoke behind her, and she said, 'I've got to go. They're calling us. Shostakovich five waits for no man. Love you.'

'Me too,' he said, seeing McLaren hovering in the doorway. 'Chicken!' she laughed, and rang off.

Freddie Bell's gaming empire was run from his headquarters offices over the Lucky Bells Casino on Leicester Square. Above the offices there was reputed to be a penthouse flat of surpassing magnificence where Freddie himself lived, when he was not at his manor in Gloucestershire, his stud in Wiltshire, his castle in Aberdeenshire, his villa in Monte or his apartment in New York. The man was *seriously* rich. He had casinos wherever they were legal, 'arcades' on high streets and sea fronts, fruit machines in every pub and chippy, betting shops, hotels and motels, plus an interest in several London theatres and a promotional company that specialised in musicals and operas. Atherton had done his homework before heading for Leicester Square. Despite naming his casino empire after himself, he preferred to be called an impresario, which suggested either a desire to become respectable or delusions of grandeur; although, Atherton thought, he was so rich and powerful it probably wasn't possible for him to be delusional about it. In his younger days, though, he had been so famous for settling disputes with his fists, it had been suggested his empire ought to have been called Seven Bells rather than Three.

The Lucky Bells was his largest casino in the UK, though he had one in Las Vegas that made it look like a corner shop in Droitwich. All the same, it was big, and Bell owned the whole building on a long lease, which given the value of real estate in central London ranked it high among his assets. It had the gaming rooms downstairs; entertainment suites, restaurants and control room on the first floor; and the offices of Three Bells Entertainment Enterprises Ltd on the second. It was one of the grand old buildings in Leicester Square, stone faced, with a fancy frieze all round under the roofline depicting dryads, puff-cheeked Bacchuses and fat bunches of grapes, and false columns between the vertical window lines which ended in busty caryatids. All rather louche and appropriate, Atherton thought. The casino wasn't open yet when he arrived, but he found one door at the end unlocked and went in. With its prosaic main lights on and the cleaners patiently mowing up and down the vastness of hideous carpet, its night-time glamour was exposed as tawdriness, its luxury fake, glittery and naff. It was sadder, Atherton thought, because it had obviously cost a lot of money to get it to look like a WAG's dream. To have spent so much on chandeliers like *those*, and a carpet like *that*, made the crime against taste all the greater.

He had hardly had time for more than a cursory glance when he was fielded by a man already in dinner jacket, whose dead-fish eyes and bulging unsuitedness to his suiting marked him instantly as a bouncer – or security specialist as he no doubt liked to be known these days.

'We're not open, sir.'

'I've come to see Mr Bell,' Atherton said, showing his brief. 'He's expecting me.'

The flat eyes sharpened an instant, memorising Atherton's appearance. He turned his head slightly, revealing the curly black wire behind his ear, and spoke to his lapel. Atherton could hear the faint bat-squeak of the reply, and saw the nearest security camera up on the ceiling turn minutely towards him. He half expected to be patted down and was rather disappointed to be seen as so little of a threat.

'Would you come this way, please, sir,' the man said, leading Atherton towards the back where, behind a screen wall, there was a bank of lifts. He unlocked one with a key from a bunch chained to his belt, showed Atherton in, pressed 2, and stepped out before the door closed. 'Someone will meet you at the lift,' he said.

Someone did, and it was a relief for Atherton that it turned out to be a smart and pretty woman, who smiled and offered her hand in a friendly way and said, 'I'm Lorraine Forrest, one of Mr Bell's assistants. He'll see you right away, if you'd like to come this way.'

Atherton suppressed the obvious riposte as she walked off, revealing a very nice posterior in a tightly fitting skirt, and made himself wonder instead if she shortened her name to Rain. It was a belter of a name in these eco-nutty days.

He caught her up. 'What's he like?' he asked, in a low voiced, chums-on-the-way-to-the-headmaster manner. 'I mean, I'm a bit nervous, what with all this.' He waved his hand to indicate the Empire. 'He's a multibillionaire. What's it like to work for a man like that?'

'He's very nice,' she said, giving him a humorous look, 'and I like working for him, and I don't think you're the slightest bit nervous, so stop trying to yank my chain. Here we are. Go in, and he'll be there in a second.'

She shoved him in a motherly sort of way through the door into a vast office, rather dim because of the low ceiling, the tinted glass in the huge windows and the acres of purple carpet on the floor. It was deafeningly quiet. Despite looking down on Leicester Square, with its crowds and fairground rides and all London's traffic nearby, there wasn't a sound from outside – quadruple glazing at least, Atherton thought. There was no sound of air conditioning, either, though the air was neutrally cool and odourless. There had been something of an air-brake type of resistance when the door closed behind him, which gave him the hint that the room was sound-proofed and there-fore probably miked as well. Standing still, he allowed his eyes to wander casually round the room and spotted four good sites for hidden cameras, which probably meant there were more than four. They were watching to see what he'd do when left alone. Freddie Bell was taking no chances, and given his wealth and the nature of his business, it was probably just as well. Atherton looked straight at the suspect light fitting and gave a big grin. No harm in letting them know he knew.

The right-hand wall of the office was covered floor to ceiling with bookcases, and given that the books were all matching sets of leather-bound hardbacks, he guessed that there wouldn't be much choice if you actually wanted to read one. Sure enough, immediately after his grin, one whole section swung inwards, revealing a false door, and Freddie Bell himself walked in and closed it behind him.

'Inspector Atherton?' he said.

'It's Detective Sergeant, actually. But thanks for the promotion.'

'What, I don't merit the top man?' Bell said jovially.

He advanced across the hampering carpet but did not extend his hand. Atherton was tolerably acquainted with his appearance from newspapers and the television, but those media could not convey the sheer animal presence of the man. He was not unusually tall, probably five-ten or eleven, but he was massively bulky, as if he had been designed on a grander scale, perhaps for a planet with a different gravity. His shoulders bulked under his suit jacket as if they'd been borrowed from a Hereford bull. His hands were huge, decorated with a heavy gold ring on the third finger of each, and a watch so massive you could have clubbed seals with it. His head seemed bigger than normal, but his features were big enough to fit it, with a thick nose and a prominent underlip, and blue eyes under strong, fair eyebrows. His light brown hair was cut in a fashionable disarray that must have cost hundreds each time to get it to look so casual: it stood out slightly from his head, which gave the impression that it was being forced outwards by the tremendous pressure from inside the skull that held the brains of this huge and successful empire.

All in all, Atherton thought, you could see what he was – a man who had made his own fortune from nothing and was increasing it all the time, a man in control, a man of power. His suit was fabulously expensive and well cut, his shoes and tie were to swoon for; but strip him of all that, and place him in any surroundings, and Atherton would have bet he would still have looked like an emperor. The power came from inside. Atherton was suddenly glad he had not had to shake hands.

Bell looked to be in his late fifties, although he could have been older but very well preserved. His face was firm and pleasantly tanned, and Atherton supposed it was handsome in a tough Daniel Craig sort of way. He did not have to suppose that women would find Bell attractive – that was well documented. But to talk of Candida Scott-Chatton fancying a bit of rough was to miss the point entirely. This was a rich, powerful and clever man; and after being married to her earl (who by all accounts was a bit of a wet), then mistress of virtuous Ed Stonax, and having worked in the charitable sector all her life among fluffy volunteers and the terminally well-meaning, she might well have been pining for stronger meat and drink even without knowing it. And Atherton could see that it would be intoxicating – if you could keep it down.

Nine

Green Unpleasant Land

'Well, Sergeant, what did you want to talk to me about?' said Freddie Bell. He did not look at his watch, nor say, 'I'm a busy man,' as lesser men would. He stood quite still, an extra stillness in this unnaturally quiet room, as though like a black hole he drew all sound and movement into himself. Atherton could feel the astronomical mass of him and almost wanted to take hold of something to keep himself from sliding helplessly across the carpet like a pin towards a magnet.

Was that why they called them magnates? he wondered frivolously. He took a grip on himself and got to the point. 'Ed Stonax,' he said.

'Ah,' said Bell, his eyes searching Atherton's face briefly. 'I read about the murder. Terrible thing.' His voice was dark and gritty but without accent, except a sort of man-of-the-people ordinariness. He had grown up in t'north but had long ago shed any regional markers. 'Some punk broke in and robbed him. But you've got the man – didn't I see on the TV you've arrested someone?'

'Yes,' said Atherton.

'Well, it doesn't look as if you need my help, then.' One of several telephones on the massive desk rang, and he said, 'Excuse me. I have to take this.' He went round the desk so that he could answer without turning his back on Atherton, and kept his eyes fixed on him as he said, 'Yes?' and then listened. 'Let him go to a hundred, then cut him off. No. Tell King and Morris to stand by. OK.'

He put the phone down, sat down, and gestured Atherton to a chair in front of him. 'So, what is it, then?'

'Can you tell me when you last saw him?'

'Month, six weeks ago. He came to see me here. Had a brief chat, then he was on his way.'

'What did you chat about?'

'This and that. Time of day. Nothing in particular.'

'He came to see you, and then didn't have anything in particular to say to you? I find that hard to believe, such busy people as you both are.'

Bell made a restless movement. 'He asked me about Salford Quays. Big retail development in Manchester.'

'I've heard of it. What did he want to know?'

'He asked how much a development like that would stand to make for an investor. I told him it depended on how much you had to pay for the land.'

'Why did he ask you that?'

'I don't know. I said did he have something in mind and he said no, he was just interested. Then he asked me about government investment – Salford had quite an injection for the infrastructure – and I said he should come and see me when I had more time and I'd tell him what I knew. Then he pissed off.'

Atherton could make nothing of all this. 'Did he often ask you for investment advice?'

'No. Doubt if he had anything to invest. Anything else?'

Atherton took the plunge. 'Candida Scott-Chatton,' he said. Bell's expression, bright and watchful like a cat at a mouse hole, did not change. 'I understand you're seeing her.'

'Yes. What about it?'

He wasn't going to offer anything. Atherton was going to have to ask. 'I wondered how you felt about the fact that she was also still seeing Ed Stonax.'

'Why should I feel anything about that?'

'Well, there was an occasion some years back when you got rather riled about a similar situation. A fight outside the Ram pub in Manchester, a young woman called Sharon Railton, a – shall we say? – business rival called Gus Oldfield. Oldfield ends up in hospital with a knife wound. Ring any bells?'

As he spoke, he saw Freddie Bell relax, and was intrigued. What had he been afraid of, Atherton wondered, that was worse than having this bad episode from his past brought up again?

'That was ten years ago,' he said, 'and you know perfectly well that the police found no knife and Gus refused to press charges. It was just a bit of high spirits, a friendly tussle, and the press got hold of the wrong end of the stick, as usual. There was nothing between me and Sharon Railton and she was free to go out with anyone she pleased as far as I was concerned. And Gus accidentally wounded himself when he slipped over and fell on some broken glass.'

'It was a very neat wound for broken glass,' Atherton said. He had read the files. Frustration on the part of the police breathed from every line. Despite the fight taking place outside a popular pub at chucking-out time, following a violent argument inside about the girl, the witnesses had all melted away when questioned. No-one had seen anything.

'Gus said himself that was what happened, Sharon confirmed it, and I don't know why you're dragging all this up again. I'm a peaceable man. I've never gone tooled up. I don't need to.'

'A man as powerful as you,' Atherton said, 'with so many loyal employees, certainly doesn't need to.'

But Freddie Bell only laughed and shook his head. He ought to have been – or at least have pretended to be – annoyed at the suggestion, but he wasn't, which bothered Atherton more than a bit. 'It's no good sizing me up for Ed Stonax's murder. You'd never get me to fit. Apart from everything else, I liked Ed. He and I worked on several projects together, and I gave him money on more than one occasion for his campaigns. Why on earth would I wish him harm?'

'Men have fallen out over less tasty dishes than Candida Scott-Chatton.'

'She's a grown woman, she can choose for herself who to go out with. And I'm not so infatuated I can't cope with her seeing another man as well. I knew it was Ed she was in love with, and good luck to it. *I* didn't want to marry her. I'm not the marrying kind. Besides, it was Ed who suggested it.'

'Ed Stonax suggested you started seeing his woman?' Atherton said with derision; and yet he felt uncomfortably that it was going to turn out to be true. Freddie Bell might have literally fought his way out of the mean streets and have built his empire on ruthlessness and sometimes questionable acts, but he had crossed the line now into a world of such wealth that it guaranteed its own respectability. He looked massive and unshakable, like a national monument.

'Look,' he said, easing himself in his chair as if for a long chat, 'I'm going to tell you the whole story, because I can't afford to have you lot tramping about all over my business and my private life. This is the truth, and you can believe it or not, it's up to you.'

'Fair enough,' Atherton said.

'I've known Candida for a long time,' said Freddie Bell. 'I always quite fancied her. She isn't as strait-laced as she looks, you know. That girl likes a bit of fun. She could drink you under the table, and get her in the right mood and she's got a stack of filthy stories that would curl your nose-hair. A lot of those public-school, rich-daddy, *Tatler* girls are like that. Butter wouldn't melt and all that, but they go like trains in the right company. Anyway, Cand was married to that twerp Bannister when she was eighteen and only just out of school. It was her parents' choice, and she went along with it because she didn't know any better, and he wasn't bad looking. But he was so wet he was a non-starter, and he must have bored her to tears. So she started doing her charity work, just to fill her life. And it gradually took over. That's how I first met her, at a fundraiser, and we hit it off like nobody's business. We saw a bit of each other over the years, on a casual basis. We kept it private, because she was still married, and I didn't want any scandal. I had plenty else on my mind in those days. Then, thank God, Bannister ran off with that girl, Candida met Ed, and everything looked set fair. I still thought she and I might have a little fling now and then if the occasion arose, but if it never happened, so be it.' He shrugged. 'In actual fact, it didn't. For a couple of years I hardly saw her, except at the occasional function, just to nod to each other. But I was cool with that. I've never lacked for female company.'

'So I understand,' said Atherton.

'Then that business of Ed's came up,' Bell continued.

He paused, for the first time looking away from Atherton, his eyes reflective. 'They wanted him out, and the bloody fool wouldn't go quietly. So they came after him, went public with those photos. Then he had to go. And he came to me. He wanted to stop them going after Candida. He asked me to step in and start dating her publicly, make it look as if she'd dumped him and taken up with me instead. Well – ' the eyes were direct again – 'I didn't mind. It suited me just then to start looking a bit more establishment. The government was talking about super-casino franchises, but they weren't popular with the voters so they needed to make them look more respectable. Mr F. Bell plus the Marquis of Alderley's daughter looked a lot better than plain old Freddie Bell with the likes of Sharon Railton tottering along on his arm, falling out of her dress, bless her, and getting mouthy drunk on screwdrivers. Bit of a stereotype was our Sharon.'

He chuckled softly in reminiscence, then shook himself back to the story. 'Anyway, Ed knew it would work for me and it would work for them. They'd get the casinos through, I'd get the franchise, Candida wouldn't have sleazy pictures of her spread round the glossies, happy result all round. And maybe it would even be Lord Freddie next January. Not that it matters to me, but Cand would have liked it. Make us less unequal. Meanwhile Ed could get on with whatever he was planning to do – which frankly I couldn't care less about and didn't want to know. I *knew*,' he added, as though Atherton had raised the point, 'that she was still seeing Ed, and I told her she was a fool – they were both fools – but it didn't *bother* me. I only thought they'd be better off staying apart until the heat was off, but she said they were being discreet and no-one would know. Fair enough, nothing ever got in the papers about it. So there you are,' he concluded. 'Now you know everything and you can chuck out any idea that I had Ed bumped off out of some sexual jealousy, or what-ever you boys call that motive nowadays. I wished them well, and that's the truth.'

Atherton felt the disappointment of deep conviction that Freddie Bell was telling the truth, and that this was the end of a potentially promising trail. He also knew his time with Bell was fast running out and that he'd be unlikely to get more than one more question in before the emperor chucked him out. And given what appeared to be Bell's ample connections with the government, he knew what it would be. It might not be anything to do with the case, but it was the thing most of all that he wanted to know.

'Why did the DTI want to get rid of Ed Stonax?' he asked. 'What had he done?'

'It wasn't what he'd done so much as what he was going to do,' Bell said promptly. 'He'd found something out and he wanted to investigate it and make it public, as if he was still a bloody journalist. I told him he wasn't working for the BBC any more, he was out in the real world where real things happen and people get hurt. He wouldn't listen. They said he could go quietly, take a nice big settlement and keep his mouth shut, or he could do it the hard way. So what did he do? Wanker.' Bell's face was hard now, and yet Atherton felt he could discern something softer imperfectly hidden in his eyes. Regret?

'So what was this thing he had found out?' Atherton asked.

'I can't tell you because I don't know,' Bell said briskly. 'And if I did know, I wouldn't tell you. It's none of my business – and it's none of yours, either.'

'Everything becomes my business in a murder investigation,' Atherton said.

'Then you're as big a fool as he was. I hate bloody Boy Scouts! I said to him, all you've got to do is keep your mouth shut. I said, who's the loser? And d'you know what he said? He said, *the truth* is the loser.' He made a sound of disgust. 'I told him to grow up. And now look where he is.'

One of the phones rang, and he snatched it up as if glad of the distraction. 'Yeah? All right, cut him off. Who? No, Lorraine's got those figures. Put him on to her. All right, I'll be through in a minute.'

He put the phone down and stood up, and Atherton was obliged to do likewise. 'That's it,' he said. 'I've got a business to run. You'll have to go.' He walked across to the door on to the corridor and opened it, holding it for Atherton, and said, 'I've told you everything I know, and I don't expect to see you or any of your little friends here again, savvy? Otherwise I might have to stop being polite, and I wouldn't like that.'

Atherton didn't like being threatened, but he had no hand to play. He said politely and meekly, 'Thank you for your time,' and Bell nodded, as if it was his due.

Atherton stepped through the door, and as it was closed behind him, Bell said, 'And tell your boss he'd better not go stirring up any hornets' nests. Keep his nose out of other people's business or he might get it bitten off.'

'Is that a threat?' Atherton said, surprised at its brazenness.

Bell gave an impatient shrug. 'It's a friendly warning. There are some people who don't like him, that I wouldn't want to piss off.' And he closed the door.

The delectable Rain Forrest was walking towards him, alerted by some means to his departure. 'I'll take you back to the lift,' she said, smiling pleasantly.

'I'm sure I can find it myself,' he said acidly.

She shook her head like a nanny with a sulky child. 'We like to know that visitors have left the building, and aren't wandering round unsupervised. Mr Bell didn't get where he is today by being careless.'

'You're beautiful, intelligent and kind,' Atherton said. 'What are you doing working for an outfit like this?'

'Like this?' she said, with what seemed like genuine surprise. 'It's a thriving international business. What can you mean? And Mr Bell is a very good boss.'

'You just don't seem like the type,' he said glumly.

She actually patted his arm. 'You did very well in there. Better than I expected.'

'You were watching?'

'Everything that happens in this building is monitored and recorded. What did you expect?'

'So I'm on tape for ever, am I?'

'Oh, I except you'll get wiped at some point in the future.'

They had reached the lift. She pressed the button and the door opened at once: no-one had used it since him. 'I'd really like to get to know you,' Atherton said, turning to face her, holding the door with one hand to stop it closing. 'Would you like to go out somewhere? Dinner tonight.' She shook her head. 'Tomorrow night?'

She pushed him gently back into the lift and pressed the G button. 'I have you on video,' she said. 'Whenever I miss your face, I can always watch that.' And she stepped back out as the door closed, still smiling and shaking her head.

'So, how was it?' Slider asked as Atherton came in. 'It must have been hard to get anything out of him.'

'I don't know when I've done anything harder, unless it was getting a kitten out of my bedroom slipper,' Atherton said. 'He was positively forthcoming.'

'Then why the air of disgruntlement?'

'He says he knew about Stonax and the woman and didn't mind, and I believe him.'

'Oh. That's a shame.'

Atherton told him the whole story, ending with the 'friendly warning'.

'I wonder who he meant by "your boss",' Slider said. 'Me? Porson? Wetherspoon? The AC?'

'I don't think it was the Home Secretary,' Atherton said. 'He's obviously got a lot of government contacts and equally obviously likes keeping on the right side of them. I'm sure he knows what was behind Stonax's sacking, but I'm equally sure he'll never tell us.'

'And you think that's important?'

'I don't know,' Atherton said. 'It was obviously a big thing in Stonax's life, but it was nearly a year ago, and if anything was going to happen to him because of it, you'd have expected it to be then.'

'Unless he was still investigating, and getting closer,' Slider said.

Atherton shrugged. 'I suppose mostly it just bugs me not knowing what he'd found out. I don't like not knowing.'

'Well, we haven't got many other lines to follow up,' said Slider. 'Why don't you look into it? Interview Sid Andrew and the woman – whatever her name was—'

'Funny how nobody remembers,' Atherton said moodily.

'And ask them what it was all about. Go on from there. And go through his papers, try and find out what he was doing these past months. We've got his diary to go through, his latest correspondence, and they've taken his computer to Jimmy Pak to examine. Enough there to keep us all busy for a day or two.'

'Right,' said Atherton, pulling himself together. 'First find out the woman's name, then find out where she and Sid Andrew have gone. A bit of phone and computer work there. And on the subject of computers . . .'

'You'd better find out how Emily's doing,' Slider supplied for him. 'She's had her head down all day, as far as I can tell – no-one seems to have seen her. In fact, I dare say she needs a cup of tea. I could do with one as well.'

They had found her a corner and a desk, in the room that housed the photocopier. There she had settled in with case notes, files, and Atherton's laptop, which he'd rigged up to a printer borrowed from the desk of one of Ron Carver's firm who was on holiday. When they went to rescue her, she looked up from a sea of papers in surprise. 'I didn't realise it was that late. I've been so absorbed.'

A good thing, too, Slider thought. Nothing like work for keeping your mind off things. He saw the realisation come back to her almost at once; but she braced her shoulders with a determination not to brood about it.

'How's it going?' she asked. 'Any luck?'

'Nothing so far, I'm afraid,' Slider said. 'I'm thinking we really need to know what your father was doing since he left the DTI. There might be some clue in that, so we're looking at his diary and computer, and we'll probably have to go through all his papers. You may be able to be of help to us there.'

'Anything I can do, you know I will,' she said. 'But this looking into Trevor Bates has been very interesting. He's quite a man. Evil, but interesting.'

In the canteen they got three teas and three slabs of bread pudding (which the canteen did very well) for sustenance, and took them to a table by the window. There was a day outside, Slider noted with vague wonder. He sat down next to Emily as Atherton had sprung into the chair opposite her, and he realised his colleague wanted to be able to look at her face. He was that far gone.

'So what have you found out?' Atherton asked her.

'Nothing really about where he might be. I've mostly been catching up on his past history, which I suppose you know all about, but was new to me. He's had his fingers in a lot of pies. He must have a brilliant brain.'

'Pity it's so misdirected,' Slider said.

'Yes. But here's the thing I found this morning that interested me particularly. You know that he was being moved to the secure remand facility by a private security company, Ring 4?'

'Yes, that's right,' said Slider. 'Most prisoner movements are undertaken by private companies. The Home Office contracts out a lot of services to the private sector now.'

'It's a good name, isn't it: ring for security? But I didn't realise they did that kind of thing. I always thought they delivered wages and collected the cash from banks, and so on.'

'They do everything,' Slider said. 'They're one of the biggest security companies in the country. They cover every aspect from guarding dockyards and moving bullion right down to domestic burglar alarms.'

'And security doors,' Atherton added. 'That's why the man who contacted Dave Borthwick pretended to be working for Ring 4. It's probably the first name that sprang to his mind.'

'I see. Well, here's the thing that really intrigued me,' Emily said. 'You said the van was held up and Bates was freed, but there's never been an inquiry into how it happened.'

Slider and Atherton looked at each other blankly, and then Atherton said, 'There must have been.'

'I've been through every record I can access, and there's nothing. No internal investigation at Ring 4, no report by the Prison Service, no inquiry by the Home Office, nothing from Woodhill – which is also privately run, of course. And what's more,' she added, before they could say anything, 'there was nothing in any of the newspapers either. Now don't you think that's odd? There was lots and lots about his arrest, rehashing the murder with all the sleazy details, because let's face it the public loves that sort of thing so the papers latch on to it. Yet when this terribly interesting murderer goes missing from the back of a prison van, there's nothing in the papers at all.'

'There must have been something,' Slider protested. He looked at Atherton. 'I don't read the papers, but you do. And you watch the television news. It must have been covered.'

Atherton was frowning. 'We were told about it personally by Mr Porson,' he said, 'but I can't remember at this distance whether I saw anything in the papers. I'm assuming I must have, but we were very busy about then and I can't recall specifically—'

'No need to rack your brains. You didn't,' Emily said with a little understandable triumph. 'I've looked up every newspaper for the day and for two weeks afterwards, and the only report is in a local paper, the *Woburn Courier*, which says that a prison van was held up on the way to Woodhill and a prisoner, Trevor Bates, escaped. And there was a stop press in the *Telegraph*. Neither gives any details of how it happened, and the *Telegraph* doesn't even mention Woodhill or Bates by name – it just says "a prisoner". And after that, nothing. Now don't you think that's odd?'

'It is odd,' Slider said, 'but I'm not sure what you're suggesting.'

'Well, look,' she said, 'the first report must have come from someone local to the hold-up, probably the local police. Someone on the local press must have had a contact at the *Telegraph*, and it made it to their late-edition stop press. But the next day the whole thing is killed stone dead. In normal circumstances there must have been a heck of a lot of people who would know who was in that van – the Ring 4 people, the people at Wormwood Scrubs where he went from, the Woodhill people who must have been expecting him – and all their wives and children and friends and secretaries, because people do talk to their families even in these inarticulate times. But nothing gets out. So either there was some very heavy duty leaning to keep it quiet, going on from the very top – which I suppose would be the Home Office?'

'Ultimately, yes,' Slider said. 'I suppose they might have wanted to suppress it so as not to alarm people.'

'But when dangerous prisoners escape,' Emily said, 'they usually put it out so as to warn people not to approach them.'

'Yes, that's true.'

'The other possibility,' Atherton said, 'which I suppose you're building up to, is that he was deliberately sprung.'

Slider looked at him in surprise, but Emily was nodding. 'It's the only thing, to my mind, that makes sense. The whole thing was done secretly, so that only the people involved knew about it – and they wouldn't tell.'

'But that's impossible,' Slider said. 'It would take connivance at a very high level. Someone very, very high up would have had to decide on it and plan it, and I can't believe—'

'Can't you?' Atherton said.

'You're being needlessly cynical. Even if there was one corrupt person high up in the Home Office, he couldn't do it all on his own. There'd be high-level police involvement.'

'But look,' Emily said, 'Bates did have connections with the government, and at a high level. He provided them with important services. Suppose it was thought to be for the greater benefit that he was got out and allowed to carry on performing those services, rather than mouldering in prison where he could do no good? That could be a good motive, even if it involved corruption in the execution. A lot of people, acceptable people, think it's OK to do evil that good might come.'

'That's true,' Atherton said. 'And there are quite a few of them in the Job. You *know* that,' he said to Slider. 'We've all known cases where the evidence has been buffed up a bit so as to put a real villain away. When you *know* someone's guilty and you just can't get enough for the CPS – well, the temptation's there. And I don't believe there's one copper in ten who would think that was morally wrong, even if they don't do it themselves.'

'We don't do that,' Slider said stubbornly.

'But others do,' Atherton said. 'And maybe *we* should, now and then. How many times have we busted our balls catching some villain, and then he walks away because the CPS won't prosecute?'

Slider shook his head in frustration. 'You can't start sub-dividing justice—'

'Oh, justice! Since when was it about justice?' Atherton said, as the frustrations of the Job burst out from years of restraint. 'Was it justice when Richard Tyler murdered his mother and his lover and got away with it because he was an MP and a junior minister and had the prime minister's ear? He swanned off to a cosy billet in Brussels, if you remember, instead of doing life in Pentonville.'

'Richard Tyler?' Emily queried.

'I'll tell you some time,' Atherton said, calming down. 'We're getting a bit off the point, here.'

'I'm glad you noticed,' Slider said.

'The point is that it might have been decided at the highest level that it was a good thing for Bates to be sprung.'

'"Might" is not evidence,' Slider said, 'though I accept your main premise.'

'I'll tell you what *is* evidence,' Atherton said. 'The fact that Mick Hutton wasn't asked to monitor the mobile number we gave Porson to give to Palfreyman.'

'There could be any number of reasons for that. Quite possibly there was just an administrative delay in asking for it. And now, of course, there's no point.'

Atherton shook his head. 'You live in such a rosy world.'

'In case you hadn't noticed,' Slider said, 'it's me he's threatening. That's not so rosy. I just can't let you rush off with suppositions that have no foundation.'

'Richard Tyler,' Emily said. 'Why is that name familiar?'

'I just told you it,' Atherton said, regaining his humour.

'He was a junior minister in the Department of the Environment,' Slider explained.

'Oh, of course, that must be it. Dad will have mentioned him.' She frowned in thought. 'Wasn't he supposed to be a bit of a high flyer?'

'They thought at one time he could become the youngest ever prime minister,' Slider said. 'We looked at him in a murder case. I was convinced he did it, but we had no evidence, nothing we could put up in a court of law. Then a couple of months later he got into some financial trouble, resigned his seat and was sent to Brussels.'

'Something about insider dealing on some shares,' Atherton said. 'They couldn't pin it on him but it was enough to have him sent into purdah for a bit.'

'Porson said at the time that would be punishment enough,' Slider said. 'The fact that he'd never be prime minister now. But Brussels, with a big salary, bigger expenses and even bigger pension, and for doing what?' Slider had seen Phoebe Agnew dead, at the hands – he believed – of her own son. And the gentle, bumbling Piers Prentiss, Tyler's lover. It didn't seem like enough punishment to him.

'Yes, I remember it now,' Emily said. 'He was made EU Commissioner for Infrastructure. The big Euro engineering projects – airports, bridges, dams and so on. He's coming back to England now, though.'

'He is?' Atherton said in surprise. 'When?'

'I don't know when – it didn't say. I read it on Reuters a couple of weeks ago. That's why the name was familiar – I knew there was something! It was a piece about the US airbase on Terceira I was reading. There's some kind of infrastructure project that the EU wants to do as a joint thing with the US – a motorway and a bridge, I think. It mentioned that Richard Tyler hoped to complete the deal as his last act as commissioner before returning to the UK – said he was going to be a special political advisor to Number Ten.'

Slider looked bitter. 'Well, there's a just reward for villainy.'

'But he'll never be prime minister,' Atherton suggested to cheer him up. 'Look, we've got to follow this up.'

'Tyler?'

'No, the Bates escape.'

'There's no "got to" about it.'

'But if we find out how he got away, it might give us a clue as to where he is.' He saw this was not playing with his boss, and added, 'Also they mustn't be allowed to get away with it – whoever "they" are.'

'If your suspicion, which is no more than a suspicion, has any truth in it, which is doubtful. Anyway, I can't spare you from the Stonax case.' Slider winced inwardly as he caught himself referring to it like that in front of Emily.

But Emily didn't seem to notice. Her face was alight with eagerness. 'Let me do it,' she said. They both looked at her, Atherton with interest, Slider doubtfully. 'Look, I'm an investigative journalist. It's what I do. I know where to look things up and I know how to get people to talk to me. They'll tell me things they would never tell a policeman. Let me do it, please! Let me take it off your minds while you get on with finding out who killed Dad.'

'I can't agree to it,' Slider said at last, though with a little reluctance. If there was some connivance at Bates's escape, he badly wanted to know about it.

'You don't have to,' she said, and jumped over his difficulty for him. 'In fact, you can't actually stop me, you know. Once I leave here you won't know what I'm doing, and as a free citizen I can exercise my right to ask questions of anyone I please.'

Slider sighed. 'If you put it that way. But be careful.'

'Of course.'

'And understand that it will be without any official sanction whatsoever.'

She smiled suddenly, and it was good to see, like the first breaking of sun through clouds. 'I never work any other way,' she said.

Ten

Trapped Nerd

Joanna phoned from a curry house in Leeds at six o'clock.

'We're just getting something to eat between rehearsal and concert. There's a whole crowd of us here, so don't worry.'

'I'd worry for the audience,' Slider said, 'with half the orchestra breathing out balti and vindaloo. I hope you're not playing "Blow the Wind Southerly".'

'Ha ha. You'd have made a great musician,' Joanna said. 'How's it by you, anyway?'

He told her what little progress had been made, but on a last minute decision did not tell her the idea about Bates being sprung, in case it worried her more. 'Where are you staying tonight?'

'The Holiday Inn, and I'm sharing a room with Sue, so I won't be alone. And a few others are staying as well, so we'll be in company. It'll be a chance to tell Sue about Jim and his new infatuation.'

'Do you think she'll mind?' Slider asked, imagining Joanna spending the evening soaking up sobs and handing out Kleenex. It didn't sound like a fun occasion to him.

'Bound to, a bit, but I don't think it'll break her heart. It was her who decided they weren't suited, and I'm sure now that she's right. She needs someone more down to earth – and someone who'll appreciate her, not try to make her live up to him.'

'Ouch,' said Slider.

'Well, Jim can be a bit – challenging,' she said carefully. 'Much as we love him. Anyway, I suspect there's a new interest in her life, which is always the best cure. I told you there's quite a few of us here – in the curry house, I mean – which includes most of the brass section, and John Saxby, one of the trombones, is at our table and being very attentive to Sue.'

'A trombone player?'

'Don't be snobbish. He's really nice and quite gentle and thoughtful under that rough ey-oop exterior. He and Sue would be very good together.'

'Matchmaker.'

'I want my friend to be happy. I'd better go – someone else wants the phone. Wait, here's a musical joke for you. How many clarinettists does it take to change a light bulb?'

'Dunno.'

'One, but you need a huge box of bulbs.'

'Ha!'

'Thought you'd like it. Tell Jim. And take care of yourself.'

'I will. You too.'

'I miss you so much.'

'Me too.'

'I might phone you tonight, when I go to bed. If it's not too late.'

'Phone anyway, even if it is.'

There was one last phone call before he knocked off for the evening, from Jimmy Pak, their civilian aide who specialised in computers. He reported that the computer had been delivered to him and he had had a preliminary look into it.

'The good news is that I don't think whoever took the Cyber-box has accessed it. It leaves a trace when it's used, and the last access seems to have been four days ago when Stonax was still alive. I suppose they haven't had time to work out the password yet.'

'And can you stop anyone accessing it in the future?'

'Yes, that's not difficult. I've already done that. And I've got into his main files all right. That password wasn't hard to figure. Most people use names and birth dates of their nearest and dearest when security isn't a big issue. But I've found a whole lot of encrypted files in there, and I guess that's the stuff you'll want to access.'

'Can you get in?'

'Once I've got the password. I don't suppose you have any clues to it? It would save time.'

'I'm afraid not.'

'Oh, well, never mind. I will work it out, I've never been beaten yet, but it will take time, that's all. I'll send you a print out by heading of what's in the main body of files, in case there's anything you're interested in, and then concentrate on the encrypted stuff.'

'Thanks, Jimmy. Have a good evening.'

'Kidding? I'm just starting work. Night's the best time for me. I sleep in the morning when people start making a noise.'

Slider put things away and locked his desk, thinking of the little shaggy-haired figure hunched over a keyboard under a pool of light from a desk lamp, clicking and mousing away through the silent hours like the shoemaker's elves. It was an odd sort of life – but then that's what most people thought about his.

Atherton found himself suddenly shy when he and Emily got back to his house, and she seemed a tense and ill-at-ease too. It could be the moment when what had happened so far backfired, when she felt repelled by the memory of what they had done and blamed him or herself for it. The knowledge that the relationship was on a knife-edge made him realise very clearly how important it was to him, and for once in his life he didn't know what to do. He had developed a thousand ploys to cover every situation he normally found himself in with a woman, but he couldn't use ploys on her. And he had never been in this situation before. He was terrified of getting it wrong, and the terror paralysed him.

Fortunately the siameses dashed into the breach, thundering into the room with competing loud remarks about the lateness of the hour and the absence of food in their dishes. Vash shinned lightly up Emily and sat on her shoulder, shouting chattily into her ear like someone talking to a deaf person, while Tig did his Wall of Death challenge, racing round the room at top speed without touching the floor.

It broke the gathering ice, and Atherton offered up a silent thank you to the absent Sue for having forced him to take them on.

'Hungry?' he asked Emily.

'Very,' she said. 'I don't seem to have had any lunch.'

'That often happens with police work. I read a thing about the First World War, where soldiers always said if anyone offered you food you should eat it, even if you'd just had a meal, because you never knew when the next meal was coming. I'll see what there is in the fridge.'

She drifted into the kitchen after him, looking dead tired, and bleak around the eyes. The thing to do, he thought, was to keep her occupied. 'Would you mind feeding the kits?' he said. 'Their food's in the cupboard under the sink, in the big plastic bucket-thing.'

She did as he asked wearily and without comment, but in a moment was laughing as Tig and Vash climbed over and around her with the fluidity of ferrets, trying to get at the food before it got to the dishes. 'They're impossible! Look at this one, trying to jam his head into the bucket! Get out, you silly animal. Let me fill the bowl first! How much should I give them?'

'A scoop in each bowl is fine. And if the water bowl's empty, could you fill it from the tap, please?'

By the time she had done these things, he was ready to say, 'How about chicken, bacon and avocado salad? The avocadoes are just about ready now.'

'Lovely.'

'And I've got a bottle of Meurseult in the fridge. Would you like a drink beforehand? I could do with a gin and tonic. Would you make them while I get the bacon on? And put some music on?'

So he kept her gently occupied, until Rachmaninov's first symphony laid its firm opening notes down into the silence, and she came back to the kitchen door with two tumblers and offered him one. He thanked her and left the bacon to get some ice out and drop a lump into each drink. Then he paused on the brink of saying *cheers*, tripping over another of those invisible obstacles, because it wasn't quite the right thing to say, was it?

She obviously felt it too, because she said, 'Is it right to be like this? Food, music – a drink?'

'You know it is,' he said.

'But it seems wrong to want to enjoy them. Isn't it disrespectful? I ought to be in mourning.'

'And you are. Aren't you?'

She nodded. She knocked her knuckles against her chest and said, 'It's like a sort of sump of misery in here. I want to cry and howl, and I'm afraid to. I'm afraid to let go.'

'That's natural,' he said. 'It's your own self defending itself. It's too much to think about now. When the time comes that you can cope with it, you'll do it. Your father would understand that.'

Her hand went up automatically to the locket and took hold of it: it fitted nicely into her closed palm, and Atherton imagined the smooth, warm feeling of it. Comforting.

'Yes, he would,' she said. 'He was always so good about feelings. It can't have been easy bringing up a teenage girl alone, but he coped with all the moods and floods and sulks and always managed to make me feel normal. You know?'

'You weren't normal?'

'It wasn't normal to live with your dad instead of your mum. But apart from that—' She hesitated.

'Anyone who is a bit out of the ordinary by definition can't be normal. And that includes anyone who is more intelligent or more talented or more gifted than the rest.'

She looked relieved. 'You do understand. Not that I'd say I was gifted or anything,' she said, back-pedalling automatically, 'but I was brighter than the other kids in the neighbourhood. And they knew it too.'

'Kids always do. That's why this business of not streaming never works. They always have an exact knowledge of the hierarchy, however you try to disguise it.' He turned away to turn the bacon. 'It just makes it harder for the bright ones, if you don't let them be with other bright kids. They get bullied.'

'Did you?'

'Oh, yes. Beaten up regularly,' he said lightly.

'It makes you lonely,' she said, as if commenting generally.

'And being lonely gets you into all sorts of inappropriate relationships.'

He turned back and took up his glass again, and she said, 'I've done that. Dad was so good about it. He always managed to make me see how inappropriate without setting my back up. You know how you always immediately want to do the opposite of what your parents tell you? Then, when I got a bit older, he said I should use as a rule of thumb whether I'd want to bring whoever-it-was back to meet him.' She smiled. 'That really narrowed the field!'

'I bet it did,' he said. His feelings were in such turmoil he had to turn away again, and concentrated on cutting and peeling the avocadoes. After a moment she put her glass down and took the second one and a knife and peeled along beside him. The cats finished their biscuit and sprang up on to the draining board to clean their whiskers and watch, their eyes on the chicken skin.

She said, 'I'm not sorry about last night.'

'Thank God for that,' he said. 'I'm not either. Are we OK, then?'

She didn't immediately answer, but then said, quietly, and with a hint of the tears she was denying access to, 'I think Dad would have approved of you.'

Slider drove home by a circuitous route, watching for motor-bikes and black Focuses, and naturally enough there were plenty of both to keep him in a state of jitters. He was beginning to wind his way towards Turnham Green when he remembered that there wasn't any food in the house. He thought of stopping at a supermarket, but the mental image of himself cooking in the empty flat was not convincing, so finally he stopped in Chiswick High Road, parked in a fortuitously empty space by the kerb, and walked down to the Chiswick Chippy and bought himself a rock and chips. There was a street bench on the pavement a little down from where he was parked, and he sat down there and opened his package and ate the fish and chips from the paper, while covertly watching the traffic and the passers-by.

He saw the black Focus go past twice. It wasn't the same reg number that he had sent in before, but he was pretty sure

it was the same car from the tinted glass and the way it
slowed and idled a moment as it got to his part of the street.
What innocent driver goes past the same spot twice at that
time of night? He got out his mobile and rang through to
the traffic division, gave the watchers the new number and
urged them to send a patrol out right now. Then he slowed
his consumption rate, lingering over each chip, and even
eating the crumbs of batter in the bottom of the bag. They
had used to call them 'crackling' when he was a kid. When
the fish and chip van came round, if you hadn't got enough
money for chips you could get a pennorth of crackling to
munch on.

He saw the unmarked patrol go by, but the Focus didn't
come past again. Had they seen him get his phone out and
guessed why? He got up, dumped the vinegary paper into
the nearest bin, and went to his car, and when the patrol
came by again he signalled to them. They stopped beside
him and wound down the window.

'I think he's taken fright,' Slider said. 'Maybe saw me
phoning. But he might still be in the area.'

'We'll cruise around a bit, do a couple of passes by your
house. Maybe we'll spot him.'

Slider drove home, feeling weary and sick of the whole
business. Was Emily's theory right? If it was, it was the worst
thing of all. He had given his life to the Job, and if the
honesty and probity of those above him was going to come
into question, then – well, it would be time for him to leave.
He parked a way from his house, looked carefully for motor-
bikes before getting out, locked the car and crossed the road,
walking on the opposite side, keeping to the shadow of the
hedges and sending out his senses in all directions.

He saw nothing, heard nothing, until he got to the house.
That morning when he locked the front door he had put a
minute scrap of paper between the door and the jamb, at a
point where the fit was too tight to allow it to fall unless
the door was opened. The paper was no longer in place. As
he fumbled out his key, he saw it in the corner of the porch,
gleaming a warning at him. He let himself in carefully,
listening, smelling, but the house was silent and seemed as
usual. And yet, someone had been there. What had they

done? Was it Bates, or one of his minions? Were they searching for something, or doing mischief? He remembered Bates's area of greatest expertise: listening devices. Had he put in a mike somewhere? Or was that paranoia? What could Slider have to say that Bates could possibly find illuminating?

He closed the door behind him and, without putting on the light, walked slowly down the passage. The sitting-room was the first door, and it was just slightly ajar. He frowned. How had he left it? Not closed, that was for certain. They rarely closed that door. In fact, he rather thought it had been wide open that morning – wider than it was now, anyway. He eased out the side-arm baton that, feeling faintly foolish, he had slipped into his belt under his jacket before leaving the office. He didn't feel foolish now. With the tip of it he pushed gently at the door, and felt a resistance. Was there something lying behind it? He got closer and pushed again, more firmly, and the door yielded. At the same moment there was a sensation of movement in the darkness above him, an indecipherable sound, a sharp pain in his head and shoulder, and then blackness.

Now someone was shaking his shoulder, a man's voice saying, 'Sir, are you all right? Sir?'

Slider groaned and opened his eyes and the light hurt. How was it light? Was it morning? No, it was electric light, he saw now, and he was lying on the floor in his own flat, in the doorway of the sitting-room, and his head and shoulder hurt abominably.

'All right,' he said, and the shoulder-shaking stopped. Slider squinted up. It was the traffic patrol man – what was his name? Willets, wasn't it? – with his partner behind him, looking anxious. Slider struggled into a sitting position. 'What happened?' He remembered the blow in the darkness, and the details of Stonax's death came back to him. 'Was I coshed?'

'Booby trap,' said Willets. 'We watched you go in as we went past, and then when we passed again and there were still no lights on, Wright said we ought to check if you were OK. You didn't answer the door, and when I looked through the letter box I heard you groan, so we broke the glass panel in the door and let ourselves in.'

Now there's broken glass to get fixed, the domestic part of Slider's mind worried. 'Booby trap?' he said.

'A bucket resting on the top of the door,' said Willets. 'A metal one.' He gestured, and Slider turned his head, wincing, to see a large, heavy, old-fashioned galvanised bucket lying on the carpet. 'Someone doesn't like you, sir,' Willets concluded, with questions sticking out all over his face.

Fortunately, Slider thought, he had not gone barging straight in, so the bucket had not hit him directly, but struck his head glancingly and the tip of his shoulder on its way down. The old schoolboy trick. Bates was making a fool of him. Had he meant to kill him? Well, probably not, but he wouldn't have minded if he had.

'Need to get forensics in. You didn't touch anything?'

'Only the door, and then you,' said Willets. 'I think you ought to go to the hospital, sir. There's quite a bit of blood.'

Slider became aware, now, of a stickiness around his neck and collar.

'Can't leave the place,' he said.

'We'll take care of it, sir,' said Willets. 'I've already phoned it in. Wright will take you to the hospital and I'll wait here and preserve the scene. You really ought to get that looked at.'

A veterinary-sized painkiller and three stitches later, Slider was functioning again, needing a clean shirt more than anything. Mackay, who'd been doing night duty, was beside him in the cubicle, reporting that nothing else in the flat seemed to have been disturbed, that there were no finger-marks on the bucket, only glove smears, that the forensic team had finished and gone, and that a carpenter was even then boarding up the broken panel in the front door.

'Do you want a bug sweep done, guv?' he asked. Slider had mentioned his initial thought that Bates may have put in a listening device.

'No, don't bother. I think the booby trap was the reason for the break-in. I suppose my door locks were child's play to him.' He only thanked God that Joanna had not been there.

'Well, I don't think you ought to go back there,' Mackay said anxiously. 'Not tonight, anyway.'

'I need clean clothes,' Slider said, 'and some shut-eye. And he's not going to do anything else tonight, is he?'

'Well, at least have a uniform on the door,' Mackay urged. 'Renker was there when I left. Let him stay on guard while you sleep.'

Slider agreed to that, rather than argue, which was becoming increasingly difficult as his brain kept trying to check out into the land of nod. He knew that his old friend O'Flaherty was the night relief sergeant at the station, and he wouldn't mind leaving PC Renker on nursery duty. And it would be a brave villain who tried to get past big Eric Renker in a confined space.

Eleven

Fainting in Coils

'Why didn't you call me?' Atherton demanded, the next morning.

'I thought about it, but I didn't want to disturb Emily with more tales of violence,' Slider said. He felt as if he hadn't slept for a week.

'She's going to find out anyway,' Atherton pointed out.

'Better to hear about it in daylight than in the middle of the night,' Slider said from experience.

'Well, you can't stay there now, anyway. Who knows what he'll do next? You'd better come and stay at my place tonight.'

'And interrupt love's young dream?'

'Facetiousness is my thing. It doesn't work for you,' Atherton informed him. 'If you're worried about the proprieties you can have my room and I'll sleep on the sofa.' And, of course, creep up to Emily in the spare room once the lights were out.

Slider couldn't bear to argue any more. His head hurt too much. 'Thanks,' he said. 'I'll come, just for tonight.' When Joanna got back he'd have to think of something else. But at least he'd get one evening of Atherton's cooking. Those fish and chips had given him heartburn, though that probably wasn't their fault, but a result of the subsequent dramas. As a long-serving policeman, he didn't usually have any difficulty digesting grease. 'It's Porson I feel sorry for,' he said, to turn the attention away from himself. 'The old boy really feels it.'

He had reported in to Porson as soon as he arrived, and found the super pale and shaken.

'I'm just about sick of this,' he said once he had ascertained that Slider was not seriously hurt. 'They've tied me up hand

and foot. Bates is SOCA business now, and you know what these SO units are like. Jealous as fishwives, and if you tread on their toes, you're in all sorts of grief. I've been told categorically not to pursue him, and my pension's on the line, laddie, as you well know. But I'm not having my officers put in jeopardy and do nothing. What are SOCA doing? Sitting round scratching their targets. So you can go after him with my blessing, and anything you want, just ask. If it costs me my pension, well, that's not an absorbent price in the scheme of things. Only,' he had added, rather spoiling the magnificent defiance, 'don't let the Stonax case slip, will you?'

'No, sir.' Slider hesitated, wondering whether to voice any of Emily's and Atherton's conspiracy theories. He was beginning to have a suspicion of his own, though against his will. Why had the Stonax murder been left with him? Usually high-profile cases were whisked away to the specialist units for the greater glory of some desk jockey with a degree in looking good. He had been led by the nose to conclude that Borthwick had done it, but what if it was not the villains who were doing the leading, but the 'them' of Atherton's paranoia?

But if the idea that such things could be would make him sick, they'd make Porson sicker. He had become, since his wife died, something of a shabby tiger, but he was not yet tamed. Slider decided to say nothing, at least yet, and to ask instead for something deliverable.

'Could you get the traffic unit to find that Focus as a matter of urgency? I've got another reg number for it, so the likelihood is that they're going to change it again, but there aren't that many black Focuses with the same dint in the same place. I'm pretty sure it's one of Bates's close cronies driving it around, and if we get him, we might get a lead on Bates.'

'Consider it done,' Porson said. 'I'll sit on them and put a rocket under their arses, don't you worry. Anything else?'

'I can't think of anything at the moment,' Slider said.

'Come to me if you do. Now, what are we going to do about Borthwick?'

'The report on the oil marks was waiting on my desk when I got in,' Slider said. That was another surprise, that it should have come through so quickly. Conspiracy was like oranges

– once you got the smell in your nose, you couldn't get it out.

Porson evidently agreed. 'They must have priorised it,' he said. 'You don't normally get presidents for non-human fluids. So what was the result?'

'It's a match for the sample taken from Borthwick's bike,' Slider said. 'He says he's never been in the flat at all, so that, plus the victim's watch, make a pretty firm basis for a charge.'

'Yes,' Porson said, starting his lope up and down in the space between his desk and the window. 'And then you'd have to try to trace the movements of that motorbike the old dear saw, which means watching endless CCTV tapes, and God knows what else besides trying to prove he did it when we know he didn't. Which all adds up to a lot of running around with our heads up our blue-arsed flies.'

'Displacement activity,' Slider said, as Porson continued to pace.

'We've got to do it, and we've got to make it look good,' Porson decided. 'It's a pity that oil report came so quickly. But we can hold him pending more evidence. I'll think of something to tell the muppets. He's still co-operating?'

'Yes, sir. I think he's quite enjoying it. Bit of a holiday for him. He likes the food.'

'The man's sick! He hasn't asked for a solicitor? He'll have to have one, otherwise the press'll cotton on and start moaning about human rights. But it's got to be one we can trust.'

'I'll find one, sir.'

'And get him what he likes to eat, and whatever he likes to read. Keep him happy. Meanwhile find out who *did* do it. What lines have you got to follow?'

'We're trying to trace and interview people who were in the pub the night Borthwick says he met the man, Patrick Steel.'

'No luck on the name, I suppose?'

'No, sir, but I don't want to waste too much time on it because it's almost certainly a false name.'

'I'll get one of Carver's firm to chase it up, take it off your books. Go on.'

'We're looking into Stonax's past life, and talking to friends and colleagues to try to find what he was busy with recently. It seems likely his death was connected with one or the other.'

'Or both. Could be two halves of the same coin. Well, get on with it, then. And let me know if you get anything on Bates.'

Joanna rang him from the hotel room at half past nine. 'I've just had an enormous breakfast,' she said. 'Egg, bacon, black pudding, the lot. I shall have to play standing up. There's not room in there for breakfast and the baby if I sit down.'

'How is baby Derek?'

'Oh don't! If we start calling him that it'll stick.'

'Only if the wind changes.'

'Don't talk to me about wind! You were right about the curry yesterday. Derek-stroke-Gladys is fine. Listen, about tonight – I can't see the point in staying in a hotel. I'd much sooner come home after the concert.'

'No, I don't want you to do that,' Slider said, wishing he didn't have to tell her, and wondering how shocked she would be.

'I know you think I'm made of tissue paper,' she said, 'but Huddersfield isn't that far, and the traffic will be light that time of night, and I'm used to driving back after concerts. I'd just sooner sleep in my own bed.'

'Well, I'm afraid that's not possible anyway,' he began, trying to assemble the right words.

She jumped right in. 'Oh God, something's happened! What is it? Tell me. Are you all right?'

'I'm all right,' he said. 'Don't worry. Remember the baby and try to take this calmly.'

'You're making me more nervous telling me to be calm. *What happened?*'

'Someone broke into the house yesterday and set up a booby trap, which I sprang when I went home. It was the old schoolboy trick, a bucket balanced on the top of a door.'

'For God's sake,' she said, sounding more bewildered than anything.

'I don't think it was meant to hurt me seriously. I got a

cut on my head and a bruise on my shoulder but I'm all right, apart from a headache.'

'Oh, *Bill!*'

'Please don't cry. I'm all right.'

'I have to cry, it's my hormones. Was it Bates?'

'I suppose so. It's his sort of speed. He likes making a fool of me and wants to scare me.'

'Well, he's scaring me, so tell him he's succeeded and he can stop.'

'Anyway, you can see why I don't want you to come home tonight. I'm going to stay the night at Atherton's, so you'll be better off at a nice, comfortable hotel. Then tomorrow come here when you get back and we'll decide what to do. We might have caught him by then, you never know,' he added in the vain hope of cheering her up.

But she was a sensible woman, he thanked heaven, and did not waste more time on useless remonstrance. 'All right, if it will take a weight off your mind, I'll stay. Oh, Bill, I do miss you! Please be careful.'

'I am being. Truly. That's why I'm not sleeping at home tonight.'

'I have to go. Rehearsal starts at ten thirty.'

'Drive carefully,' he said.

'That's the least of my worries,' she said.

The preliminary report came in from the electronics expert, Phil Lavery, on the security door at Valancy House. He had found a device, and it was, he said, a straightforward timer which caused a short-circuit at the desired time, disengaging the locks as would happen normally during a power cut. The interesting thing about it was the timer itself, which was a tiny transistorised thing not much bigger than a watch battery.

I have not come across one like it before, he wrote, and suspect it may be of Far Eastern origin. I do not recognise the handwork signature, but I will research further on both that and the timer, and report as soon as I have more information.

It was not much help, Slider thought. Most new electronic stuff did come from the Far East these days. The hope was that someone in the trade would recognise the handwork, because people who put together devices like that all had their own way of doing it, and it was generally as personal as a signature. Unless the 'bloke in the van' was clever enough to disguise his work. It sounded as though 'Patrick Steel' was clever enough, but he'd had to hire someone to do the actual work and it was possible that man was not. Get him, get to Patrick Steel. Was he the brains behind the thing or was he fronting for someone else? What they didn't know was legion. No, they needed to find the *reason* for all this. Find the why and you find the who.

Hart came in with papers under her arm and a cup of tea in her hand. 'Brought you this, guv,' she said, setting the cup and saucer down. She reached into her pocket, and placed a bottle of aspirin beside it. 'And Norma sent you these. She reckoned you might need 'em by now.'

'You're very kind,' Slider said. His head was aching again. 'And thank Norma for me.'

'We don't reckon you shoulda come in today,' Hart said, eyeing him in a motherly way. 'You look pale. You musta been concussed, and concussion's not something to mess around with.'

'It's all right,' Slider reassured her. 'I'm not messing around with it, I'm having it properly.' There had been a time when, according to Joanna, Hart had fancied him and hoped to get off with him. He'd never seen it himself, but he didn't want to encourage anything. 'What have you got there?' he asked briskly.

'Stonax's diary,' she said, drawing it out from under her arm. 'I was working backwards, and then it occurred to me to go forwards a bit, and I found he had an appointment today with a "DM". Look, here, DM at half twelve.'

'So why hasn't DM come forward to tell us that?' Slider said. 'He must have seen on the news or in the papers that Stonax is dead.'

'That's what I thought,' said Hart. 'Unless he was some kind of crim, but it didn't seem likely, with Stonax being such a Boy Scout. So I looked back and found a meeting with a Daniel Masseter a couple of months back, beginning of

July. I done a bit of a trawl through the files and everything, but I couldn't find any reference to Daniel Masseter anywhere, not so much as an address or phone number. If Stonax kept any info on him, it was either in that file we think's gone missing—'

'Or it's in the encrypted part of the computer,' Slider said.

'Or both. Anyway, I thought it was worth a bit of a goosey, so I put him in the computer and started searching. Luck would have it, I started with police records and found he'd been in trouble a couple of times doing environmental protests – Hartlepool, the Able UK ship recycling thing?'

'Yes, I remember. The company that got the contract to break up US naval derelicts.'

'Yeah. Well, he chained himself to some gates, apparently, and when they cut him loose he threw a brick and smashed someone's windscreen, so they nicked him. And he was nicked for obstruction in that Essex oil refinery protest. And quite a bit in between.'

'But those were both years ago,' Slider said. 'The Hartlepool thing must be – what – four years ago? And Jaywick two years ago.'

'Yeah, so what's he been up to since then? That's what I wondered.'

'Maybe it would explain, if he'd had trouble with the police in the past, why he didn't come forward to say he had an appointment with Stonax.'

'Maybe. But a more compelling reason, I reckon, is that he's dead.'

'What?'

'Yeah. I wanted to see if he'd been visible recently, so I put him in a news filter, and up he come straight away. *Reading Observer*, local lad killed in an RTA. He was apparently knocked off his motorbike on a country road near Pangbourne – it's a sort of cut-through to the A4. Locals say people use it as a rat run and drive too fast – it's only really a country lane and some of it's single track with passing places. Anyway, he was found by a woman going to work early morning two weeks ago. Him and the bike was in a ditch, there was skid marks across the road, and his neck was broken. Local police reckon from the damage to the bike he must have been sideswiped by a car. They put it down as a hit-and-run driver.'

'And it could have been,' said Slider.

'That's the beauty of it. *Reading Evening Post* did quite a bit on it, tragedy of young life cut short, blah de blah – I printed it out in case you want it – and made out he was some kind of planet-saving hero because of his "well known environmental activities". Then the next day the *Observer* come up with his police record and they dropped him pretty sharpish.'

'I think,' Slider said, 'we need to have a word with his nearest and dearest. Have you found out who they are?'

'Yeah, his nearest, anyway. He lived with his mum on a housing estate in Reading. Don't know if she's his dearest – news reports don't mention if he had a girlfriend.'

'Well, you'd better go and find out, then,' he said, and was rewarded with a wide grin.

'Thanks, guv. I won't let you down.'

Slider drank his tea, swallowed two of the aspirin, thought for a bit, and then rang his best snout, Tidy Barnett. Tidy's sepulchral tones answered at the second ring. ''Ang on a minute, Mr S. Someone 'ere. We ain't secure.' There were various indeterminate sounds as Tidy removed himself to a more secluded spot, and then he was back on. 'What can I do you for? I 'ope it's not about this big business in 'Ammersmith, cause I'm not up to all that. I've 'ad me ear out for you, naturally, but nobody don't know nothing about it.'

'It is about that,' Slider said, 'and I was hoping you could help me with one of the minor players. He fixed the security doors of the flat to unlock themselves at a certain time. Used a transistorised timer, maybe Chinese in origin. Know any electronics experts who might do that sort of thing?'

'Not my street, Mr S,' Tidy said regretfully. 'I could put you on to someone who might 'elp. Ever 'eard of Jack Bushman?'

'Solder Jack? He's not still around, is he? I thought he went to Australia.'

''E did, but 'e's back. Didn't like it out there. Been back years. He's straight now, which is maybe why you ain't 'eard of him. He's got a shop, Ladbroke Grove way, on the KPR. He was into all that miniature stuff. You could try him. Otherwise – well, deceased was a nobby bloke, and it sounds like a nobby murder. You need special snouts. Me and mine is no use to you on this one, guv.'

'Thanks, Tidy,' Slider said, and rang off. He sat thinking for a while, and then, on an impulse, rang his old friend Pauline Smithers. She was Detective Chief Superintendent Smithers now, and back at the Yard after what had seemed to her like an interminable – though successful – stint on child pornography. The trouble with crime like that was that you could never wrap it up and be done with it. As soon as you cleared out one stinking gutter, you'd get word of another. He was glad for Pauly's sanity that they'd moved her on.

They had been in uniform together way back when the world was young, and had always had a soft spot for each other. Then she'd got promoted and married the Job and a while later he'd got married to Irene, his first wife, and that had been that. He had often wondered, idly, how things would have turned out if they had hooked up, as had once seemed quite possible, even likely. She had never married, though he was not vain enough to attribute that to a broken heart. For women, the upper echelons of the police force were harder to tackle than Annapurna, and those who made it were rarely able to have emotional lives.

Which he thought was a shame, because Pauline had been a good egg and a perfectly normal woman.

He called her number. It rang for a long time before she answered, and when she did, she spoke before he had a chance to. 'I'm in a meeting,' she said in a normal, if slightly severe, tone; and then added, very low and urgently, 'I'll ring you back. *Don't* ring me.' Then she was gone.

He had rung her on his mobile. As soon as he rang off, his land line rang.

'Hello, Mr Plod.'

A weary sort of anger surged through him. 'What do you want?'

'I'm just calling to see if you enjoyed my little joke last night,' said Bates.

'Why do you insist on talking like a villain in a B movie?'

'Oh, dear. You sound a bit tetchy. Head aching?'

'I always hated practical jokes, even when I was a child. For an adult to practise them is contemptible.'

'Contemptible, is it? And there was I trying to be kind to you. I could have killed you, you know. I could have filled the bucket with sand. By the way, are you trying to trace this call?'

'Of course,' said Slider.

'Well, you might as well amuse yourself, but you'll never be able to. My skills, small as they are, are sufficient to run rings round your mediaeval tracing capabilities.'

'They didn't have telephones in mediaeval times. A man of your education ought to know that.'

He chuckled. 'Keeping me talking, eh? I don't mind. Time is not of the essence to me.'

Slider tired of it. 'Well, it is to me. What do you want?'

'Just to let you know that if you enjoyed that little joke, you'll love the next one. Do you like Guy Fawkes Night?'

'Not particularly.'

'Well, you'll find my little surprise *divine*. Divine as in see you in heaven.'

'Or in your case, not,' said Slider.

But Bates had gone. McLaren came to the door a few moments later and shook his head. 'Same story, guv. Bounced round the satellites. Mick Hutton reckons you'd need to keep him talking for fifteen minutes to have a chance of tracing it – and even then, he wouldn't be there with his stickies on the receiver.' He eyed Slider sympathetically. 'What did he want this time?'

'Dear Mr Slider: threat, threat, threat, threat. Yours sincerely.'

'Bloody hypocrite. I'm going to get a sarnie. Can I get you one?'

'God, is it lunch time already?'

'Going down the stall outside the market,' McLaren said temptingly.

'Go on then. I'll have a sausage sandwich. With tomato sauce.'

'Got it,' said McLaren, and wheeled away.

He passed Atherton coming the other way. 'Word, guv?'
Atherton asked. Slider nodded him in. 'Emily's gone off on
her travels. We got her a hired car this morning and she's
gone to see the Ring 4 people. Not,' he added, 'that you
know that, because she isn't doing it officially and we've no
idea where she is.'

'What *do* we know, officially?' Slider asked. He heard
himself sounding tetchy and reached for the aspirin bottle,
before realising he had taken them too recently to take more.
His shoulder was aching, too. He rubbed it carefully.

'I've been looking up the Sid Andrew business,' Atherton
said. He observed his boss's actions but guessed sympathy
would get his nose bitten off. 'The girl in the case was called
Angela Barlow. She was a junior press officer in the DTI –
that's a civil service appointment, not a political one. Quite
a looker, twenty-eight when it all happened, secretarial background, interest in journalism – what bright girl these days
doesn't want to be a journalist? – been in the job just under
two years. She seemed to disappear without trace after she
got sacked, and with the media interest in her, I thought she
probably would have gone to earth. I mean, those pictures
were pretty explicit, and the popular press's appetite for all
things salacious being what it is—'

'So where did she go?' Slider cut in.

'She went home to her parents,' Atherton said.

Slider read the bad news in his eyes. 'And?'

'She's dead. Committed suicide last January.'

Slider slammed to his feet. 'That's it,' he said. 'We're
going to find out what this whole Sid Andrew thing was
about. We're going to go and see her parents, and then we're
going to and roust him.'

'Maybe it was just shame,' Atherton said, playing devil's
advocate. 'We've only got the Stonax supporters' word for
it that the thing was a set up.'

Slider didn't glance at him as he walked past. 'We'll find
out,' he said. 'And then we'll know.'

Twelve

Thickening

It didn't take Emily long to discover the local journalist from the *Woburn Courier* who had been responsible for the story of Tyler's escape. She found Chris Fletcher at the magistrates' court in Milton Keynes, and persuaded him outside for a chat.

'I'm sorry to interrupt your work,' she said when they reached the open air.

'Dunt matter,' he said equably. 'I was busting for a smoke, anyway. Do you?' He proffered the pack and she shook her head. 'Mind if I do?' He didn't wait for her reply, but knocked one out, shoved it in his mouth and lit it like a starving man falling on bread. He was young, mid-twenties, she thought, and staggeringly badly dressed, with a tweed jacket that was far too big, a tie that looked as if it might have been used to tie up a dog, a grubby shirt with a crumpled collar, and cheap, scuffed shoes at the end of what looked like his old school trousers. The dress code for the magistrates' court had evidently fallen hard on him. He had a snubby, rather pallid but not unattractive face, and spiky fair hair ending in an unfashionable mullet. His fingernails were badly bitten and his fingers badly stained with nicotine. Being a journalist at this level must be really stressful, she thought.

'I won't keep you long,' she said. 'I'm just interested in a story you filed back in July about an escaped prisoner—'

'Oh, God, yes, that!' he jumped in. 'I thought I'd got it made! Big city here I come! But it all turned out to be rubbish and I got a rocket from my editor. He kicked my bum so hard I couldn't sit down for a week.'

'Would you tell me what happened?'

He was so eager to talk she didn't have to give him a reason for asking. The fact that she was Press seemed to be enough for him.

'Well, it was just luck I came across it, really, because I was going home one evening and there's this cut through round the back of Apsley Guise – I live in Husborne Crawley?' She nodded as if she knew what he was talking about so as not to slow him down. 'Anyway, it's just a lane and there's never much traffic on it, so I wasn't surprised to find myself on my own. Then I come round a bend, and there's a barrier across the road. I was on my bike – I've got this mini Moto. It's useful for getting about to stories, easier to park than a car – not that I could afford a car anyway on what they pay me.'

'Right. You came across a barrier?'

'Yeah. Well, I didn't want to go back, so I pushed the bike round it. And round the next corner there's a local cop I know, Colin Gunter, and he stops me. I look past him and I see a big Ring 4 van and some more police and a couple of patrol cars. So I says, "S'up Col?" and he says, "You can't come down this way. There's a prison van been held up." So then he tells me this prisoner was on the way to Woodhill, the van got held up and he's on the loose. So I go back and phone the story straight in, and I ring the *Telegraph* news desk as well. I've been doing that for a while, any time I hear anything good, because I'm hoping to make a name with them, and then they'll give me a job.'

'Why the *Telegraph*?' she asked out of idle curiosity.

'It's what me dad reads. Anyway, the *Courier* puts my story in, but it's hardly gone to bed when I get a call from Colin to say it was all a mistake, there was no-one in the van, it just broke down, and someone was having a laugh with him, telling him there was an escaped prisoner. I was well gutted, and the next thing the editor calls me in and chews my arse off. It was too late to stop the story, but nobody else had run it and in the end he just left it, cause he said it would look worse to print a retraction. And that was that. I never heard anything more about it.'

'How did your editor know the story was wrong?'

'Someone rang him from Ring 4 – the controller down in

Luton – Trish Holland, I think her name is. Apparently this bloke *was* going to be moved, and then it was all cancelled at the last minute. That's why they thought he was in the van, I s'pose. Anyway, it's a shame, because it would have been a lot of fun if he really was on the run. We had one over the wall last year and we got three days' front pages out of him before they caught him.'

'The *Telegraph* didn't print his name, I notice,' she said.

'Well, it was only a stop press, and I s'pose they wanted to check it before they ran it properly. Lucky for them they did. Unlucky for me, though – I'll never get a job there now.'

She felt rather sorry for him, with his forlorn hopes and his lost scoop. She said, 'The real news is always local. That's the news that affects peoples' lives.'

'Are you local press?'

'Yes,' she said, and it was true, though New York was a rather more seething metropolis than Woburn.

The control centre at Luton was sited in a modern block on a small industrial estate, and Trish Holland was a middle-aged woman with a cosy figure and hard make-up. She allowed Emily into her presence with the ease most people seemed to accord to the press, but she grew defensive when she learned the subject for discussion.

'There never was an escape,' she said angrily. 'It was all in the mind of that stupid reporter from Woburn. I suppose he thought he was having a joke. Everyone seems to like poking fun at Ring 4. I'd like to see them do a job like ours.'

'Yes, and I want to do an article exactly on that point,' Emily said warmly. 'I want to put Ring 4's side of things. It's all too easy to make cheap jokes without knowing the facts.'

She ceased to bridle. 'You're completely right there. Facts were pretty thin on the ground in that story. It wasn't even one of our vans.'

'The reporter says he saw the Ring 4 logo on it.'

'Doesn't matter. All of our vans were accounted for. And it's easy enough to hire a suitable van and fake a logo. Film companies do it all the time.'

'That's true. But you did, in fact, have a movement order for Trevor Bates?'

'Yes, he *was* going to be moved, to Woodhill, and we had the usual paperwork to collect him from Wormwood Scrubs—'

'The paperwork was all correct?'

'Of course it was. A copy was sent to me and it was completely in order, otherwise I wouldn't have put it through. Then at the last minute I was notified that he wasn't being moved after all, so I cancelled the movement, and that was that. Far from having escaped, he was never in transit at all. He's still in Wormwood Scrubs, as far as I know.'

'Who was it who notified you of the cancellation?'

'One of the directors of Ring 4, Mr Mark. He'd said he'd been notified by the Home Office of the change of plan. He faxed through the paperwork, I stood down the team, and no movement of any sort was made that evening.'

'Well, thank you, that's all very clear,' Emily said. 'I'm certainly glad to have heard your side of the story. Fortunately it never made it to the national press.'

'No, and that boy will be more careful in future, after the wigging I gave his editor. But it's all of a piece with the general attitude that Ring 4 is fair game.' She went on to complain at length and in detail about various other bad stories Ring 4 had had told against it, and Emily listened for as long as she could bear it before apologising and extracting herself. She needed to get back to her computer to do some more checking.

Hart had discovered long ago in the Job that the recently bereaved rarely resent people coming and asking them questions. It accounted for how often people could be seen on television screens talking about their loss at a time when the uninitiated would have expected them to be prostrate, with the curtains closed. The big, savage grief generally held off for some time, and arrived when everyone else had got tired of the subject and gone away, leaving the bereaved unsupported.

Mrs Masseter lived in a tiny house in a dismal, raw new estate outside Reading. The estate was as featureless as the fields it had replaced, but not nearly so green or pleasant. Each little yellow-brick house had a paved-over front area to make up for the lack of a garage, and the tiny back gardens were mostly still nothing but bumpy developer's grass between the cheap orange fencing, except where young inmates had already trampled them bare. The approach roads were laid in a series of unnecessary twists and cul-de-sacs, presumably to make the place look friendlier, and here and there along the pavements puny saplings were struggling to survive, shackled like starving prisoners to thick posts. Elsewhere empty holes showed where two out of three had already been uprooted by vandals. You can't be nice to some people, Hart thought.

The Masseter house was tiny, the front door leading straight into a single sitting/dining-room with a kitchen alcove off it and French windows leading into the garden. Halfway along one wall an open-plan staircase led up to what could only be, Hart judged from the dimensions and some experience, two tiny bedrooms with a bathroom in between. Mrs Masseter was shapeless, grey-haired and hopeless, though probably only in her late fifties. She was pathetically eager to talk to Hart, and had her sitting on the sofa with a cup of tea listening to her life story before you could say knife.

Not that there was much to tell. The most important thing that ever seemed to have happened to her was her husband running off with the teller from the Halifax in Castle Street, a dyed blonde divorcée who was fifty-five if she was a day (the age seemed an additional affront to Mrs Masseter, as if she could have borne a twenty-year-old rival much more gracefully). The running off accounted for why she was living in this place, which was all she could afford once the value of the family home was split between her and her husband.

'The law's a terrible thing,' she said, 'when it can turn a person out of her own home just so her husband can buy a place for his fancy woman. The solicitor told me it was because Danny was grown up, so I was only due half the house. I said Danny's still going to live with me – because there was no way he'd live with his dad and *that woman* – but they said he was nearly thirty and that's all that mattered. He counted as a grown-up so he was reckoned to fend for himself. But my Danny's *never* been able to look after himself. If it wasn't for me, he'd never have a clean shirt to his back.'

The other important thing that had happened in her life

was Daniel's death, but she didn't seem to be coming to grips with that. She spoke about her son in the present tense, as though death was some kind of trip he had gone off on, and from which he would be returning eventually with a haversack full of dirty clothes for her to wash.

'He's always going off on his protests,' she said proudly, when Hart got the conversation round to him. 'He's a member of all those things, Greenpeace and Friends of the Earth and what have you. He really *cares* about things, animals and the environment and global warming and all that. And unlike *some* people I could name, he puts his money where his mouth is. His dad's always griping about him not having a job, but I say to him, our Danny *does* have a job – saving the planet. And you can't have a more important job than that, can you?'

'He's had some trouble with the police in the past, hasn't he?' Hart asked.

The question didn't seem to bother Mrs Masseter. 'Well, it's bound to happen, isn't it? I mean, the police have got to be on the side of the landowners, stands to reason. I'm not blaming you, dear, because I can see it's your job. You can't afford to worry about right and wrong. But Danny has to do what's right for the planet and that. If it means clashing with the police – well, there you are. More tea? Help yourself to sugar. No, my Danny would never have got into trouble in the normal way. He's a good boy and he'd never break the law, except in a protest. But he has to do what's right, and he does, whatever it costs him. He's that sort of boy.'

'Do you know what he was involved with just lately? I gather he'd been back home?'

'Yes, since he came back from Scotland, about three weeks ago.'

'What was he up to in Scotland?'

'Oh, I don't know, dear,' she said. 'It was something to do with—' She screwed up her face with effort. 'Oh, he did tell me. Something about water, was it? And Cadbury's? Oh dear, I can't remember. Cadbury's came into it, and Beryl somebody. Not Beryl Reid, but something like that.'

'Cadbury's?' Hart queried. 'Their factory's not in Scotland.'

'I'm sure he said Cadbury's. Anyway, I know it was Scotland

because he'd been going up and down for months now. To tell you the truth, I don't really understand a lot of what he goes on about, with his scientific words and all that. But I do know he said this one was very important and secret and the less I knew about it the better. He said it was high-powered stuff and it was going to cause a stink when it got out. Quite excited about it. And it's the same one he's been on for ages.'

'Are any of the organisations involved? You know, Greenpeace and so on?'

'I don't think so. He never said they were. In fact – ' she frowned again, considering – 'he seems to be doing this one all alone. Usually there's his friends tramping in and out – scruffy lot, and don't some of 'em smell! But their hearts are in the right place, I suppose – and having meetings in his bedroom and making leaflets and placards and I don't know what. But there's been none of that this time, so I suppose he's been doing it on his own. If it was deadly secret, maybe he couldn't trust anyone else.' She stared at nothing for a moment, and then said, 'Except he did have this journalist person who was going to help him, a high-up, he said, who'd been in the government.'

'Ed Stonax?' Hart asked.

'Could have been,' she said. 'Yes, I think that was his name. He was into all that eco stuff himself, this journalist, which was why Danny went to him. He sent him a load of stuff just recently – documents and that.'

'Danny sent it to Mr Stonax?'

'Yes, and sent it registered post, so that shows you how important it was. Danny was going up to London to see him after, only he had his accident.' For a moment she faltered, as the jagged spike of the accident refused to fit into the woolly shape of her reality. 'He sent me flowers,' she went on. 'When he heard about it.'

'Mr Stonax did?'

'He rang to see why he hadn't heard from Danny, and I told him. And the next day these flowers arrived. Those big lilies that smell. Ever so posh.' She looked round vaguely as if she expected to see them. 'They don't last long, that sort, but they're nice.'

'That was kind of him.'

'Danny always said he was a real gentleman. A right proper sort. He was upset when he heard about the accident. It wasn't Danny's fault, you know,' she added anxiously. 'He wasn't a tearaway. He wouldn't have been speeding or anything. He was never in trouble that way. You can check if you like – never even had any points on his licence. It was a hit-and-run driver, they said – your lot said, only the locals, I mean. Hit-and-run.' She paused, staring again. 'So I suppose they'll never find out who it was.'

She looked strangely stunned by the end of the last sentence. Hit-and-run, Danny with a broken neck and never coming home again, were things outside her experience. At some point she would have to come to terms with them, but for the moment her mind was defending itself like anything against realisation.

'Would you mind if I had a look at Danny's room?' Hart asked.

Mrs Masseter jerked out of a reverie, and smiled as though she was glad to do so. 'You can have a look, and welcome, but if it's his papers or anything to do with his protests you're interested in, you won't find anything like that. Your lot have already got them.'

'My lot?'

'The police. A policeman came that same day and said they wanted all his papers and his computer. It was quite late when he came. Mike – my husband – had just gone, and I thought it was him come back when the doorbell rang. But no, he'd gone off home to be with *her*. Said she'd be upset, though what she'd got to be upset about I don't know.'

'This policeman—' Hart prompted.

'He was one like you,' Mrs Masseter said, and as Hart was thinking he must have been black, she added, 'not in uniform, I mean. A plain-clothes one, a detective, whatever you call yourselves.'

'Did he give his name?'

'Yes, it was Inspector something.' She frowned. 'I'll think of it in a minute. It was an ordinary name, like Black. I think it began with a B. Or a G. Was it Green? Anyway, he said he wanted Danny's things, and he went upstairs, and come down with all his papers in plastic bags – two lots he had to do, to take 'em all. And he took Danny's computer – not the television bit, but the box bit that sits under his desk.'

Hart had a bad feeling about it. It was just not the way things were done. She got out her brief and showed it to Mrs Masseter again. 'Did he show you his identification, like this?'

'No, he just said he was Inspector whateveritwas – was it Sampson? No, not Sampson, but something like that. Strong, was it? Anyway, he said could he have Danny's papers.'

'Did he say why he wanted them?'

'Well, no. I suppose it was some police thing. I mean, Danny wasn't in trouble. I suppose it was because of the accident he wanted them.'

Hart rolled her mental eyes. 'And you didn't ask to see his identification?'

She frowned a little. 'Well, it would've been rude, wouldn't it? Like calling him a liar. Strong. I'm sure now he said his name was Strong – Inspector Strong.'

'But if you didn't see his ID, how did you know he was a policeman?' Hart asked in despair.

'Well, he said he was. Anyway, who else could he have been?'

Who indeed, Hart thought. 'Would you mind if I just had a look at his room anyway?'

'No, dear. You go ahead. It's the one at the front.'

Hart climbed the narrow, cardboard stairs, turned carefully on the midget-sized landing, and took the one step necessary to bring her to the open bedroom door. The room was about eleven foot square, with a window on to the street, and a street lamp directly outside which must have flooded the room all night with yellow light through the thin curtains. They were patterned with lions, and matched the duvet cover on the single bed under the window, smoothed out and pulled taut by a mother's hand. There was no dust anywhere, the carpet had been hoovered, and there was very little lying about. Either he had been a very tidy boy – boy? He was nearly thirty, she reminded herself – or his mother had put everything away.

The walls were bare except for two posters neatly put up with Blu-tack, one of an African elephant on the veldt, the other the famous view of the earth from outer space, all blue and white and romantic.

Along one wall was a cheap desk unit with shelving above and a wheeled office chair in front of it. On the desk the VDU, keyboard and printer sat forlornly, their wires fed down the trough cut in the back and leading to nothing but the footprints in the carpet where the box had stood. She couldn't know, therefore, anything about the computer, but the printer was a very good one and the screen a new-looking nineteen-inch flat. In contrast to everything else about this house, it looked as though nothing had been stinted on the IT front.

But all the shelves and the drawers were empty. 'Inspector Strong' had taken no chances and cleared everything out. At the end of the desk there was a CD player with speakers, but there were no CDs anywhere to be seen. Strong must have taken those as well, perhaps on suspicion that a computer data disc might be hidden among them.

There was hardly room for anything else, except an upright chair with a haversack resting on it. Hart looked inside just in case, but it was empty except for half of a Snickers wrapper and a box of Bluebell matches. She lifted up the liner at the bottom and searched in the corners of the pockets, but there was nothing there but ancient crumbs and fluff. And that left only the beside table on which stood a bedside lamp with a frieze of cut-out elephants round the shade, a travelling alarm clock, a set of house-keys attached to a rubber fried egg, a water flask on a strap of the sort runners carry, and a paper-back book. Presumably it was what Danny had been reading in bed.

Hart picked it up. *Elephant Song*. Either Inspector Strong hadn't seen it – which was possible because it was behind the flask and not visible until you reached the table, and he must have been in a hurry – or he hadn't thought it important. She flicked through to see if anything had been scribbled in it, but the pages were clean. But there was something – a piece of paper, folded into a long thin strip as though it was being used as a bookmark. She opened it out. It was a printed letter from Reading Borough Libraries. *The following book(s) are overdue. Failure to return the book(s) may lead to increasing fines.*

There was only one title: *Analysis of Risks Associated with Nuclear Submarine Decommissioning, Dismantling and*

Disposal. Unsurprisingly, it had an asterisk beside it and was marked 'Special Loan – Reading University Library'.

Well, how's about that for light bedtime reading, Hart thought to herself. She turned the paper over. On the blank back of the form, in a scrawly, unformed handwriting in blue biro, was a sort of list.

> Clydebrae
> Scottish War Museem St Vincent St
> Clyde Maritime and Shipping Museem (Govan)
> public records office Argyle St
> universty? Meekie book
> Hager Loch (Museem?)

Then a word so scrawly she couldn't read it properly. It looked like Newark. And at the bottom, scrawliest of all: cad ber.

Hart grinned to herself. He couldn't even spell Cadbury's, the dipstick, never mind know where the factory was!

She took the piece of paper with her and left the sad, empty little room to its thoughts.

Mrs Masseter looked up eagerly when she stepped off the bottom of the stairs. 'All right, dear? I've kept it nice and clean and tidy, not that there's much left since your Inspector Strong came. I'm just boiling the kettle again – you'll have another cup?'

'I found this in a book beside Danny's bed,' Hart said, showing her the paper.

She turned it automatically from the written to the printed side, and unexpectedly blushed. 'Oh, I know, there's been another of them just this morning. Asking for their book back, and I don't know what to do – that inspector must have taken it with the other books because it's nowhere in this house, that I do know. But if it's a library book he oughtn't to keep it, did he? I don't want to get into trouble about it. Could *you* ask him to send it to them, dear? Only I don't know where he is or anything.'

'There's some writing on the other side,' Hart said patiently. 'Can you tell me if that's Danny's writing?'

'Oh, yes. Just some of his nonsense.'

'Would you mind if I kept it?'

She looked doubtful. 'Well, if you think it's important. Only there's the library book to think of.'

'I'll have a word with Reading Library,' Hart promised, and Mrs Masseter's face cleared like fast-forwarded clouds parting.

'Thank you ever so much,' she said. Her only son had been killed and she was shut in the human equivalent of a hamster cage without him for the rest of her life, but she was so relieved the library weren't going to chase her for an overdue library book.

In an access of pity, Hart stayed for another cup of tea, which was not like her.

Thirteen

'Orrible Merger

Angela Barlow's parents had little to add. They received Slider and Atherton with polite reserve, a well-to-do retired couple in a nice house in a leafy suburb, with a large garden, a Labrador, and a flotilla of framed photographs on the piano. Outside, blackbirds hopped across the neatly manicured lawn; and inside, the nice people whose lives had seemed so immutably pleasant less than a year ago revisited, at Slider's behest, the bewildered grief that had come upon them when their daughter had killed herself.

Angela had been their youngest, of four. All the children had received good educations and had done well. Angela had studied anthropology at university, largely, it seemed, because she didn't have any particular career in mind. But she had worked hard and got a good degree, and immediately after graduating had done a secretarial course, because she thought the skills would be useful. The Barlows plainly felt pride in this evidence both of good sense and good will. 'She didn't just go on the dole like so many of her friends and wait for a job offer to come round.' Mr Barlow said. 'She actually got out there and *did* something.'

After the secretarial course she had done some temporary work, and then asked them to fund her in a journalism course. 'Journalism was her real interest,' Mrs Barlow said. 'And I'm sure she would have been a great success, because English was always her best subject at school, and she wrote very nicely. She had several things published in the school magazine.'

Mr Barlow seemed to feel an embarrassment. 'It's not quite the same thing, dear,' he said.

She looked hurt. 'I'm just saying she was good at writing.'

'I don't think these gentlemen want to know about that sort of thing.'

'I'm interested in everything you want to tell me,' Slider said gently.

Angela's photograph was looking at him across her mother's shoulder from the top of the piano and it made him feel both angry and sad, as such reminders of lives lost always did.

The Barlows resumed. Degree, secretarial diploma and journalism course notwithstanding, no journalism jobs presented themselves for their daughter, and after several months at home, driven by the example of her successful older siblings, Angela had taken a job at a PR agency rather than remain unemployed. She had quite enjoyed it, but after three years had wanted a change, had seen a recruitment advertisement for the civil service for press officers, and had decided it would at least be closer to journalism than where she was.

'She thought it would give her good experience, and lots of useful contacts, so that she could make the move to journalism in a year or two,' said Mrs Barlow.

'And did she do well in the job?' Slider asked.

'I think so. She seemed to be enjoying it, and was quite excited about her prospects. She went to live in London, of course, and we didn't see so much of her after that. She was very busy, and only managed to get home once or twice a year. Of course, she had a very lively social life, from all accounts, so she didn't really have time—' She stopped abruptly and gave her husband a haunted look.

'We didn't know,' he took up gently, 'how lively it was. We can't understand how she was so led astray. It could only have been high spirits, because there was never any bad in her. She was a good girl and a good daughter. I suppose her liveliness must have got her into bad company without realising the danger she was in. And then – then it all broke like a storm over our heads. It was so sudden. We never had an inkling anything was going on until those terrible pictures appeared in the papers.'

'You didn't hear from Angela beforehand that anything of the sort was likely to happen?'

'No, of course not. I don't think she knew any photographs had been taken. They were – they were—'

'We know,' said Slider, to save him having to describe them. 'I'm so sorry. It must have been a terrible shock for you.'

'We felt she must either have been very drunk at the time, or have been taking some drugs. We hoped the former rather than the latter. She'd never taken drugs before, to our knowledge, but I understand it's quite common in those circles – cocaine and so on.' He paused, almost enquiringly, but Slider did not commit himself. 'But either way,' Mr Barlow resumed, 'she had let herself down very badly. And then they sacked her. We didn't know about that at first.'

'She didn't tell us, because she was too ashamed,' said Mrs Barlow.

'Then she telephoned and said she wanted to get away from London and asked how we'd feel about her coming home.'

'We said *of course* she should come, this was her *home*,' Mrs Barlow said, with a speed and emphasis that suggested to Slider it had not been as automatic as all that at the time. Harsh words were probably spoken and harsh thoughts certainly harboured before the black sheep was taken back into the fold; and harsh regrets were now desperately trying to rewrite the script.

'And did she speak to you about what had happened?' Slider asked.

Mrs Barlow shook her head. 'She didn't want to talk about it. She was terribly depressed. She said, "Mummy, I've let you all down." She was most worried about what her brothers and sister felt about it all. Well, they were shocked, of course. And it's only natural that they should want to distance themselves from it at first, while the scandal was fresh, because they all have partners and children to think about.'

'But they would have got over it,' Mr Barlow said. 'It was just that Christmas.' His face was drawn, reliving some domestic horror. Slider could imagine the scenes. 'Well, that Christmas wasn't easy. And Angela grew even more depressed. And then one day . . .'

He couldn't go on. He rested his forehead on his knuckles in a curiously awkward attempt to hide his eyes.

Mrs Barlow took the story up with a desperate courage, looking straight at Slider and Atherton as if daring them to pity her. 'One day she said she was going out for a walk.

It was snowing, and I said put something on your head, you lose forty per cent of your body heat through your head. She said, "Don't fuss, Mummy," and went out. And later – well, they found her hanging from a tree in the wood down by the stream. The police came, and—' Now she couldn't continue.

Slider asked, 'Did she leave a note?'

But she had not, and the lack of any word from her seemed to be one of the things that made it harder for them.

Soon afterwards, Slider and Atherton took their leave. 'Sid Andrew next,' he said grimly as they got back in the car.

'If you can get him to talk to you,' Atherton said. 'He's Lord Sid now.'

'By God, he'd better talk,' Slider said. 'That girl may or may not have been pushing the boat out, but if she wasn't an innocent victim of all this, my nose is a nectarine.'

'Which it ain't, my dear old guv,' Atherton said gloomily, and then exclaimed, with transferred emotion, 'God, I hate the suburbs!'

Despite having taken the name of his birthplace for his title, Lord Leuchars, the former Sid Andrew, preferred Northamptonshire for his home on leaving the House of Commons, and had bought himself a handsome Victorian mansion and twelve acres within handy reach of the M1, which of course as well as leading north also led south into the heart of London. They did not have to penetrate the leafy solitude of Blisworth Manor, however, for his lordship was at that moment chairing a meeting of one of his quangos, the Forestry (Sustainable Uses) Advisory Committee, in the library conference room at the Swan Hotel in Bedford.

The staff of the hotel (which depended a great deal on businessmen and conferences for its profits) were naturally unwilling to disturb well-paying delegates, but Slider was in no mood to be brooked and said either they could fetch him out quietly or he'd go in and get him noisily.

So very shortly afterward, Lord Leuchars came out into the corridor, giving them a glimpse of the handsomely panelled room and a dozen comfortable men around a mahogany table before the door was shut.

'What's all this about?' Leuchars demanded shortly, though

not as irritably as he might have, for the committee had lunched extremely well before resuming their meeting.

Sid Andrew was a short, wide man, so wide he gave the disconcerting appearance of having been flattened, like a cartoon character run over by a steamroller. His head was rather large for his body; his face was red, with a spreading nose indicating a lifelong devotion to the bottle. It was also much scarred around the lower cheek and jowl by youthful acne, which made shaving difficult, so there were little tufts and sprigs of iron-grey whisker here and there in the craters, which gave him an unfortunately unwashed appearance. He had shaggy white hair, always unkempt, and thick black eyebrows over pale, watery, red-veined eyes. Atherton had never seen him close up, and thought again of pretty Angela Barlow. It must surely have been someone's idea of a joke to pair them in sexual congress.

'I'd like to talk to you in private,' Slider said when he had introduced them. 'Is there somewhere we can go?'

'What makes you think I want to talk to you?' he growled. He had never lost his accent – indeed, he wore it, with his working-class background and his trade-union credentials, almost aggressively as badges of honour.

'You *will* talk to me,' Slider said quietly, 'and either we can do it the easy way or we can do it the hard way. I imagine there are things you wouldn't want said in public.'

'Aw, bloody hell, what now?' he said, scowling. His vinous breath wafted towards them as he sighed, but he looked into their faces, shook his head wearily, and then said, 'Wait a minute, then.' He went back into the room, and they heard him say, 'Fellas, I'm gauny have ta love ye and leave ye. Wally, can you take over this lot?' before the door swung shut of its own weight. Half a minute later he was out again, walking by them briskly saying, 'You'd better come to my room.'

His room was in fact a suite, with a large sitting-room over-looking the river and the glimpse of a bedroom beyond. He waved them to a sofa and headed straight for the mahogany bar in the corner. 'Snifter?' he offered.

'Thank you, no. Not on duty,' Slider said.

'Well, I'm having one. Let me know if you change your mind.' He fixed himself a large brandy and soda, came back and sank ungracefully into a chair facing them, and said, 'Well, what do you want? Shepherd's Bush? I don't know anyone in Shepherd's Bush.'

'It's concerning the death of Ed Stonax.'

'Oh, is that it?' Leuchars rolled his eyes. 'I half suspected you lot might start digging up old grievances when I read he'd snuffed it. He was a nasty piece of work, let me tell you, so don't waste any of your sympathy on him.'

Slider could see he was loquacious with drink – and possibly nervousness – which was all to the good. 'Nasty in what way?' he enquired.

'In a bloody bigoted, middle-class, self-satisfied-prig sort of way, if you want to know,' he said, and laughed. 'I'm not sorry he's dead, so you can make what you like of that. Thought himself too good for the rest of us, big-headed bastard.' He pronounced it with the short 'a', which made it sound more vicious. 'But he was stupit, like all those elitist do-gooders, so everything that happened to him was his own fault. What d'you want to know about him, anyway?' He took a swig of his drink and said, 'Christ, I could do wi' a cigar!' He jabbed a stubby finger upwards to the ceiling. 'Smoke alarms every-where. You don't know how to disable 'em, do you? Christ, what do they teach you in copper school anyway? I can't believe our lot brought in these fucking no smoking laws. What the fuck was all that about, eh?'

'Mr Andrew,' Slider began.

'It's Lord Leuchars to you, Jimmy!' he exclaimed, his face reddening. His accent grew stronger with his anger. 'It's no' much, but it's all I've got tae show for forty years service. An' I fuckin' earned it, so don't you disrespect me, boy.'

'No disrespect intended, I assure you,' Slider said sooth-ingly. 'It was a slip of the tongue. What I really wanted to ask you about was the business of the photographs with Ed Stonax and Angela Barlow.'

Unexpectedly, he chuckled. 'Oh, that old thing! It was a bloody laugh, was that. You've seen the photos, have you? Brilliant!'

'The purpose was to get Stonax sacked from the depart-ment, I suppose?'

'He wasn't sacked, he resigned. Eventually . . .' He chuckled again; and then the smile disappeared as if wiped. 'Mind you, if the stupit bastard had gone quietly when they first showed him the piccies, he'd have saved himself a shitload of trouble. But he started bellowing that it was all a big set-up and he was being framed, so he just made things worse for himself.'

'But he was framed, wasn't he?' Atherton asked.

Leuchars looked at him for the first time. 'Of course he was. That was the whole point. My God, you've seen that girl – what a piece of tail! And look at me! Christ, son, she wouldn't have touched me with the far end of a bargepole. That was what made it so fucking funny. And Stonax, of all people, the original altar boy!'

'The photos were faked, then?' Slider said, feeling relief and rage in about equal proportions.

'We were never all three in the same room together,' Leuchars said. 'Brilliant work,' he added, though a little morosely. 'Even I'd have sworn they were real.'

'Why did you pick on Angela Barlow?' Slider wanted to know.

'She'd been partying a bit too hard, done too many lines o' coke, made mistakes, been indiscreet. She looked like being trouble somewhere down the line so it was a chance to get rid of her. She hadn't got a boyfriend, lived alone, so she'd be easy to see off. And she'd been in the service less than two years.' He shrugged, and took another swig. 'I wouldn't have worried about employment laws, but they said it made it just that bit easier. Course, if Stonax had gone quietly, her part would never have come out. She'd have taken the settlement all right and no-one any the wiser.'

'And what about you? You got kicked out as well.'

'I got my pay-off,' he said indifferently. 'Mind you, it's no as much fun as being in the Commons, I'll tell ye that. And I can never go back to Fife after the scandal. But what the hell.' He finished the brandy and heaved himself to his feet. 'Sure I can't tempt you gentlemen?'

His gait across the room was just a trifle unsteady, and he came back with another large one, almost dropping into the armchair. 'Where was I?'

'You can't go back to Fife,' Atherton prompted.

Andrew winked. 'Aye, and I'll tell you what – you'd be a

fuckin' moron to want to.' Another swig. 'So what is it you want to know?'

'What it was all about,' Atherton said. 'What Stonax had done to make you go to so much trouble to get rid of him.'

Andrew nodded, going over to serious mode, and said, 'You've heard of the Waverley B Shipyard?'

Slider, who hadn't, said, 'Pretend we haven't, and tell us from the beginning.'

'Waverley B was one of the biggest shipyards on the Clyde. It was owned by Dansk, the Danish shipbuilders, but they wanted out. They could never make a go of it. It was always an unlucky yard. Plagued with accidents, absenteeism, a lot o' bad feeling. But – ' a feeble rage seized him – 'they were gaunnae close the fucking yard, with two thousand jobs down the toley, just before the last election, with the Nats creaming us at three by-elections within three months, and the polls all tae cock!'

'Not good,' Atherton commented, since he seemed to want something.

'You bet it wasnae good.' He drained his glass, and held it out to Atherton abruptly. 'Get me another of these. I can't get up.'

Slider nodded minutely, and Atherton did as he was asked. Andrew nursed the glass tenderly and went on. 'Well, we couldn't persuade Dansk to hold on. But then I had a stroke of genius. Anderson-Millar – you know who they are?' It was an ironic question.

'Ships, planes and tanks,' Atherton said tersely.

'Right. Well, they'd been wanting to merge with BriTech, who did all the military electronics for the Ministry of Defence, and we'd been blocking it. Too much defence provision in one company. The Monopolies Commission was my baby, of course, as head of the DTI. So my brilliant idea was that we drop our objections, let the merger go ahead in return for Anderson-Millar buying the Waverley B and keeping it open. And it worked. It fucking worked!'

'It did?'

'We won the election, didn't we?' he said aggressively. 'But Mr God Almighty Stonax wasn't happy. He'd been in on the meetings and he thought the AM-BriTech merger wasn't good for the nation. Without competition we'd end up having to pay too much for our defence kit – that was his beef. When he couldn't stop it, he threatened to go to the press with it, cause a stink – maybe force another election if the stink was big enough. Well, we couldn't let him do that. So we had to get rid of him – and do it in a way that would stop his mouth. Hence the pictures. The fancy artwork. Destroy his reputation. Disgraced ex-journo chucks mud, it doesn't stick like it would from Mr Clean. We thought the threat would be enough – ' he shook his head in wonder – 'but he wouldn't roll over. We had to leak the photos to the press, and then threaten to do the same to his kid and his burrd before he caved.'

He took another slug of brandy, and Slider said, 'I'm glad you're being so frank and helpful over this matter—'

'Nothing you can do about it now, is there?' Andrew interrupted. 'Election's over and done with.'

'There's the little matter of blackmail,' Atherton said.

Andrew wasn't moved. 'You could never prove it. Anyway, Stonax is dead, the girl's dead, and I'm not going to press charges, am I?'

'Yes, you were the third victim. Why was that? It can't have been pleasant for you. Had you upset them in some way?'

He tried to shrug it off for a moment. 'I've done all right out of it. I got ma title, all these quangos, directorships – I'm earning ten times what I got as a minister.'

'But the public humiliation,' Atherton suggested gently. 'You had to take the rap for something you hadn't done – and when you were the one to solve the problem for them.'

It was enough to break through the crust into the self-pity reserves beneath. 'You're fucking right! You're no wrang! Money's all very well, but I'm nobody now. I was an MP and a minister, I was in the *cabinet*, for chrissake. I had *power*, and now I'm Jimmy nobody! Nothing I do makes any difference to anyone now. Lord Leuchars? I'm a joke!'

'So why did they turn against you?'

'They blamed me for hiring Stonax in the first place. I was the one suggested we ought to get a media star on the press team, I was the one who picked him out of the applicants. So I had to go down with him. And I'll tell you something else. They didn't want me to get the credit for winning the election. Oh, no. That was reserved for bloody Tyler, the wonder boy.'

Slider felt a prickle, like the sting of electricity, along his scalp at the name. 'You mean Richard Tyler?'

'Aye, who else? There was only the five of us in on the whole thing – me, Tyler, Molly Scott from the number ten office, Stonax to work out the press angles for us, ha ha, and Stuffy Paxton from Anderson-Millar.'

'Sir Henry Paxton,' Atherton supplied.

'Aye, him.' He made a sour face. 'Him and Tyler were thick as thieves. I bet they worked out the stitch-up between them.'

'But Tyler wasn't DTI,' Slider said, remembering aloud. 'Tyler was Department of the Environment, wasn't he? He was the junior minister there.'

Andrew shrugged. 'Tyler was Paxton's liaison with the government. I dunno where they knew each other from. All I know is Tyler ended up getting the credit and I ended up getting the sack. There's no justice.'

He seemed to be sinking now, literally deeper into the chair, and figuratively into a drunken gloom. Slider hastened to ask his next question. 'So what has Stonax been doing since he left the department? What has he been investigating? Has he been following up the Waverley B business?'

'*I* don't know,' Andrew said. 'Nobody tells me anything any more. I wouldn't be surprised if he has. Never could keep his nose out of things that weren't his business. But there's nothing to follow up. The election's over, the yard's closed anyway, and AM are selling it. What's to investigate?' He closed his eyes. 'Tell ye what, fellas, I'm just gauny have a wee nap, 'cos I've got a helluva headache coming on.'

It was clear they would get nothing more out of him – and Slider doubted he had any more to tell, so they left him in peace. As they left, Atherton kindly removed the brandy glass from his slackening fingers and set it on the coffee table, before it could tip over and wet his trousers. At least that would be one less thing for him to worry about when he woke up.

Fourteen

A Legend in His Own Lunchtime

They had to pass Emily's cubbyhole on the way to the office, and she was already back, beavering away on the laptop. She looked up as Atherton paused in the doorway and the look that passed between them, brief as it was, shook Slider. It was not that it was a look of unbridled passion: that wouldn't have been so very surprising, knowing Atherton's past record. It was that it was a look of acceptance, accustomedness, belonging, the sort of look you usually have to be together for some years to achieve. Somehow in three days they had passed from strangers to companions. It had happened that fast for him and Joanna, but their circumstances had been much more favourable. He hoped desperately, for his friend's sake as much as Emily's, that the whole murder-bereavement thing didn't rear up and bite them when things calmed down a bit.

'I've got a lot to tell you,' she said. 'I've been finding out things.'

'I never doubted you would,' Atherton said.

She half rose, looking from him to Slider. 'D'you want me to tell you now?'

'I need tea,' Slider said.

'Canteen,' Atherton translated, and they headed for the stairs.

As they climbed, and while they queued at the counter, she described how she had found Chris Fletcher and what he had told her; when they were seated with their cups, she got on to Trish Holland.

'I'm sure now that Bates was sprung deliberately,' she said, 'and how it was done. The beauty of it is that nobody misses him. Wormwood Scrubs thinks he's at Woodhill. Woodhill assumes he's still at Wormwood Scrubs. And as far as Ring 4 are concerned, he never went anywhere. After a bit of useful confusion at the site where the van is found, it's confirmed that it wasn't a Ring 4 vehicle and there was never a prisoner in it.'

'But then why get the police in on it at all?' Slider asked.

'I think that was a bit of insurance, in case anyone *does* miss him at any point. Then they can say, oh, yes, he escaped, but we suppressed the news for public-safety reasons. You can justify anything on health and safety grounds. But I don't think his name was meant to get out. That was probably a mistake: the story was supposed to get the one outing as a deniable unnamed prisoner. The fact that his name *was* mentioned might account for why the escape filtered down through police levels to your superintendent. But it was never in the public domain. I'm sure if you asked in the prison service they wouldn't know anything about it.'

'But *how* was it done?' Slider asked.

Emily looked pleased to be the one to be telling him something, rather than vice versa. 'All you need is someone who can produce the right documents in the first place, someone who knows what they look like, the wording and everything, and knows the protocol. That suggests someone in the Home Office or with access to someone in the Home Office, but it needn't be. It could be anyone who's ever had anything to do with prisons or moving prisoners. With modern computers and printers, making the documents isn't hard as long as you know what to put on them. And then, of course, you need someone with influence inside Ring 4, someone who can give the orders without being questioned.'

'Who did you say this Holland woman said cancelled the movement?' Atherton asked.

'She said it was one of the directors. She said his name was Mr Mark.'

'Mark?' Atherton and Slider looked at each other.

'I looked him up,' Emily said with exquisite relish. 'Thomas Mark, director and, more recently, major shareholder. He owns forty per cent of the shares – transferred to his name by their previous owner, Trevor Bates.'

'Thomas Mark, Bates's driver and right-hand man,' Slider

said bitterly. 'We couldn't implicate him when we took down Bates, and he disappeared off the radar.'

'The transfer was affected before the date of Bates's arrest,' Emily said. 'Obviously he suspected he might be in trouble and was taking care to lay off his assets.'

'And Bates was so arrogant,' Slider marvelled. 'So sure we couldn't touch him, right to the end.'

'He was right in a way, wasn't he?' Atherton said. 'He must have known that he'd be got out. Maybe he'd worked out the plan already, just in case. But who was his man on the inside – the inside of the Home Office, I mean?'

'You said he had government connections,' Emily said, 'so I've been looking that up, too. Bates owned a company called OroTech. He built it up himself from scratch. It was mostly electronics and IT, but it had a large property division called Key Developments, some residential, but mainly large-scale property development.'

'Yes, we knew property was his other interest.'

'It was under OroTech that he provided services to the US government. I've got a friend on The Hill who's just confirmed that.'

'Thank God for open government,' Atherton said. 'We could do with a bit more of that over here.'

'Anyway, OroTech also had a very nice contract with the UK government for IT services, which originated from—'

'Let me guess: the Home Office,' Slider interrupted.

'Not even close,' said Emily. 'It was the Department of the Environment, and the junior minister responsible for the contract was Richard Tyler.'

Slider had no idea where to put this information. His brain whirred out of gear. Emily looked at him anxiously.

'I am right, aren't I? That is the name you said, the man you couldn't get because you didn't have enough evidence. I thought it was interesting they were linked in that way. One villain proving the other, so to speak.'

'Yes, Tyler was the name,' Slider said. 'And there's an old saying, hear a new name and you'll hear it again within the day. Tyler's not exactly a new name, but we've heard it once already today.'

Between them, Atherton and Slider told her the story of

the framing of her father. She listened soberly, and under the table Atherton advanced his knee to touch hers comfortingly, because it couldn't be pleasant to have all that brought up again. At the end, she said, 'Coincidence? It must be, mustn't it? This Bates person can't be connected with Dad in any way, can he?'

'I wouldn't have thought so,' Slider said. 'Obviously, from what you say, Tyler and Bates knew each other and if Tyler had given Bates a nice fat government contract, I'm betting from what I know about him that there was something in it for him. But other than that I can't see how Bates could be connected with your father's death. And from what Sid Andrew said, the whole departmental thing your father got into trouble over is finished and done with. The election is history.'

'Hmm,' said Emily thoughtfully. 'Well, you don't mind if I go on looking into him, do you – Bates, I mean? His business connections seem to have spread a long way and infiltrated some interesting places.'

'As long as it doesn't upset you to do it,' Slider said, 'it can only be a help to us.'

'It helps me to keep busy. And I've got the bit between my teeth now,' she said. 'It's the reason I became a journalist, because once I start on a story I can't stop until I get to the end – until I know everything.'

'It's much the same being a detective,' Slider said, and seeing Emily's instant glance towards Atherton, realised he had probably hit on the thing that they had in common; and which, given a fair breeze, could allow them to make a go of it.

Slider and Atherton walked back to the office, dropping Emily on the way at her cubbyhole. 'They *can't* be connected, can they?' Slider said. 'The two cases?'

'Only one is a case,' Atherton reminded him. 'We aren't investigating Bates's escape.'

'If only we could get hold of the movement order,' Slider said. 'I'd like to know who was behind that.'

'Well, they'll never let us even ask for it, so you can forget that. And we still don't know what Stonax was investigating.'

They turned in at the door, and at once Hart got up and came towards them. 'I reckon there was definitely something fishy about Daniel Masseter's death, guv,' she said.

Hollis, who was also in the office, drifted up to listen, and they all perched on desks while she told them about her visit to Mrs Masseter's house, and the bogus Inspector Strong who took away Masseter's papers and computer. 'I've checked, and the local police never went back at all, because as far as they were concerned it was an ordinary RTA. They just handed it over to Victim Support. And nobody from the CID knew anything about it.'

'So whoever killed him went back and seized his papers and computer, to stop anyone finding out what he was investigating?' Slider said.

'That's what I reckon. It's a pattern with Stonax, innit?'

'Except that they didn't take his computer.'

'No, but they took his Cyber-box; maybe they thought they could get in that way. And it wouldn't have looked so much like Dave Borthwick done it if they'd nicked the computer, would it?'

'Yes, I was forgetting we had our sacrificial lamb downstairs,' Slider said.

'We've had a bit of a breakthrough on Bates,' Atherton said. 'Or rather, Emily has.'

He told of her discoveries, and at the end, Hart said, 'Bloody Nora, what a cheek, eh? Makes his gofer head of the company that's going to move him about if he gets caught! Makes you proud to be British, dunnit?'

Slider shook his head. 'We don't seem to be any further forward with the Stonax case – and let me remind you all that that's what pays our wages.'

'I think I'll have another look at the Waverley B business,' Atherton said. 'See if anything strikes a chord.'

'Waverley B?' Hart queried. 'What's that when it's at home?'

'Shipyard on the Clyde.'

'The Clyde? That's in Scotland, isn't it? Mrs Masseter said Danny had just come back from Scotland.'

Atherton's eyebrows rose. 'It's a big place. But there may be a connection. Sid Andrew said all that Waverley B business was over and done with, but what if Stonax had found something else that was fishy, and Masseter was helping him with it?'

'See what you can find out,' Slider said. 'Given that both

of them are dead in violent circumstances, it's tempting to think there's a link.'

Porson listened with keen intelligence to the new developments.

'Tyler,' he said in disgust. 'Well, I can't say I'm surprised. A leper doesn't change his spots. But Andrew isn't wrong – you can't prove any of it now.'

'No, sir. But I'd like to know what Stonax was up to the last few months and whether it had anything to do with Tyler in any way. He's been out of the country, but that doesn't mean he's been out of play.'

'Hmm. And Tyler knew Bates. Well, birds of a feather gather no moss.'

'We knew Bates had government connections.'

'Yes. But if you're right about this escape, it doesn't begin and end with Tyler. There's got to be collusion on our side too.' He stared bleakly out of the window, still for once. 'I should have taken early retirement. I've been in the Job too long. If there's one thing I can't stand, it's a bent copper. Give me an old-fashioned, honest criminal any day.' He sighed and pulled himself together. 'Well, keep at it. Do everything you can, and I'll back you up, but don't throw the winds to caution. Remember however far you row out, you've got to row back. What are we going to do about Borthwick?'

'We can't let him go, sir,' Slider said. 'The press'll be all over him like a rash, and he's not the sort to keep his mouth shut.'

'You think he'd be in danger?'

'Whoever's behind Stonax's death, it looks as if they killed Masseter too, so one more wouldn't turn their stomachs.'

'You want to charge him?'

Slider hesitated. 'We've got enough to cover ourselves, and I don't suppose he'll complain. He's pretty docile. I just want to make sure he's safe.'

Porson hesitated too. 'It's an awful lot of paperwork and man hours. I'd sooner spend 'em in a different shop. Look, it's the weekend coming up. We'll keep him till Monday and see what happens, make a decision then. Has he seen a brief?'

'Yes, sir. Kevin Swan.'

'Swan? Good choice. He's sound enough.'

'He understood the situation.'

'All right. I'll square the magistrates. But you'll have to get a move on, because that only gives us another forty-eight hours, and still waters wait for no man.'

And I'm nowhere near a solution, Slider thought as he went away. He wondered what Bates was up to, why Pauline hadn't called him back, if Joanna was all right. She'd be in rehearsal just now, so he couldn't call her. Instead, when he got back to his office, he called Jimmy Pak.

'I haven't got anything to tell you,' he said. 'I'd have rung you if I had.'

'I know,' said Slider. 'It's just frustration. I needed to bother somebody.'

Pak laughed. 'At least you know yourself. Self knowledge is the key to—'

'No more proverbs, thank you. I've just had a skinful upstairs. Tell me what's happening.'

'I've got more respect for him than I thought. It's really hard to crack. I'm trying every combination I can think of but no good so far. He must have been really cautious, or have something really important to hide.'

'Both, I think. He knew he was dealing with pretty ruthless people.'

'Right. Well, the safest password is a completely random sequence of letters and numbers. Breaking that is just chance. But people hardly ever use completely random sets because they can't remember them. So they use birthdays, family initials, pets' names, that sort of thing. If they do have a random set, they usually have to write it down somewhere. You've got access to his paperwork?'

'Yes, all but the file that was stolen.'

'If it was written down in there you're in trouble. Otherwise, you'd better start looking for it. I'll keep on trying, but it'll speed things up if you can find it.'

'I would like to speed things up. What am I looking for?'

'A set of eight, numbers and letters mixed. Look in his diary, address book, personal papers, that's the most likely place.'

'Right. I'll leave you in peace, then.'

'Do that, man. Luck!'

'Luck yourself.'

He passed on the instruction to the troops who were toiling through Stonax's effects, and then sat behind his desk staring at the sea of papers with what felt like a brick of ignorance in his head. It was no good. He couldn't even think. He needed to get out.

As he passed through the outer office he said to Swilley, who was nearest, 'I'm going out for half an hour. Hold the fort, Norma.'

'Boss, oughtn't we to know where you're going?' she called after him. 'Just in case?'

'A man's snout is sacrosanct,' he called back over his shoulder.

The Kensington Park Road – always known as the KPR to local residents – had in Slider's memory been a shabby, run-down street of peeling stucco, cracked windows and blowing rubbish, the fine old houses divided up into the lowest sort of bedsits. Now, since so much smart money had come to Notting Hill, it had been bought up and done up, and was exactly the right place for a man to set up in the burglar alarm, window lock and security camera business. Jack Bushman's shop was just up from the Westbourne Grove turning, a discreet and narrow place with a smart fascia in green and gold, polished wood flooring and a retro wooden counter which Slider guessed played well with the locals. Solder Jack himself was standing behind the counter doing something to a piece of equipment that looked like the inside of a radio. His eyes sharpened as he saw Slider, but his welcoming smile did not waver and, most tellingly to Slider, the hands holding the piece of kit did not disappear under the counter.

'Hello, Jack, how's it going?' he asked pleasantly.

'Mr Slider,' he said. 'It's going well, thank you.' He was a tall man, well set up, with a big, handsome head topped with thick hair, swept back, in which there was the odd thread of grey. His face had the lines of experience in it now. It was the sort of firm, large-featured, fatherly face that inspires trust, especially in women, and a bit of age did it no harm at all.

He had been straight for – oh, it must have been ten or twelve years now, Slider reflected; and it was interesting that the thought of Jack knowing the inside secrets of all the locals' security arrangements did not bother him. Poacher turned gamekeeper. But of course, Jack knew that he would be the first to be asked his whereabouts if anything went down, and there was nothing better for keeping a man straight – apart from his own intentions.

'Just passing?' Jack asked, his eyes taking in the Jiffy bag Slider was carrying and moving politely away to his face again.

'It's not an entirely random visit,' Slider said.

'Not trouble, I hope?' Jack said, but it was without alarm. He had the calm eyes of a man with a clear conscience. His accent, Slider noted, had gone upmarket quite a bit too, obviously to fit in with his new clients.

'It's a lot of trouble,' Slider said, 'but for me, not for you. I've got something here that I wonder if you'd have a look at, tell me what you think.'

'Always glad to help.'

Slider drew out the evidence bag containing the device from Valancy House, and passed it across the counter. Jack took it up and looked at it, turning the bag in his hands. 'Can I take it out?'

'As long as you don't dismantle anything. It's been tested for prints.'

'Wouldn't get anything useful off surfaces this small,' he said with professional confidence. 'But I'll put gloves on anyway.'

He had a box of disposables under the counter. 'How come?' Slider asked.

'Some devices it's not a good idea to get grease and acid on,' he said. Gloved, he removed the device from the bag, stuck a jeweller's glass in his eye, and examined it minutely, using a pair of tweezers to move the wires out of his line of sight. 'Very nice,' he said. 'Simple, but all the best devices are. What was it used on?'

'Security door. One of those buzz-in jobs in a block of flats.'

'Old one?'

'Pretty old.'

'So the locks cut out if there's a power failure. The modern

170   *Cynthia Harrod-Eagles*

ones use a conventional lock with a key or a numbers pad as a back-up. What did you want to know about it?'

'Whether there's anything about it that would tell you who made it.'

He removed the eyeglass and lowered the device on to its bag. 'I've been out of that game a long time,' he said.

'I know. But you've kept up with things. Your opinion has got to be better than mine, anyway. Tell me what you think.'

'Well, it's simple. But elegant, almost. A lot of people could do it, but they wouldn't all bother to take the trouble someone's gone to with this. This was done by someone who cared what his work looked like. So he was intelligent, skilled, and right far up his own arse.'

Slider almost laughed at the descent into vernacular. 'Self absorbed? Self obsessed?'

Jack nodded. 'A nutter. Why bother? The way this wire's held with a tiny brass screw. Anyone else would just stick it with a touch of solder. Do the job just as well. The bloke who did this is watching himself doing it. Playing to his favourite audience. Probably masturbates a lot,' he concluded, straight-faced.

'Anything else? What about that timer?'

'It's nice,' Jack said with genuine admiration. 'I've not seen one like it. Chinese. All the new miniature stuff is coming from China now. Used to be Taiwan, but its mainland now – they're catching up in everything. And since they took Hong Kong back they've got no trouble with distribution.'

A heaviness had settled on Slider at the mention of Hong Kong. It seemed to be leading him towards the conclusion he had started to suspect, but didn't want to.

'Got a name for me?' he said. 'Strictly between us. It never gets back to you.'

Jack shook his head slowly. 'I don't know,' he said. 'I'd have said straight off one name in particular, but he's inside. Not for this sort of thing, though.' He met Slider's eyes. 'Trevor Bates. He was legit, as far as this sort of thing goes, but he got banged up for some personal stuff.'

'I know. I did the banging,' Slider said. Jack's eyes widened slightly, but he forbore to pursue the point. 'How did you know him?'

'I didn't, not personally, but I've come across him a few times at trade fairs and so on. I saw him once put something together as a sort of demonstration – a listening device. It was on his stand at the Surveillance and Security Trade Fair at Olympia. Fascinating, watching his little fingers twinkling away. Didn't like the bloke – him with his silly red hair down to his shoulders. What did he think he looked like? But he was good. And his company imported all those Far East novelties. He had connections out there.'

'I know.'

Jack surveyed his face. 'You thought it was him,' he said.

'I didn't want to. It creates all sorts of complications.'

He gestured at the device. 'Bad trouble?'

'The worst.'

'Sorry.' Carefully he replaced the device in the evidence bag and began peeling off the gloves. 'I tell you what, though, it doesn't altogether surprise me. If ever there was a bloke up himself it was Trevor Bates. Little runt of a bloke,' he added with all a large man's contempt, 'and they're often the worst. Napoleon complex, you know? Got to be better than everyone else to make up for it.'

'You may not be wrong,' Slider said.

Outside, he walked back to his car in a brown study, only to find a traffic warden in the process of writing him a ticket.

'Didn't you see the notice on the dashboard?' he said, pointing out the battered POLICE ON CALL sign he had stuck there when he was forced to park on the double yellow.

She was unperturbed. 'I don't take no notice o' dem tings. People write hall sorts o' notices, hanyting to get out o' payin'.'

'But I really am a policeman,' he said, showing her his brief.

'Dat don't mean hanyting to me,' she said magnificently, continuing to write. 'Once I start de ticket, I got to finish. "I started so I'll finish",' she concluded, and tee-hee'd merrily.

Slider was just going to say something moderately savage when a roar of a motorbike, now hard-wired into his brain, made him jump for cover, carrying the woman with him. They had been standing together on the road side of the car; he flung her almost bodily before him into the gap between the bonnet and a white van which was obviously destined to be her next port of call. She was a hefty woman and about his own height – useful in altercations, he supposed vaguely – but his adrenaline made him strong as well as fast, and the motorbike roared past as she shrieked and clutched him and they both banged into the van doors, setting its alarms going, and reeled off on to the bonnet of his car.

The van blocked any forward vision, and by the time he had regained his balance and got out from behind it, the bike was long gone.

'Don't you touch me!' the woman shrilled angrily, brushing herself down. 'You can't touch me! I'll call de police!'

'I am the police,' he reminded her. 'Did you see the number?'

'People all against us! But you shouldn't park wrong if you don't want a ticket. Hit not my fault. I just makin' a livin'.' She burst noisily into tears. 'People all de time takin' a pop at us, callin' us names – hittin' us. I'm sick of it. I'm callin' de police on you dis time. I got your number.' She shook the parking ticket at him. 'You not get away wid it!'

'I just saved your life,' Slider said, exasperated. 'That motorbike tried to kill me, and you with me. Did you see the number?'

But she had backed away from him on to the pavement, and one or two passers-by were starting to take an interest. She noticed them, and began to play to the gallery. Her sobs increased in volume and she said to the world in general, 'He attack me! For no reason! I just doin' my job! A helpless woman!'

Slider decided on the better part of valour. Fortunately, traffic wardens were not popular, and with her size she looked anything but helpless, despite her boo-hooing, so no-one was exactly leaping forward to get involved. But that might change at any moment, and he got in his car and drove away before someone discovered his chivalry and got involved.

Fifteen

A Tale of Two Kitties

Hardly had Slider regained his desk when Bates rang him. There was a change in the man. The self-conscious calm and confidence were gone. He sounded angry for the first time.

'All right, Plod,' he almost snarled, 'I'm done with you. I'm done playing with you.'

'Whoever asked you to?' Slider retorted, too wearily angry himself with the whole thing to be much afraid. 'Starting to repeat your effects, aren't you?'

'Don't interrupt me! You've been warned to keep your nose out, and you won't listen to warnings, so I'm going to have to put you out of the game. Permanently.'

'If it means I don't have to go on listening to you quoting from bad gangster movies any more—'

'Oh, you think you're quite the hero, don't you?' Bates sneered. 'Well, the next time you hear from me will be the last, all right. I'm going to get you – and then I'm going to get that woman of yours. And in the split second when you realise you're about to die, which is all you'll have, I hope you'll think of her and remember that it's you who've condemned her to death.'

Slider was cold to the pit of his stomach at this direct threat to Joanna, but there was only one way to talk to people like Bates, who got pleasure from intimidation. 'Oh, sod off,' he said, and put the phone down.

What had made him change, he wondered, as he sat staring at the telephone, squatting on his desk like a malevolent toad. Something had put the wind up Bates. Was it his visit to Solder Jack? Had Bates had him followed, seen him go in, guessed what it was about? He was intelligent enough to put two and two together; and if that was it, it rather confirmed Jack's diagnosis, that it was Bates who made the device for the door at Valancy House. If Tyler was behind the murder, it would be natural for him to consult his electronics-expert friend. Was Bates afraid that Slider was closing in on him? He did so hope that Bates was afraid.

Maybe it was Bates himself who had followed him. Bates on the motorbike, who had twice tried to kill him. It would explain how he had called the moment Slider got back to his desk – following him back to the station and giving him just enough time to get upstairs. He felt a sort of perverse relief at the thought, because if Bates was actively following him, he couldn't also be following Joanna.

He checked the time. She'd have finished her rehearsal by now. He rang her mobile number. It rang too long before she answered it.

'You had me worried,' he said.

'Sorry, I'm driving. I had to pull to the side of the road in the approved manner before I could pick you up. Trouble with dating a cop.'

'I'll have to get you a hands-free set.'

'They'll be banning those, too, soon. Talking is distracting. What's the matter?'

'How do you know something's the matter?'

'I can tell from the quality of your silence.'

'I just had another comedy phone call from The Needle.'

'Oh. The usual? Don't be alarmed – be very afraid?'

'That sort of thing.'

'Any further along with catching him?' she asked in a studiously calm voice.

'I wish I could say yes. He *must* have a safe house some-where local, but where?'

'I'm glad you're going to a safe house tonight, anyway.'

'Ditto. You've got a hotel room?'

'Yes, and Sue's staying on with me, which is noble because she'd sooner go straight home. Like all of us.'

'Offer to pay for her, and I'll give you the money.'

'It's not costing her anything. You pay for the room in

these places,' Joanna pointed out. 'But I will stand her a meal, if she'll let me.'

'Good. Well, be careful. I don't think anyone's watching you, but keep an eye out. And I'll see you tomorrow.'

'Yes, thank goodness. We miss you. Little Derek keeps asking after you.'

'How?'

'In Morse code. With his feet.'

'Come to the station tomorrow when you get back. Don't go to the house.'

'Are we ever going to be able to go home?' she asked, and sounded upset.

'Of course we are. As Mr Porson says, it's a long road that has no turnstile, and every dog has his Daimler.'

'I wish I'd thought of that.'

'I can't think of it now.'

Slider left his car in the yard and let Atherton drive him home, with Emily following in her hire car. He was dog-tired, and the headache that had been hovering like a thunderstorm over the hills all day seemed to be settling in for the night. He needed an early one.

'Do you mind if we don't talk about the case tonight?' Slider said, breaking the silence as Atherton pulled into his road and started looking for a parking space. 'I need a break from thinking.'

'Good idea. The unbent bow, and all that sort of thing. You look pretty terrible, s'matter of fact.'

'I couldn't look terribler than I feel.'

'I think we should have a large drink followed by a superb meal and listen to a bit of soothing music. Luckily, I nipped out and bought some stuff this afternoon.' He pulled up parallel to the car in front of a parking space, and before he could change gear, Emily nipped into it forwards. Slider saw in the wing mirror on his side her grin through the windshield. Atherton made a threatening gesture in his rear-view and drove on. 'It's good to see her show a bit of spirit. I keep worrying that she's going to have a relapse and sink into gloom and guilt.'

'It will probably happen when the case is closed,' Slider said. 'Then it'll all come home to her.'

'And then what will happen to me?' Atherton said. 'She might hate me.'

'There's always that,' Slider said.

Atherton glanced at him. 'A comforting reassurance would have been nice.'

'You could always go back to Sue.'

'No, once the trust has gone out of a relationship, it's no fun lying to them. Ah, here's a space. And not even in the next county.'

Atherton's arms being full of groceries, he gave Emily the key and she opened the door and went in first, to receive two half-grown cats full in the chest. They pronged their way up on to her shoulders, purring like JCBs.

'They've really taken to you,' Slider observed, easing in behind her.

'I'm a good twiddler,' she said.

Slider was too tired to ask what she meant, and let that one go.

Atherton kicked the door closed behind him. 'Can you make us all a drink while I unload this lot?' he asked her.

'Of course. Get thee to thy kitchen, scullion. Bill – is it all right if I call you Bill? Why don't you sit down, because you look as if you're about to fall down?'

Blessedly soon he was in the fireside chair, a large gin and tonic in his hand, and one of the cats – he had no idea which one – on his lap. Emily put on a Brahms' serenade, one of Slider's favourite pieces, and sat down on the floor, as Joanna had liked to do before she got too big, with a cat on her shoulder, to talk to him. Her interview skills were soon apparent, as she got him talking about himself, despite his tiredness and his natural reticence; and at the very moment when he noticed he was talking about himself, she changed the subject with graceful ease to architecture, which he must have mentioned in passing was an interest of his.

'When you say architecture, I suppose you mean ancient rather than modern?' she invited.

'Most modern architecture seems to me to be a mixture of ambition, distraction, uglification and derision,' he said. 'But there are honourable exceptions. I think the Gherkin is a wonderful design, for instance. But I wonder whether even a really *good* joke will go on being funny century after century, whereas if you look at the great churches—'

'Is that where your real interest lies?'

'I'm not exclusive. But something like Salisbury or Durham – mankind at its absolute best.'

'I suppose in your job you need an injection of mankind at its best now and then, to make up for mankind at its worst.'

'It helps,' he said.

'We had an absolutely lovely church in our village when I was a little child. I used to go and sit in it sometimes, because I liked the smell and the silence.'

'You didn't go to services?' Slider asked.

'No. Dad was a furious atheist. He was too pig-headed to be religious. Would never be told what to do. People think because he was so good he must have been religious too, but he wouldn't even have us taught about Christianity. I had to study it for myself, later.'

'Why did you bother? If you weren't brought up religious?'

She smiled. 'It was a very embarrassing incident from my teenage years, just the age when you feel social gaffes the most. I was about fifteen, I suppose, or sixteen. I went to stay with a girl I knew from school, at her parents' house. They were very well off – big house, servants and every-thing – and they were Catholics. Well, I was already worried about what was going to happen on Sunday, when they had this big dinner party on Saturday night. All grown-ups except for Jen and me, and what with all the knives and forks on the table, and wine and everything, I was in a state of panic, terrified I was going to do the wrong thing. Then suddenly someone put a little bowl of water in front of me, beside my plate. Well, I had no idea what it was for, but I knew they were Catholics, so – I dipped my fingers in and crossed myself.' She sighed and shook her head at the memory. 'It was the most mortifying moment of my life.'

Atherton came in. 'Nearly ready. You two look very cosy.'

'We're swapping embarrassing moments,' Emily said. 'Can I do anything?'

'You could lay the table.'

Slider's phone rang. He didn't recognise the number, and was in two minds about taking the call, but Emily had got up and left him to get cutlery from the kitchen, so he answered, a little gingerly in case it was Bates again.

It was Pauline. There was a lot of noise in the background. 'Where are you?' he asked.

'At a garage. I'm sorry I couldn't call you back before, but I never know at work who might be listening. I tell you, it's a bloody reign of terror these days. I'm thinking of getting out.'

'Oh, Pauly, is it that bad?'

'You don't know the half of it. What did you want?'

'As one of my snouts said, it's a nobby murder of a nobby bloke. Ed Stonax.'

'I've read about that,' she said, and, curiously, there was relief in her voice. 'And seen it on the telly. Could hardly miss it. But I thought you'd got your man.'

'There's more to it than meets the eye. I wondered if you'd heard anything.'

'Not a thing. Sorry. So that was it, was it? I knew it couldn't be a social call.'

'Would you welcome a social call?' he asked. 'When I said it was Stonax, you sounded relieved. What did you think I wanted to talk to you about?' She didn't answer at once, and he said, 'You've always helped me when I was in trouble.'

'And a lot of good it's done me! Look, Bill, there are things going on at the high levels that I don't approve of. Well, that's putting it mildly. I'm not supposed to know about them, of course, but sometimes being a woman has its advantages. Sometimes they'll say things in front of you, or in earshot, because they just don't see you. You're part of the furniture, you know?'

'What have you heard?'

'I don't know the ins and outs of it. But I'm guessing one of your old cases has come back to haunt you – am I right?'

'Yes.'

'Well, watch out, that's all I can say. Someone's got it in for you, and that boss of yours won't be able to protect you.'

'Can't you be more specific?'

'I've said too much already. Go back over your old cases,

put two and two together, try to keep out of sight. That's all I can say. And please don't call me, not at work or at home. I love you, Bill, but you're bad news.' And she was gone.

Atherton popped his head round the door enquiringly. Normally he wouldn't ask, of course, but given the Bates situation . . .

'Who was that?'

Slider decided on the instant not to pass it on. 'Someone who doesn't want to talk to me,' he said.

'Smart of them to ring and tell you. Want to open the wine?'

By the time Slider had eaten and drunk his share of the wine he was utterly spent, and hardly had the strength to fall asleep. But he slept like the dead, secure in the knowledge that if the bad men broke in to get him, the cats would get them first; and in the morning he felt a lot better, stronger, clearer-headed, more optimistic. They drove in together in convoy, Slider keeping a look out for motorbikes and black Focuses, and looking forward to seeing Joanna. If he knew her, she'd be up at sparrow's and on the road early.

Atherton and Emily went to their respective computers to continue their researches. Slider got on with necessary paper-work while the troops filtered in. When everyone was there they'd have a meeting to establish where they had got to.

It was Norma who got to him first. She brought him in tea and an apricot Danish, and said, 'Boss, I've got something, but I don't know if it's anything.'

'Anything could be anything. Fire away.'

'Well, you know I've been going over all Bates's known associates with Fathom?'

'Yes.'

'They all check out – most of 'em were normal employees and business connections. He didn't seem to have any friends, and we know what his sexual preferences were like.'

'Did you check with the pro's he used to go to?'

'Yes, and with a lot more besides.' She grinned suddenly. 'I put Fathom on to that. Thought he may as well start at the deep end. Sent him round all the brothels and establishment whores in the area. It's not likely Bates'd take one off the street.'

'Right. I'm sure Fathom was extremely thorough?'

'I hope so. But anyway, none of them have seen hide nor hair of him since we nicked him the first time. And nobody seemed to know he was on the loose, either. They all thought he was banged up awaiting trial – some even thought he'd had the trial and was doing his time. So wherever he is and whatever he's been doing since he escaped, he hasn't been having fun.'

'I'm glad to hear it,' Slider said grimly. 'So what was the thing that wasn't anything?'

'Well, the only suspicious contacts we had were his bodyguard, who's safe in Pentonville, his butler Archie Gordon, and his driver Thomas Mark. We had nothing on those two, as you know, and Gordon got out and went to Spain. His mum and dad have retired there, near Barcelona, and he's living with them and the local police say he's not been in any trouble.'

'And that leaves Mark.'

'Who disappeared as soon as Bates was arrested and hasn't been seen since. Well, I've just been trawling every source I could think of, and it occurred to me that maybe Mark had family in the area, so I went into the BDM register, and found his birth certificate, and it turns out his mother's maiden name was Steel.'

Slider jumped as if he'd touched a live wire. 'The man in the pub! Don't tell me – his father's name was Patrick?'

'Well, no,' Norma said, reluctant to deny him anything, 'it was John. But it's possible, isn't it, that when he had to give a false name to old Dave Borthwick in the pub, that that was all he could think of.'

'It's certainly possible. We've got a photograph of Mark, haven't we?'

'Yes, boss. Not a very good one – he's in the background of a picture of Bates. We never had a mugshot of him, because he was never arrested. But you can see who it is.'

'Get a print-out and get Fathom to take it down to the cells, see if Borthwick recognises him.'

Hart appeared behind Norma at the door, wondering what the excitement was about. 'Guv? Something up?'

'Thomas Mark's mother's maiden name was Steel,' Norma said as she pushed past her.

Hart's eyes widened. 'Wait a minute!' she exclaimed, and dashed off to her desk.

The word spread from person to person and the room buzzed with renewed vigour. A breakthrough made everyone feel better. Fathom came back, his fleshy face pink with exertion, to say, 'He thinks it's the same bloke. He's not sure. He says it's hard to tell from a photograph.'

'God, the useless twonk!' Swilley exclaimed.

'But he thinks it's him,' Fathom said eagerly. 'And in a line-up – in the flesh . . .'

'Yeah, we've got to get hold of him in the flesh first, haven't we?'

'Crop it and get some copies made,' Slider said, 'and take them to the people who were in the Sally that night. Start with the staff and then try the customers.'

'Guv?' Hart looked up from her desk as she put the receiver down. 'I was just on to Mrs Masseter. Asked her if the inspector who took away Danny's things might have been "Steel" instead of "Strong", and she jumped at it. Said yes, that was the name all right.'

Slider's blood sang. 'When Fathom's got the photo ready, send it over to the local police, ask them nicely to take it round to her, see if she can identify him.'

'So, boss,' Swilley interjected, 'are we saying that Bates and Mark are connected with the Stonax murder? That the two cases are linked after all?'

'I think we are saying just that,' Slider said. 'It's not a coincidence that Bates has turned up here and now.' He told them about his visit to Solder Jack, without mentioning his name, and Jack's immediate fingering of Bates as the possible manufacturer. 'So Bates makes the device to open the door, and Mark persuades old dipstick Borthwick to let him install it,' he concluded. 'I wonder, could Bates have been the "man in the van" that Borthwick never saw? The one Mark said was going to do the actual fitting?'

'Bates would be careful not to be seen,' Norma said. 'That would be why he'd put Mark up as the front man in the pub, make him do the public work. But who did the actual murder? Mark? I can't see Bates getting his hands dirty.'

'He's killed before, with his own hands,' Hart said. 'Susie Mabbot, the prostitute.'

'By accident,' said Swilley, 'or at least in hot blood. The other deaths we think are down to him he may have had someone do for him. You don't get to be a master criminal by doing your own dirty work.'

'If Thomas Mark is mixed up with the Masseter death,' said Hollis, 'maybe he was the one that did both of them.'

Slider interrupted. 'But even if Bates and Mark were implicated in Stonax, or Stonax *and* Masseter, we still don't know why. What the hell was it all about? There's got to be a reason, and it's got to be a bloody good one, if I know my Bates. And we still don't know *where* he is – or they are. Norma, does Mrs Steel still live in the area?'

'She's dead, sir. Both the parents are. I checked that right away. I'll have a look to see if there were any brothers or sisters, but it'll take a while.'

'Do it. Mark seems to be the only friend Bates has in the world.'

Mackay, who had been answering the phone across the room, called out, 'Guv, they've found the car. The black Focus. They think it's the same one because it's got the damage in the right place. The number's different from any of the ones we've reported, but the number it *has* got is from a scrapped car.'

'Where did they find it?'

'A traffic warden called it in, illegally parked in a residents' bay without a permit. Duchess of Bedford's Walk.'

'Sinning above its station,' Slider commented.

'Where's that?' asked Hart, who hadn't lived in Shepherd's Bush all her life.

'Just off the Campden Hill Road,' said Swilley, who had. 'And just round the corner from Aubrey Walk, where Bates's house is.'

'Creatures of habit, criminals,' said Slider. 'Even the ones who think they're uncommon criminals. And overconfidence has brought down the mighty before. Get the car in, go over it with a fine-toothed comb. One nice dab or one long red

hair inside would be very nice. And a bit of something interesting on the tyres or the wheel arches would be even better.'

'Don't get your hopes up,' Hart said.

'I don't think my hopes know where up is,' Slider said.
'Also get a paint sample and photographs of the damage and
send them through to the Reading police. See if they can get
a match with the damage to Masseter's motorbike. If we can
get Mark it may lead us to Bates.'

Sixteen

Armageddon Too Old For This

Joanna arrived early, in buoyant mood, and bearing gifts: bacon rolls for herself, and doughnuts for everyone else.

'I left so early I didn't get breakfast before I left,' she said. 'God, it's good to be back!'

Everyone clustered round for the goodies, including Emily, whose presence by now caused no surprise or comment. 'I've found some things out about Bates's company. Should I tell you now?' She addressed the comment to Slider, but obviously with the rest of the team in mind.

'Go ahead,' he said. It would save repeating it all later.

'Well, you know he had this electronics firm called OroTech? His own baby, built up from nothing over many years, so he was virtually the sole owner.'

'Virtually?'

'Ten per cent was owned by someone else, the shares registered to a holding company. I thought it was interesting that he would give up any part of his company, because from all I can find out he was pretty much of a control freak, but when I looked at the date of the transfer, it was within six weeks of his being awarded the government IT contract. So I wondered, you see, whether it was a quid pro quo.'

'You give me the contract, I give you a hand in the profits?' said Atherton. 'Sounds feasible. Obviously it must be Tyler.'

'Don't jump to conclusions,' Slider said. 'If it was, Emily would have told us. What's this holding company?' he asked her.

'It's called Vollman Zabrinski. It's a sort of offshore wrapper, if you like, but I can't get in to check individual holdings, and obviously they won't answer my questions.

It would have to be a police inquiry.' She looked from Slider to Atherton and back.

'I'll ask Mr Porson,' Slider said. 'Might have to go through Interpol, though, which will take time. Anything else?'

'Oh, yes,' Emily said. 'Two years ago OroTech split off its property division, Key Developments. And shortly afterwards it did a merger with British Electronics Systems, or BriSys, and the two became BriTech.'

Atherton clapped his hands together in satisfaction. 'Which then tried to merge with Anderson-Millar and was snubbed, until Sid Andrew came up with his brilliant idea.'

'I wonder, though,' Slider said, 'whether it really was his idea. He didn't seem all that bright to me. Maybe it was Richard Tyler's invention, and he just let Sid do the fronting, and Sid got ideas above his station. He did say Tyler got the credit, while he got the sack.'

'Whoever thought of it, it does mean than Bates was in on the whole Waverley B business,' Atherton said, 'and we've got even more connections between him and Tyler.'

'I wonder if Stonax – I mean, Mr Stonax, sorry . . .' Swilley corrected herself with a blush. Emily made a negating gesture with her hand. 'I wonder if he knew about the Bates-Tyler connection.'

'Or if he didn't before, maybe that was what he was working on after he left the DTI,' Joanna suggested. 'Did he never mention any of this to you?' she asked Emily.

'Not a thing. Which now I think of it was a telling point, because he used to like talking to me about his campaigns and investigations. But this one he played really close to his chest, so I ought to have known it was something serious.' She sighed. 'But if he didn't want to tell, he wouldn't have. You couldn't force my dad to do anything he didn't want.'

The same thing occurred to everyone simultaneously – that he had been forced, by a threat to Emily – but no-one said it. She obviously thought it too, because she looked unhappy and lowered her eyes for a moment.

Swilley spoke, mostly to break the awkward silence. 'So what's become of the Waverley B shipyard in all this?'

'Sid Andrew said AM-BriTech were selling it,' Slider said.

'That's not strictly true,' Emily said. 'They closed the yard as soon as their merger went through – which was pretty cynical, but I suppose that's business for you. The gates closed at the end of May last year.'

'And the election was in April,' Atherton said. 'That's pretty cynical too. And now it's going to be developed. I've seen the plans on the internet. It's in a fabulous position, you see – on a sort of promontory sticking out into the Clyde, so it has water on three sides. It's close to Glasgow – City of Culture, isn't that what they call it now? – which is bursting at the seams with young money looking for somewhere to spend itself. It has good transport links. And there's even an old railway line they're talking about reviving. That was hinted at on the website, and it would mean a public money injection. "Infrastructure investment" is what they call it these days.'

'And what's it going to be?' Joanna asked.

'A mixture of leisure, retail and residential,' Atherton said. 'Shops, galleries, hotels, restaurants, small retail units – craft workshops and the like – and some swanky flats with river views.'

'Like Salford Quays,' Joanna said.

'I was just going to say that,' said Hollis. 'Have you been there?'

'We went out there when we did a concert in Manchester last year,' Joanna said. 'We had some time to kill between seating rehearsal and concert, so we thought we'd go out there for a meal. It was quite impressive, but a bit sad, I thought.'

Hollis nodded. 'Like when they turn the great old mills into yuppy flats.' He had been born in Oldham, where now there was nary a mill.

'Still,' said Joanna, 'a generation breathes easier.'

Slider looked at Atherton. 'That name rings a bell. Didn't you report that Freddie Bell said Mr Stonax asked him about Salford Quays?'

Atherton nodded. 'He asked what sort of money there was in a development like that, and Bell told him it depended on how much you had to pay for the land.'

'You're building up to something,' Joanna said. 'I know that look.'

'The Waverley B development – or the New Clydeview Centre as they're going to call it . . .'

'What else?' said Joanna.

'The development is being done by Key Developments, Bates's company which he took care didn't get taken over in the takeover. And since he's also a large shareholder in AM-BriTech, I dare say the price charged for the land won't be too heartbreaking.'

There was a silence as these facts were absorbed. Then Swilley said, 'So is that it? Is that the whole conspiracy? That Bates and Tyler were doing some fancy financial foot-work together to make a profit out of the old shipyard?'

'Isn't it enough?' Atherton asked. Their old resentment seemed to prickle the air for a moment.

Swilley frowned. 'I don't see how that makes a case for killing Stonax – sorry.'

'Please, you don't have to mind me,' Emily said. 'I know he's dead. That's why I'm here, to try to help find out why.'

'OK, I'll stop saying sorry,' Swilley said. 'What I'm saying is that Ed Stonax knew about the fix that went in over Waverley B and the election, and that's what they got rid of him from the department for. Developing a site as a leisure complex is what goes on all over the country all the time, and apart from maybe the "infrastructure investment" you were hinting at, Jim, having Tyler's fingerprints on it, there's no extra scandal for anyone to disapprove of. The development would bring regeneration to what was presumably a run-down area, and surely that's a good thing all round? OK, a few people are going to get extremely rich on the back of it, but blimey, we all know that happens. It's not something to kill anyone for.'

'And what about Danny Masseter?' asked Hart, who had come to feel rather proprietorial about him. 'Where does he fit into it?'

'And why was Bates sprung – if he was sprung?' Hollis asked. 'Couldn't be just to enjoy the fruits of his labours, could it?'

'He was a friend of Tyler's – isn't that enough?' Atherton said.

'I wouldn't have thought Tyler had any friends,' Slider

said. 'Not of the sentimental sort. But you're right, Norma – this doesn't tie up all the ends. In fact, it leaves me with just as many questions as I started with.'

Hart's phone rang, and she went over to answer it. She came back smiling. 'That was Reading,' she said. 'Mrs Masseter recognised Mark from the photograph as the bogus Inspector Steel.'

'Good,' Slider said. 'So we've got him for impersonating a police officer, obstructing the course, and burglary, just for starters. Get his description and photograph out to all units. He's to be arrested on sight.'

'And if the car damage matches the motorbike,' Hart said happily, 'we can have him for murder.'

'You've got to link him with the car first,' Mackay reminded her.

'We'll do it. Poor old Danny,' she said. 'By Grabthar's hammer, I will avenge you.'

'By what?' Slider said.

'Best not to ask,' said Joanna, who had seen the film.

'I'm sorry to have to tell you this,' Joanna said when she and Slider were alone, 'but I have to have some more clothes. I didn't pack all that much because it was only two days. I have to go back to the flat.'

'Not on your own,' Slider said.

'You went on your own,' she reminded him.

'And look what happened to me.'

'Yes. You didn't manage to avoid it, so how will your coming with me make things better?'

'I saw the warning signs, without which I could have been much worse hurt.'

Joanna looked anxious. 'It's not that dangerous, is it? It was only a prank – the bucket? Painful for you, but not life-threatening.'

'His threats have escalated,' Slider said, choosing his words carefully. 'I don't know, I've never known, how seriously he means them, but I can't take chances, especially not with you. If you tell me what you want, I'll go and get it.'

'Not on your own, to quote somebody I know and love,' Joanna said. 'You'd never find half what I want, and you'd get the wrong things. Besides, the whole thing about threats is that they are blackmail, and you don't give in to blackmail. It's my flat and I won't be kept out of it by some creep of a criminal.'

'Bravely spoken,' Slider said, but he didn't smile. 'All right, we'll both go – but you're to do exactly as I say, if anything happens.'

'OK,' Joanna said, making certain mental reservations. Probably he could read her mind – they had been together a long time – but there wasn't much he could do about it.

Slider drove by a roundabout route, and this, and his constant checking in the mirrors, began to work on Joanna's nerves. He had been hurt before – the memory of it chilled her – and Atherton had been seriously wounded some years back, so badly wounded that his nerve almost went and he was on the verge of leaving the Job. Being pregnant made you feel differently about all sorts of hazards. She had never given a thought to the hazards of falling over until the baby started to show. Now being at the top of a flight of stairs gave her pause. She didn't let it stop her using stairs, but she *thought* about it. She wondered suddenly if, once the baby arrived, she would ever feel the same again about ponds, electrical sockets, bleach bottles, large dogs and any number of other pieces of previously ignorable life furniture. She had given a hostage to fortune in loving Bill, but it was the baby that had made her realise all the ways in which the ransom could be levied.

But you can't give in to it, she thought, otherwise there was no point in being alive at all. She wondered, though, how often Bill had been afraid for her, how often he was afraid for his other children. He never spoke of it, but that would be Bill anyway. Men's courage was different from women's. What they had decided to put up with come what may, they didn't see the need to talk about. She reached across and laid a hand on his thigh as a huge gust of love went through her. He took his hand briefly from the wheel and laid it on hers in acknowledgement.

There was a parking space right in front of the house, for once in a blue moon, and for a moment he wondered if that

was ominous. Then he told himself not to be a fool; and not
to appear one, either, by driving past it and parking further
away, which was what he would have done had he been
alone. But after all, if they were following him, they knew
by now where he was going – would have known it as soon
as he turned into the road. He parked, told Joanna not to get
out until he opened the door, checked all the mirrors minutely,
then got out and went round to her side. The day-empty
street mocked his precautions. A car went past and he tensed,
but it was a silver Peugeot with a young woman driving it.

'OK,' he said, letting Joanna out. He helped her to her
feet, and as her face reached a level with his, he saw that
she was nervous now. 'This is silly,' he said. 'I'll buy you
some new clothes.'

'You will not,' she said. '*That* would be silly.'

He walked up the path with Joanna behind him, scanning
the house for any signs of change, scanning the path for any
hint that anyone else had been there. He got the key out,
inspected the lock and the door, turned it cautiously, and let
himself in.

The door opened without resistance, and a tiny alarm bell
rang in his head before he realised what it was: there should
have been a heap of junk mail impeding it, but there was no
mail at all lying there. How many days in the year was there
nothing in the post? He couldn't remember a single one,
except for bank holidays. He had stepped in as he thought
this. The windowless hall passage was always dark, and
Joanna, stepping in behind him, reached automatically for
the light switch, just at the instant that his nose and brain,
working separately, suddenly joined forces in a flash of
horror. His hand shot out, grasping her wrist, and he turned
her with its leverage and pushed her with his whole body
back out of the door.

'Gas!' he said as he ran her back down the path. She stumbled because he was pushing her, but he had his arm round
her now and bore her up as well as along. Out of the gate,
across the pavement. There was a big plane tree growing
opposite the next door house, and he pushed her into the
shelter of its trunk. 'Stay there,' he snapped and flung himself
at the boot of his car.

'Bill! What are you doing?'

He rummaged frantically in his tool kit and found a big screwdriver.

'Bill!' Joanna cried, her voice rising in terror as he headed back to the house. 'Bill, don't!'

'Stay there!' he flung over his shoulder.

Under the small bay window of the sitting-room stood the white meter box. He flung himself to his knees with frantic haste, wrenched open the flap with the screwdriver, and twisted the shut-off lever closed. Then, with the horrid sensation of the sweat of fear in his armpits, he ran back to Joanna, reaching for his mobile.

She was so white he thought she was going to be sick. But her fear turned itself nimbly into anger. 'How dare you? How dare you risk yourself like that?'

'I had to turn off the gas,' he said. 'Thank God the meter box was outside.' She began to cry. He conducted her across the road, further from the house. It could still go up, though the worst was averted now the gas was shut off at the main. 'I have to ring the bomb disposal squad,' he said. 'Hush, it's all right.' He put his arm round her, and let her cry on his shoulder while he spoke to them. It was just her hormones, he told himself.

The subsequent fuss took a big chunk out of the day. The road had to be sealed off and the house and the ones either side had to be evacuated – though fortunately, because of the time of day, that only involved one old lady and a cat, the rest of the flats being empty. Then the squad went in to do a sweep. There were two triggers, it turned out. One was the light switch by the front door – it was damn lucky, said Cattishall, the head of the squad, that Slider's reactions had been so fast.

'It's lucky I've got a good sense of smell,' Slider countered.

The other trigger was in the kitchen, and was particularly cunning and nasty. It was a friction device fixed in the runner of the sash window, so that if Slider had smelled the gas and come in without using the light, as soon as he pushed up the window – the natural first action – it would have acted like a match striking a matchbox. All the gas taps had been left fully open and there was a considerable volume of gas inside the house.

'Makes you nostalgic for the old shilling-in-the-meter days,' Cattishall said. 'It would have run out before too much harm was done.'

Once everything had been made safe, Slider and Joanna both went in to pack up everything they thought they might need to take with them, before the flat was boarded up completely. Packing a suitcase, Joanna was calm, but unhappy.

'I hate this. I'm sick of it. How can people be allowed to ruin your life like this? It's my home! I hate that blasted Bates.'

'You're not meant to like him.'

'Oh, Bill,' she said tragically, 'when will it all be over?'

'When we catch him,' Slider said.

Seventeen

No Tern Unstoned

The landlord of the Sally identified Thomas Mark from his photograph a little doubtfully, but one of his bar staff said much more definitely that she had served him. She had noticed him because he was talking to Dave Borthwick, who was a regular, and he looked so far out of old Dave's class that the anomaly had amused her. Not that she said anomaly, of course. She asked Jerry Fathom, who had been doing the asking, what was happening with old Dave.

'I never would have thought he had the balls to do something like that. He just used to come in here and sit with his couple of pints. He seemed like an ordinary bloke.' She gave herself a pleasurable shiver. 'To think all the time I was serving a murderer! Anyway, what's this bloke got to do with it?'

'Well, I can't tell you anything at the moment,' Fathom said, 'but when the case is all over, I could tell you all the details, if you'd like to come out with me one night.'

For a moment the thought of being in the know flickered greedily through her eyes, and then she looked properly at Fathom and said scornfully, 'Get bent!'

The forensic sweep of the black Focus had revealed a number of fingermarks, though none of them belonged to Bates.

'But they might well belong to Thomas Mark,' Slider said, when he was back in circulation in the afternoon. 'We haven't got his on record to compare them with, but when we find him, it'll be another nail in his coffin.'

There was also a lot of mud under the wheel arch and a sample was being analysed to see if it matched the mud in the lane where Masseter was killed.

'But I think we can assume, for working purposes, that it was him who killed Masseter, because otherwise what was he doing up there and why did he take away the papers and computer?'

'Why did he do that anyway?' Hart said.

'Well, let's come back to Masseter later,' Slider said, unwittingly driving a thorn in her heart. 'Let's look first at what we've got linking Bates to the Stonax murder.' He could call it that with impunity as Emily was out of the room, still beavering away on the computer, with Atherton's assistance.

'At about the same time Ed Stonax was killed, the next-door neighbour Mrs Koontz sees a motorbike courier come out of the building with a large Jiffy envelope in his hand. The bike had a white box on the back with a circular logo on it, with, she says, a "little telephone" in it, which is the logo of Ring 4. Also a file was missing from Ed Stonax's filing system. So it's a promising inference that the courier was the murderer and that he took away the file.'

'After smearing oil on the victim's pockets and cuffs, which he got from Dave Borthwick's bike, to make it look as if Borthwick did the job,' Hollis added.

'And leaving some faint oily smears on the filing cabinet,' Swilley said.

'I suspect those weren't intentional,' Slider said. 'The residue left after sullying Stonax. But he won't have cared much. If the file was that important, presumably he will have thought getting hold of it made him invulnerable. And anyway, it was Dave's bike's oil, so if found he knows it goes to Dave's account.'

'Yes, but who is "he", boss?' Swilley asked. 'We know Thomas Mark set up the lock disabling, but was he the one that did the murder?'

'I think the one thing we can be sure of is that he didn't do the actual killing,' said Slider. 'Remember we had the footmark by the filing cabinet, and it was too small to be either Borthwick's or the victim's. Now I don't know Thomas Mark's shoe size, but he's a big man and I think we can take it as read that his feet will match the rest of him.'

'Which leaves – Bates,' said Swilley.

Slider nodded. He had been coming to this conclusion

ever since his talk with Solder Jack, who had reminisced that Bates was a 'little runt of a man' with 'little fingers twinkling away'.

'Bates is not a tall man,' he said. 'He's quite slight in build, too, though he keeps – or used to keep – himself very fit. And he has small hands – very useful for fiddling about with miniature circuitry – so he probably has small feet as well.'

'But could a small man have coshed a tall man that easily?' Fathom asked.

'I've got a picture in my head. Let me run it by you,' Slider said. 'The courier lets himself in by the disabled front door, pops down and gets some oil on one of the gloves from Dave's bike, and goes up to the flat with a large envelope and a clipboard. He rings the doorbell. Stonax answers it. "Could you sign for this please?" says the courier. He hands over the clipboard, and then says, "Oh, I'm sorry, I seem to have mislaid my pen. Have you got one?" Stonax turns back into the flat to get one. As soon as he's taken a step away from the door, courier says, "Oh, it's OK, here it is," and takes a step forward himself to hand it to Stonax. Stonax bends his head over the clipboard—'

'Right!' said Swilley. 'That's how you get him to put his head within reach! And when the courier whacks him he drops the pen and then falls on top of it.'

'But why all the pen malarkey anyway?' Hart said.

'The courier needs to get him to step away from the door. If he fells him actually in the doorway, he won't be able to get the door closed without moving him, and that will take time and make noise. The courier's purpose is to get in and out as fast as possible without alerting anyone. It takes just seconds to empty his pockets and take the watch, and a few seconds more to find the right file. He stood still by the filing cabinet just long enough to leave his impression in the thick-pile carpet. The hall carpet outside the front door was far too thin and old, and the vestibule has a tiled floor, and he didn't stand still anywhere else.'

'Then he pops Stonax's watch in an envelope and puts it under Borthwick's door, shoves everything else in the Jiffy bag, and walks calmly out to his bike,' said Hart.

'To be seen by Mrs Koontz,' said Mackay, 'which is no bad thing, really, because Borthwick has leathers and a helmet with a dark visor, so it helps shove it on him.'

'So you think the courier was Bates, then, boss?' Swilley said.

'There's been a car and a motorbike all the way through,' Slider said, 'and it seems logical that if Thomas Mark was driving the car, Bates must have been on the bike. He was careful not to be seen by Borthwick, or to leave any fingerprints, because he's on our files and Mark isn't. But Jack Bushman instantly thought of Bates as being the likely manufacturer of the device that disabled the Valancy House door.'

'*Likely* manufacturer,' Hollis said. 'It seems to me that while we've got a lot of supposition that fits the facts, and we've got Mark definitely implicated, we can't actually prove Bates was there at all. He's worked it out right well.'

'I know,' said Slider. 'That's the problem. We need to know what was in that file. That's probably where all our evidence is. If we knew *why* Stonax died, we might be able to prove *who* did it. Because at the moment we can't connect Bates with Stonax at all.'

'Unless we can get Mark to roll over,' Hollis said. 'And given that Bates has put him in the shite up to his oxters, he might well do that.'

'But we've got to find him first,' said Hart.

There was a gloomy moment of silence.

'What about Bates's escape?' Mackay said.

'What about it?' Slider said.

'Well, he had to have had someone on the inside. What if that someone was Tyler, and offing Stonax was the quid pro quo?'

'You're saying he got Bates out of jail to do it?' said Hollis. 'It's an idea.'

'Why wouldn't Tyler do it himself?' Swilley said. 'We know he's willing to kill, *and* to do it with his own hands.'

'But he wouldn't do Stonax himself,' Mackay said. 'Too risky. He's got too much to lose now, and he can't hope to be let get away with it again.'

'And he's out of the country,' Hart added.

'No, he isn't,' Swilley said. 'I came across it on a website when I was checking Bates's contacts. He doesn't take up his new appointment until October, but he came back in July. There was a photograph of him attending a performance at the Royal Opera House.'

'He could have been just visiting,' Hart said.

'But his term in Brussels ended in July, and he'd want to get himself set up, find somewhere to live and everything,' Norma said.

'Find out,' Slider said. 'Find out if he's here, when he came, and where he's living. If he did come back in July, it makes a lot more sense.'

Atherton had gone through page after page of Waverley B references without gaining any insights, except that it confirmed what Sid Andrew had said, that it was an unlucky site. Industrial relations seemed to have been particularly bad, and there were stoppages and strikes as well as an unusually high absentee rate. He was staring at the screen in frustration when all the hairs stood up on the back of his neck and his nostrils twitched as he caught Emily's scent. She had come up behind him, and now leaned lightly on his shoulder to look at the notes he had made, which were lying on the desk beside him.

'Are you working back chronologically?' she asked.

'Not particularly,' he said. 'Just going through references as I find them. Why?'

'Nothing here dates from before the fifties. But all these old shipyards on the Clyde go back to the nineteenth century at least. They were all terribly proud of their history.'

'True. Well, there must be stuff. I just haven't come across it yet.'

'Or maybe it changed its name,' she said, 'and the history is under the old name.'

He made that an excuse to look at her. 'Come to think of it, "Waverley" is a bit of an Edinburgh name for a shipyard on the Glasgow side.'

'Yes, it does seem rather tactless. They should have called it St Enoch at least.' She looked down his notes again. 'I wonder if they're calling the new leisure centre by the old

name? That would be a smart move if you wanted to endear
it to Glaswegians.'

'Clydeview? But it's a bit of a girl's blouse of a name for
a horny-palmed shipyard.'

'Yes, it sounds more like a suburban bungalow.'

'Wait a minute, though,' Atherton said, sitting up straight
so suddenly he almost knocked her out. 'What about
Clydebrae? The first word on Danny Masseter's list.'

'It was underlined,' she said, 'as though it was a heading.'

'Wait here,' he said, and dashed off to get it. When he got
back Emily was sitting in his place at the keyboard, so he
dragged up another chair, more than happy to work with her.

She had already put in 'Clydebrae' and had got a number
of references to Clydebrae Street, Govan. There was a map,
showing a road that ran up to a small promontory on the
Clyde and stopped there. There seemed to be nothing on it,
but it was named in very small letters, Clydebrae. Emily's
fingers flew, found a better map, scrolled across and found
the Waverley B shipyard next door to the promontory, sticking
out much further into the water.

'Why would they build a road to nowhere?' she said.

'An estuary is like the seaside,' Atherton said. 'The water
is an object in itself. It's never nowhere.'

She was looking at the other Clydebrae Street references.
There were photographs on one. 'It's terribly derelict. Looks
as if it hasn't been lived in for years. Derelict tenement
blocks, a few breeze-blocked houses, and you can see there
must have been houses here, where it's all flat. They've been
knocked down. I wonder when?'

'There were big slum clearance projects in Glasgow in
the fifties and sixties. People moved out to new estates.'

'Or maybe it's part of the leisure centre development? But
now, look here.' She had gone in to another reference. 'You're
right. They wanted to redevelop it in 1962. Here's a plan of
a new council estate. I wonder why it never came off?' She
scrolled on. 'The Scottish Ornithological Union notes that
there are now no more red-throated divers or Forster's terns
at Clydebrae. I'm devastated. The Clydebrae ferry closed in
1959. It used to carry people across to Partick, where the
thistles come from.'

Atherton looked up. 'It doesn't say that?'

'Of course it doesn't.'

He looked down again at the list. 'It looks as if he was interested in history, anyway. Scottish War Museum. Clyde Maritime and Shipping Museum. Public records.'

'Maybe he'd found what you've found – that he couldn't get further back than the fifties.'

'What's this Meekie book?'

'If he was going to look for it at the university, it must be something rare.' She put in 'Meekie' and started working through the results, which were startlingly unhelpful and nothing to do with shipping. 'Did you know that a meekie is a person with an abnormally large head?' she said. Patiently she scrolled on.

'Hager Loch,' Atherton said, looking at the next heading. 'I never heard of a Hager Loch. You carry on – I'm going to get the atlas.' He brought it back with him to be companionable, and there was silence, except for her clicking. 'There is no loch called Hager. I thought not.'

'Maybe it's not in Scotland. Do they call lakes "loch" anywhere else? What about Canada? That's very Scottish in places, isn't it?'

'But what could be the connection with Canada? I can't believe his mother wouldn't have noticed if he'd gone there.'

'Maybe it's a misspelling. He couldn't spell "university" or "museum".'

'But a misspelling of what? I can't find anything even remotely resembling Hager.'

'I'm getting bored with Meekie. What's the next thing?'

'This bit of scrawl. Hart thought it was Newark, but if we can't allow him to have gone to Canada, he can't have gone to New York either.'

'Let me see. I'm good at bad handwriting. Dad's was pretty terrible.' She studied the word and said almost at once, 'That's not an "n" at the beginning, it's a "v". That bit is the upstroke, see?'

'Vewark?'

'I don't think that's a "w" either. Look at his "m" in "Museum" – the small one. Doesn't it look the same to you? And here, and here.'

'You're right. It is an '"m".'

'So that makes it Vemark – which is pronounceable, at least,' Emily said. 'I suppose we ought to be thankful for small mercies.'

'And for big ones,' Atherton said, and the tone of his voice made her look up at him. 'Not Vemark but Vemork. Put it in. Vemork, 1942.'

'You know something?' she asked, tapping.

'There's no end to the wonder of what I know,' he said. 'It comes of having an interest in history.'

'And a brain the size of a planet?' she said. She had been around the station long enough to have heard *that* friendly jibe. 'Here it is. Vemork 1942. But it's in Norway, not Scotland. Geographically not unrelated, I admit, but if he didn't go to Canada or the States . . .'

'Well, he didn't have to go there, did he?' Atherton said. 'Only tippy-tap away on his rinky-dinky little computer. Vemork was the subject of a daring bombing raid during the war, because the Germans had taken it over. It was a source, they discovered, of heavy water.'

'Heavy water? I've heard of it, of course, but I don't really know what it is.'

'It's water enriched with an extra atom of deuterium. I don't know all the science, but I do know it's used in nuclear fission.'

'And even I know the Germans were experimenting with nuclear fission towards the end of the war. Don't they say they were on the brink of making a nuclear bomb?'

'They do,' Atherton said, though his voice was far away now as his brain processed. 'But what's Vemork and heavy water got to do with—?'

'What?'

'Hager Loch. It's just ringing bells like anything, but it's not in Scotland, it's in Germany. You asked if they called them lochs anywhere else. Try Hagerloch, all one word, in Google.'

She tapped, and read out the prompt that came up, 'Did you mean Haigerloch?'

'I think we did, Danny old bean. Spelling really wasn't your strong suit, was it – even when you were copying things down?'

'Haigerloch, now a museum,' she read. 'A heavy-water test reactor. The Germans conducted experiments in nuclear fission in a cave under the Schloßkirche in a small town in Germany. The Atomkeller – cute name!'

'It's a cute place.'

'The Atomkeller is now a museum. For opening times click here.'

'That's where the heavy water from Vemork ended up, and why the RAF had to conduct its daring bombing raid. I remember doing it at school. World War Two was just becoming compulsory, but my history teacher was a real buff, and liked to go into a lot more detail than was strictly necessary.'

'But what's all this got to do with Dad and Clydebrae and all the rest of it?' Her eyes widened. 'You don't think—?'

His eyebrows went up. 'That the reason we haven't got anything on Waverley B before the Fifties is that they changed the name, and the reason they changed the name was that they were doing the same sort of experiments there during the war?'

'Well, if they knew about Haigerloch, they'd obviously want to try to catch up,' Emily said logically. 'And they'd obviously have to keep it secret.'

'Thinking's all very well, but we need some evidence. I wonder if it's all in this Meekie book, whatever that may be. Maybe you gave up on Meekie too soon.'

'Spelling!' Emily exclaimed. 'He's a bit of a phonetic speller, isn't he? And suppose he'd only heard the word, never seen it written down?'

'M-e-a-c-h-i-e. The good old Scottish name of Meachie, sept of the Mcdonalds if my memory serves me right.'

'How can you possibly know that?'

'I don't, I'm just making it up,' he grinned. 'How do you think I got my reputation for omniscience? People hardly ever check up on you.'

'You charlatan!' She put Meachie into Google and hesitated. 'There'll be five million entries.'

'Try Meachie and Clydebrae,' Atherton suggested.

She added the word and hit enter. 'Bingo,' she said softly. 'Angus Meachie: *The Clydebrae Glory*. The Scottish maritime

Cynthia Harrod-Eagles

historian and archivist tells the story of the Clydebrae ship-yard from 1869 until its takeover in 1943 by the Ministry of Defence.'

'We'll have to get hold of that book. And I wonder what else he found out at the Scottish War Museum – the clue is in the title, folks – and the other places. If it was secret, there won't have been much in the public record office, you can bet.'

'Whatever he did find out,' Emily said, 'he will have passed on to Dad. And that's probably what was in the file they took away.'

'But your father wouldn't have had only one copy, would he?'

'Not if it was important.'

'He didn't have a safe, or a safe-deposit box or anything?'

'Not that I know of. But I still don't understand what this has to do with Richard Tyler and Anderson-Millar and all the rest of it, and why it was important enough to want to . . . to kill Dad for.'

Atherton laid his finger beside the last line of Danny's list. 'Cad and Ber. There's a full stop after each word. They're abbreviations. Dopey old Mrs Masseter said he talked about Cadbury's and someone called Beryl. If she remembered those words, he must have repeated them a lot.'

'I'm not there yet,' Emily confessed.

'Cadmium is used as a barrier to control nuclear fission. And beryllium is an isotope moderator.'

'How do you *know* these things?'

'I read a lot. But the thing you need to know about cadmium and beryllium is that they're both extremely toxic, particu-larly beryllium.'

She looked stricken. 'The Scottish Ornithological Union notes there are no more red-throated divers at Clydebrae,' she said quietly. 'Or Forster's terns.'

'Or much of anything else, I imagine. We'd better go and see the guv.'

Eighteen
The Ego Has Landed

'It all makes sense,' Atherton said to the assembled desk-squatters. 'Clydebrae was a ship-building yard until 1943, when the government takes it over. They use the site for secret nuclear experiments, trying to catch up with the Germans. After the war they hand it back for shipbuilding, but change the name in case Clydebrae has any associations for anyone. But the land is contaminated with cadmium and beryllium. Nobody realises this, but the yard is known as an "unlucky" one with a high absentee rate. Not the workers being naturally bolshie, but falling sick rather too often, and not feeling terribly well when they are at work.'

'And there are no seabirds any more on the nearby beach that used to be a bird-watching site. I wondered why there was a road to nowhere,' Emily added.

'Finally Dansk, the latest in a series of owners, decides it can't make a go of it, and decides to sell. And then the government gets involved, because there's an election coming up and the loss of two thousand jobs could just swing the seat in favour of the Nats. Anderson-Millar buy it, but they don't really want to run a shipyard there where everyone else has failed. They want to sell it for development.'

'Like Salford Quays,' Joanna said quietly, from Slider's shadow.

Atherton nodded towards her. 'Freddie Bell said the profit of a development like that depended on what you had to pay for the land.'

'But if the land was toxic and had to be decontaminated, it would add millions to the cost.'

'Could be a billion or more,' Atherton said. 'And it would ruin the cachet—'

'The what?' said Hart derisively.

'Who would want to visit, let alone live and work in, a development they knew had been built on contaminated land?' he translated for her. 'Even if they were told it had been cleaned up. It could never be a prestigious, luxury venue for the movers and shakers with that reputation. On the other hand, if you don't tell anyone . . .'

'Nobody could be that cynical,' Joanna said, shocked. 'You're talking about risking people's lives.'

Slider said, 'Two of the players, at least, have no particular reverence for life.'

'If they knew about it,' she said.

'Somebody knew about it,' Emily said. 'There was a big housing development project supposed to happen right next door after the war. But it didn't go ahead. They cleared the land and demolished most of the houses, but they never built on it. Why, when they were so short of housing? I think somebody back then knew the truth and the project was just quietly dropped.'

'It would be something to know the history of that,' Slider said, 'and who owns the land now.'

'If it was bought for council housing it must be the council,' Atherton said. 'And they've just left it empty. Maybe that was one of the things Danny was looking into.'

Hart came in. 'All Danny's protests were environmental things. He tried to get the Hartlepool ship-recycling thing stopped. And he'd borrowed that book from the library about breaking up nuclear submarines. So he'd know about the toxic chemicals that came with it.' She clapped a hand to her mouth. 'Blimey, I forgot to ring Reading Library, to get them off Ma Masseter's back.'

'What does it matter? They can buy another copy, can't they?' Fathom said, wanting to get back to the exciting bit.

'It's not like the new Dan Brown,' she told him severely. 'It costs two hundred and fifty quid a copy.'

'Yeah, and it's rubbish,' Hollis said. 'You could never make a film out of it. Guv, it occurs to me that Richard Tyler was junior minister in the Department of the Environment. So any questions about cleaning up a toxic site would come to him, if anyone. And he was supposed to be tight with Sir Henry Paxton, the boss of Anderson-Millar. Suppose Paxton had found out about the contamination, and went to Tyler quietly, saying what are we going to do? We know Tyler was in to make a lot of money out of the development, through his shares in Key Developments . . .'

'Do we?' Atherton said. 'I thought that was only a supposition until we got an answer from Vollman Zabrinski.'

'All right, we assume Tyler had the shares, and who knows what other bungs and percentages he might have through his mate Bates? So he says to Paxton, I won't tell if you don't tell. And the plans get pushed through.'

'Until Danny Masseter finds out something, and goes to Stonax because he's known as an eco-warrior,' Mackay said. 'And maybe his interest in the place is known about in eco circles.'

'And maybe also because he knows he's been in Dutch with the government,' said Swilley. 'Sorry, Emily – but Danny wouldn't want to take it to an establishment figure, and he might well think your dad had a grudge and would be more willing to listen to him because of it.'

'You don't have to apologise,' Emily said patiently.

'And it just so happens,' Atherton continued, 'that he hit on the person who already knew more than he wanted to about dear old Waverley B.'

Joanna was shaking her head, though Slider knew it was more in despair that people could be so corrupt than in disbelief of the scenario. He knew it was a far cry from working things out to proving them, but it all *felt* right, and it covered all the aspects. And it was no chickenfeed they were talking about. 'A development like that,' he said to her quietly, 'could be worth several billion. Well worth fighting for. But if the contamination story got out, it was all over.'

'But then why didn't Ed Stonax go public with it?'

'Because he didn't have all the information,' Emily said. 'Or the proof. And he couldn't go public without the whole dossier – the one, presumably, poor Danny Masseter was preparing for him. He must have asked too many questions and made someone suspicious.'

'So Tyler contacts his old friend and co-conspirator Trevor Bates, and says I'll help you get out of jail free, if you'll get rid of the problem for us,' Atherton concluded. 'Silence Masseter and Stonax before it all gets out, and make sure you get all the documents.' Out of sight of the others, Emily pressed his hand in thanks for using the word 'silence' instead of 'murder', something she still found hard to say, even in her head.

'And Bates thought he'd take the opportunity to get back at me,' Slider said. 'He thought he was invulnerable. He was too smart to get caught for the jobs he was doing privately for himself and Tyler. Dave Borthwick and a hit-and-run driver would stand up for those. And I was to go in a gas explosion – nobody's fault at all.'

'For God's sake,' Joanna muttered.

McLaren spoke up from the back through the last mouthful of Mars Bar. 'Yeah, well, it's all very nice but it's just Goldilocks and the Three Bears, innit, unless we get some evidence.'

Swilley looked at him, impressed. 'Blimey, Maurice, you come out quite sensible sometimes.'

'It's maybe not as bad as it looks,' Slider said. 'We've got Mark on evidence, as soon as we can catch him, and if the damage on the car matches the damage on the motorbike, we've got him for Masseter's murder. Mark is Bates's right-hand man, and if that's not enough, we now know Bates gave him shares in Ring 4, so that ties him in with Bates. It was Tyler who gave Bates the government IT contract, so that ties them. And if Vollman Whatnot confirm that it's Tyler who owns the BriTech shares, it gets them both tied in with the Waverley B development.'

'But we've still got nothing on the pollution, and without that, there's no motive for Stonax's death,' Mackay said.

'Well, the evidence is out there, and if Danny Masseter managed to find it, we can,' Slider said, though he didn't sound happy about it. It could take for ever – and there was always the risk that tracks would start to be covered and documents shredded. Worse still, people who had answered questions might get shredded in the process. 'We just have to hope Jimmy Pak can get into the encrypted files somehow. I'm willing to bet that's where the evidence is. Meanwhile – '

he hoisted himself off the desk – 'we have to concentrate on finding Bates, which means finding Mark. No luck on the relatives, I suppose, Norma?'

'No, sir. I can't find any at all, never mind in the area. Could be he was an only child.'

'So Bates is the only friend he has. And Tyler's the only friend Bates has,' Slider said. 'Well, I think I've had about enough. We'll call it a day and start again tomorrow.'

'Tomorrow's Sunday, boss,' Swilley said. 'Do you want us in?'

'Sunday's a good day for legwork. People are at home, you can catch them there. Tomorrow is Find Bates and Mark Day. We're going to visit every place they've ever been, every person they've ever spoken to, and find them if we have to wear our legs down to nubbins. I'll OK the overtime with Mr Porson, so you can take that look off your face, McLaren.'

'I haven't got a look on my face,' he protested.

'Oh, no, you're right, it's chocolate,' said Slider. 'That's it, boys and girls.'

They all moved away except for Joanna, Atherton and Emily.

'What are we going to do?' Joanna said. 'With all our worldlies stuffed in the car and no home to go to?'

'We'll go to an hotel,' Slider said.

Atherton and Emily exchanged a look. 'It's all right,' she said to him.

'It makes it look a bit official,' he said nervously. 'I don't want to rush you into anything.'

'If I remember rightly, I did the rushing. Come on, a friend in need and all that sort of thing.'

'Shall we leave you two to talk code in peace?' Joanna said.

'We don't want you to go to an hotel,' Emily translated. 'There are two bedrooms at Jim's house, and I don't mind sharing with him – or more specifically, I don't mind you knowing I'm sharing with him. I know it makes me look like a fast hussy, but there it is.'

'Who are we to judge?' Slider said. 'If you're sure?'

'I'm sure,' they both said at the same moment, and looked at each other and smiled.

'Well, thanks,' Joanna said. 'It'll be a lot nicer than an hotel.'

'I have to go and see Porson,' Slider said. 'Why don't you three go on ahead and I'll join you later.'

Porson listened gravely to Slider's exposition. 'It all sounds all right,' he said, 'and, my God, if you're right this is going to cause a stink.'

'It's my betting that it won't,' Slider said sadly. 'They'll cover up for him, like they did before.'

'No, laddie, he won't get away with it this time. You'd have to spin like a dervish in a washing machine to get this one to come out straight. They'll dump him hard and let him take his knocks, believe me. But we've got to have all the evidence, dot every tee, or it's all deniable.'

'If we can find out about those shares, to start with . . .'

'I'll do a bit of leaning. Anything else?'

'Reading police – matching Mark's car with the motor-bike damage?'

'More leaning. Leave it to me. Tower of Pisa job. I suppose Pak's not come up with anything?'

'Not yet.'

'Well, he's a good lad. He won't stop until he does. For now, why don't you go home? You look played out.'

'Yes, I'm going now.'

'Hang on, you haven't got a home to go to, have you?' Porson said, and he seemed to hesitate on the brink of some-thing.

'I'm staying with Atherton, sir,' Slider said. 'He has a spare room.'

'Oh, well that's all right,' Porson said briskly, and turned away. 'Off you go, then.'

Slider went, wondering uncomfortably whether the old boy had been about to offer him *his* spare room, and whether he would have welcomed Slider's company.

Atherton did an enormous stir-fry for quickness' sake, and the four of them sat around the table companionably, as if they had known each other for years, with the cats teetering on the backs of armchairs, trying to see over peoples' shoulders, and purring like food mixers. Joanna hoped so much that Atherton and Emily could survive the end of the case and the realisations that were bound to come over her then, because they seemed so right together – as right as Joanna felt with Bill.

It was inevitable they should talk about the case, and a lot of it was rehashing the supposed Waverley B plot, guessing how much money the whole thing was worth, and wondering despairingly how people could be so fixated on money.

'Because they've got nothing else in their lives,' Slider said.

'That's all very well, but Tyler, at least, did have other things in his life, before he destroyed them by his own hand,' said Atherton.

'We've got to find documentary evidence,' Slider said. 'I can't believe Bates got hold of the only copies. Where would your father keep something that important?' he asked Emily.

'In his computer,' she said with a shrug.

'He wouldn't give a copy to anyone? He didn't send you anything, like a data disc or a memory stick?'

'I'd have said so if he did,' she said patiently.

'What about a friend? Candida Scott-Chatton for instance?'

'No. He wouldn't implicate her when it was something as dangerous as this. And she'd have told you, surely, if he gave her something and told her to guard it with her life.'

Atherton looked at her sharply. She was holding the locket, warming it in her hand as she so often did. 'He did send you *something*.'

She met his eyes. 'My birthday present?'

'Why did he send it to you if he knew you were coming over? He could have given it to you in person.'

'He wanted me to have it on the day,' she said.

'Which was a week ago. And Masseter was killed two weeks ago. Allowing for the post—'

'You think he sent Emily the locket when he heard Masseter was dead?' Joanna said. 'But why? You couldn't get a data disc in that.'

'I'd have noticed,' Emily agreed, with quiet humour.

'But he did tell you it was very valuable and warned you not to let it out of your sight,' Atherton persisted.

'No, he warned me not to lose it. I was the one who decided to wear it all the time. I like it. And it reminds me of him.' Her eyes filled abruptly with tears. 'I'm sorry,' she said. Slider passed her across his handkerchief, and she accepted it and blotted her eyes, biting her lips to regain control.

Atherton said, 'I can't help thinking that he may have sent you a clue of some sort with it. Did it come in a box?'

'Yes, a jeweller's box, in a Jiffy bag. But there was nothing else in it.'

'I don't suppose you have the box with you?'

'Yes, it's in my case. But honestly, there's nothing else in it except the card that came with it, and unless you're suggesting there's a microdot . . . ?'

'Well, you never know,' Atherton said.

'I do. Where would he get access to the technology to compress all his files into a microdot?'

'But I'd like to have a look at it, if you don't mind,' Atherton said, and she shrugged and went upstairs, returning with an ordinary jeweller's box about four inches square, in red leatherette. Inside was the usual black velvet bracer, with slits where the chain would have been secured to hold the locket in place, and a square, stiff card with some hand-writing on it.

'You're right, your dad's handwriting is terrible,' Atherton said. 'What does it say?'

Emily took it back. 'It says "Happy birthday, darling. I hope you like it. It's valuable so be sure not to lose it. It will be something to remember me by, even if you're glad to see the back of me."'

'That's an odd thing to say, isn't it?' Atherton said, frowning. 'Why would you be glad to see the back of him?'

'Oh, it's a sort of old joke,' she said. 'He didn't like it when I went to live in the States, because he was going to miss me, and he said it must be because I didn't like having him hanging around me, spoiling my pitch. A joke about me being a better journalist than him – which wasn't true. He was the best there was.'

Atherton held out his hand. 'Would you let me look at it?'

'There's nothing in it except a picture of him,' she said, but she undid the clasp anyway, and handed it across.

Atherton took it, warm from her hand, smooth and pleasant to the touch. It didn't look old, that was his judgement. There's a look to old, second-hand gold. This looked quite new. And it didn't look valuable to him, either – not enough to warrant a warning. It was worth maybe a couple of hundred pounds, not more. He prised it open with a thumbnail, and inside was a photograph of Stonax, smiling and looking rather windblown with that shock of dark hair. The photograph was held in place by a thin oval bezel. He thumbnailed that off, as well, and lifted out the photograph, which he saw had been cut with scissors to fit the oval shape. There was nothing behind it but the back of the locket.

He turned the photograph over. On the back was some very small, neat writing.

BZ793A58

He handed it to Slider. 'Eight randomly assorted numbers and letters,' he said.

When Slider came back to the table from the telephone, he said, 'Jimmy Pak says there's an absolute mass of information there – notes, scanned documents, letters, cuttings from newspapers, you name it. It looks like the goods all right.'

Joanna reached over and kissed Atherton on the cheek. 'Genius!' she said. 'Old planet-brain, the boy wonder.'

'Fluke,' said Atherton. 'It was Ed Stonax who was the clever one, thinking of hiding it that way.'

'I don't know why I didn't think of it,' Emily said. 'I'm embarrassed.'

'Don't be. How were you to know?'

'But he said he had something important to tell me. I suppose when I got here he was going to tell me everything, show me the documents.'

'I'm not quite there,' Joanna said. 'He copied everything into the computer and encrypted the files?'

'The Arbuthnots heard him tapping away day and night,' Slider said.

'Then why did he keep the original stuff – assuming that was what was in the file that was stolen?'

'Insurance,' Atherton said, 'in case of a break-in. The way I see it, he wouldn't leave everything in the file, but enough to look convincing, so that if they broke in they'd think they'd got the lot and (a) not tear the place apart and (b) feel confident they'd covered themselves. He knew they were ruthless – he must at least have suspected Danny's "accident" was helped along. But probably he didn't realise just how ruthless they were. He can't have thought that they'd actually kill him – only cut him off at the pass like they did the first time.'

'If he'd known,' Emily said quietly, 'it wouldn't have stopped him.'

'But he might have gone about it a different way,' Slider said.

'So if he had all Danny's stuff,' Joanna said, 'what was he waiting for? Why didn't he go public right away?'

'Hard to say, until we see what there actually is in the encrypted files,' Slider said. 'It might be that there was something else he still needed. Or he might have been working it up into a final report. Or he may have had someone else involved and was waiting for them to act.'

'But no-one else has come forward to say they were working with him.'

'True. Well, I don't know the answer to that.'

'Of course, there wasn't any particular hurry,' Atherton said. 'It wasn't as if the leisure park was going to be built in one day, starting tomorrow. He may just have been considering what course his action should take. He had plenty of time.'

'Except that he didn't,' Emily said. There was an uncomfortable silence, which in the end she broke. 'So is this enough to get them, now?'

'I don't know until I look at the stuff. Jimmy Pak's making copies, and we'll have to go through it all tomorrow and see what we've got. And then get Porson in on it and start making up a case. But if your father took this trouble to get the information to you, I'm betting it will be significant.'

'But you still don't know where Bates is,' Joanna said. 'Not to rain on the party, but we can't go home until you get him.' She anticipated Atherton's next words and said, 'We can't stay here with you for ever, Jim. Even if you were willing to keep *us*, what about Derek?'

'Derek?'

'The baby.'

'Why on earth—?'

'Don't ask,' said Slider. 'Is that your phone?'

Atherton went out into the kitchen, where they heard him say, 'Oh, hi . . . Yes, he is. Did you want to . . . What? Good for you! Yeah, yeah, I'm writing it down. Brilliant. OK, I'll tell him. Love to Tony . . . No, I mean it. Bye.'

He came back in, grinning. 'That was Norma. She was waiting for a call back from an estate agent friend – or in her case, probably a former lover.'

'Pots and kettles,' Joanna muttered.

'Anyway, she's found – or rather he had found – Richard Tyler. He's bought a house in Holland Park Avenue. And given what property costs along there, he must have done very well out of Brussels and whatever else he's been up to since he went away. He moved in at the end of August.'

'Just about the time Bates escaped,' said Joanna.

'Holland Park Avenue's right on our doorstep,' Slider said. 'Not much more than half a mile from the station.'

'Also just round the corner from Aubrey Walk,' Atherton added, 'where Bates's house is.'

'And a hundred yards or so from where they found the black Focus,' Slider added grimly. Joanna glanced at him, and knew that expression. She felt a cold chill, though she wasn't sure what she feared. 'I said that Bates hadn't a friend in the world but Tyler – if you can call him a friend. But friend or not, he's the one person Bates can be sure won't shop him. What would be more natural than that he should hole up with Tyler? On his old stamping ground, which criminals always like, being creatures of habit. And handy for his old house if he needs a bit of equipment. I'm sure Tyler could arrange that. Tyler came back to England at the end of July, and Bates was sprung at the end of August.'

'And all the king's horses and all the king's men couldn't find him,' Atherton said. 'Well, of course they couldn't if he was under the wing of a former minister and EU commissioner.'

Joanna was still looking at Slider and reading his mind. 'Bill, no. You're not to.'

'Just a look,' he said. 'I promise I'm not going to do anything, but I just want to have a look.'

Atherton looked at him too. 'What, now?'

'Why not?'

'I'm coming with you, then.'

Slider said to Joanna. 'Just a look. And I'll feel better about leaving you because you won't be alone, with Emily.'

'Better let them get it out of their system,' Emily said to her. 'You know what boys are like.'

She was easy about letting Atherton go, Joanna thought, because their love was so new, and she couldn't yet imagine anything bad happening to him. Perhaps it was another thing to lay at pregnancy's door. But she had never tried to stop him doing what he felt he had to. It was just that the longer she knew him and the more she loved him, the harder it was to let him go.

Nineteen

Down and Out

They drove to the station in Atherton's car and left it there, to take an unmarked car out of the pool instead. It was possible, Slider thought, that they knew the number of Atherton's car as well as his, and he didn't want them to look out of the window and see it, and know they were being watched. Atherton thought he was being unnecessarily cautious.

'But since you are, hadn't we better tell someone upstairs where we're going?'

They went up to the department, where Mackay was on night duty. He was at his desk having a bunny with Fathom, who was sitting on the other side of it, evidently waylaid on his way home, since he was wearing his street clothes, a bomber jacket and a pair of lamentable cut-away leather driving gloves.

'Hello, guv. Something up?' Mackay said.

Slider explained, and Mackay whistled. 'Very nice. Very cosy, and handy for everything. No wonder Bates could follow you around so easy, guv. What're you going to do?'

'Just go and have a gander at the house,' Slider said. 'Tyler's not going anywhere, we know that, but I'd like to see if there's any sign that Bates is there. Tomorrow we can get Mr Porson to stump up a search warrant and we can go in and take the place apart.'

'Guv, let me come,' Fathom said. He looked excited. 'Please. Just in case. You might need another hand. I was just going home. I've got nothing else to do.'

It would have been like kicking a puppy. He looked at Atherton, who shrugged minutely. 'It's not going to be exciting,' he warned. 'Just sitting in a car looking at a house.'

'But I need the experience,' Fathom said cunningly. 'I have to learn.'

'All right, you can come. But you do exactly as you're told at all times, and keep your mouth shut,' Slider said.

'Deal,' said Fathom.

There was just an outside chance, Slider thought, that something might happen. And Fathom was a big lad. In a pinch, one might overlook the dorky gloves.

The Holland Park house was large, beautiful, elegant – white stucco, with a portico and steps up to the door. The tall windows of the drawing-room were lit behind drawn curtains; the upper floors were in darkness. There were also lights on in the semi-basement, which had blinds on the windows. In the original arrangement of these houses, that was where the servants had hung out. Nowadays the semi-basement was often a separate flat. Slider wondered if Thomas Mark was down there. From what he knew of both Tyler and Bates, they would have been too grand to let the minions bunk in with them.

As to whether Bates was in there at all, Slider quietly drew his companions' attention to a new-looking and very powerful radio mast on the roof.

'Now what would Richard Tyler want with a mast that powerful?' he said.

'It's the only way to get Jazz FM?' said Atherton.

'There's a satellite dish, too,' Fathom noted. 'A big one.'

'Maybe he likes Sky Sports.'

'Not the right sort of dish.'

There was a car parked on the gravelled forecourt, a black Lexus; and a motorcycle, a powerful-looking Triumph.

'And there's the bike,' Slider said.

'There's more than one Triumph in the world,' Atherton said, though it sounded a bit messianic.

'Can you see Richard Tyler on a bike? No, I feel it in my bones, Bates is in there.'

Fathom leaned forward from the back seat. 'Shall we go in and get him?' he asked eagerly. He was already reaching for the door handle in his excitement.

'Steady, lad, or I'll have to put the child lock on. We can't go prancing in there on a whim. We've got no authority to search the place, and all that would happen is that Tyler would refuse us entry and be put on his guard. By the time we got back with the right papers, Bates would be dust on the horizon and any evidence we might hope to pick up would be destroyed.'

'So you really did only want to look,' Fathom said, disappointed.

'What did you think? I'm not going to shout "Go, go, go!" just so you can get to kick the door in with your size twelves.'

'On the other hand,' Atherton said, 'we'll have to watch the place now we know there's a chance Bates is in there. Hadn't we better call it in and make it official?'

'It'll have to be twenty-four-hour surveillance. I'd better get Mr Porson out of bed. Can you radio the station and see who they can get here by way of temporary back-up – out of uniform, of course.'

Porson seemed rather glad than otherwise to be called out. Slider wondered if he had trouble sleeping. He said he would come straight in and sort out the paperwork for a surveillance request. At the station, they said they'd get someone over for surveillance as soon as they'd got them into their civvies – about half an hour, if they could hang on. Atherton said they could, and they settled down, with Fathom's tangible disappointment like a fourth person in the back seat, to watch the quiet house and wait for support to arrive.

But only minutes later there was a movement across the road.

'Someone's coming out,' Fathom said. A dark figure was coming up the steps from the semi-basement. 'Is it Mark?'

It was a man in all-over motorcycle leathers and a dark-visored helmet. Little runt of a man. 'Not big enough for Mark,' Slider said, hearing his own voice cool and far away, while his blood tingled with adrenaline. 'I'd say it was probably Bates.'

'Where the hell's he going?' Atherton complained.

'Escaping. It's my fault,' Slider said. 'I told you to radio in. Pound to a penny he's been monitoring the station radio. Why the hell wouldn't he? I just didn't think of it.'

'What do we do, guv?' Fathom asked. He was sweating

with excitement now. 'Do we grab him? Let's go get him! Run across the road and collar him!'

But the figure was already astride the bike. Even if they ran, by the time they got across there he'd be moving, and then they'd be on foot and he'd be motorised. He'd be away and gone while they were scrambling back to the car.

'Follow him,' Slider said tersely. Atherton gunned the engine. 'There he goes.'

'I'm on it,' Atherton said.

The bike swerved out of the opening and on to the road, executed a flashy U-turn round an on-coming taxi, and hammered off down the road towards Shepherd's Bush Green. Atherton was after him, while Slider radioed the information to the dispatcher. 'I bet he goes up the motorway,' Fathom said. He was leaning forward as if he could make the car go faster that way, gripping the back of Slider's seat, his breath whistling hot past Slider's ear. 'He's gonna go up the motorway. That's what I'd do. Bet he does. *Bet* he does.'

But he didn't. He went on past the big roundabout towards the Green.

'He wants to lose us in traffic,' Atherton said grimly, through clenched driving teeth. There was still a lot of it about, and it was easier for a bike to weave through it than a car. Slider was glad Atherton was driving. His reactions were years quicker and he was completely fearless behind a wheel.

'What about the bubble, guv?' Fathom suggested.

'It might help me,' Atherton agreed.

'And it might make him nervous,' Slider said. He reached out of the window on his side and slapped the blue light on to the roof. As the siren wailed he saw the motorcyclist look back over his shoulder. I'm going to look a complete plonker if it isn't Bates, Slider thought. And he had a hideous mental image of Bates slipping quietly and at leisure out if the house while they chased a nobody. But it wasn't Mark, and it would have taken time to brief an innocent extra, and there hadn't been more than enough time to get the leathers on. Besides, nobody who wasn't serious about getting away would ride a bike like that, and at that speed, through Shepherd's Bush.

Atherton squeezed the car between two frightened civilians who swerved apart and then back into their lanes, hitting their horns in sheer reaction. A chorus answered from the drivers behind who had been briefly inconvenienced. The motorcyclist was coming up to the far end of the Green with a choice of three directions to go. But the lights were red to go left towards Hammersmith.

Atherton said, 'He's going straight on, down Goldhawk.'

A gap opened up, and he accelerated with an affronted roar of the engine. Pool cars didn't expect this kind of treatment.

The rider looked over his shoulder again, one quick glance, and then instead of going straight on, at the last moment bent the bike at a fantastic angle and went right, taking the curve round the Green in front of the cinemas with the machine almost horizontal.

'Bloody hell,' Fathom said.

'Hold on!'

Tyres screamed as Atherton swung the wheel hard right, and behind them there was a screech of brakes, a blast of horn, and a crunch and tinkle as someone was forced to veer and didn't quite miss someone else. The wheels raced and then gripped again, and as the car lurched forward Fathom nutted the back of Slider's head.

'Ow!'

'Shit! Sorry, guv.'

The rider looked again to see if they had followed. It was a mistake. He had gone over at so steep an angle that the glance back was just too much. His balance went. The rear wheel went out sideways, the bike slewed left across the road and slid in a shower of sparks, hit the kerb and threw the driver off. There was a chorus of horns and brakes, and piercingly, heard even over the traffic, someone screamed. The rider rolled over and over at incredible speed, like a small black log hurtling down a mountainside. A truck, coming briskly round the corner from Goldhawk Road had no chance to brake and nowhere to swerve to. Slider felt his scalp go cold, heard Fathom swear, and saw the bike go under the wheels with a hideous series of sounds.

But the speed the rider had rolled had saved him, taking

him just clear as the truck lurched to a stop, scattering a tinkling of small glass and metal from the mangled thing under the wheels. As the traffic came to a standstill, leather-man staggered to his feet, pushing himself against the lorry's snout to make his balance. Slider caught a glimpse of the lorry driver, white and rigid behind the wheel, eyes and mouth three shocked O's, as Atherton swerved across to the kerb and stopped at a diagonal in front of all the mess.

They were all out in a second, but leather-man was already on the move. He ran, limping stiffly the first few steps; glanced round, found some adrenaline reserve, and went like the clappers, limp forgotten. They pounded after him.

'Bloody Mel Gibson,' Atherton said tersely.

There were pedestrians scattered about, halting and looking round, uncertain what was happening.

'Police,' Slider shouted. 'Stop that man.'

But no-one did. One man put out a feeble foot but leather-man easily avoided it. 'What's 'e done?' Slider heard someone shout. His whole burning attention was fixed on the fleeing black figure. The accident must have hurt him. It would tell against him. *Must* do, when the adrenaline was used up.

Leather-man's hands went up to the helmet, dragged it off and dropped it. It bounced like a hand-grenade, plastic splintering. Slider's heart sang as the long red hair fell loose and flew out behind the runner like a flag. No doubt then – it *was* Bates. The helmet business had slowed him for a second, and Atherton, pulling ahead of Slider, was almost within reach. Bates showed a white eye and dodged, round a bollard and across the road, thumping past the stopped cars of the first two lanes, dodging the crawling, gawping outer lanes.

Atherton was ahead in the pursuit, and the heavy, less nimble Fathom was falling behind Slider. Strung out in a line they pounded after the black stick-figure with the flying red mane. Atherton almost had him and he dodged again, jinked left and right and then left again – dammit – back into the traffic and across the road. Slider jerked round to throw a diagonal course and cut him off, and Fathom ran into him from behind. Slider shouted something, he didn't know what, and was off again.

Why didn't someone try and stop him? Bloody useless

civilians! Whatever happened to civic pride? Bates was doubling back towards the cinemas now. Slider's cut-across had made up a few yards. Bates looked round and for an instant their eyes locked, and Bates grinned – but he might have been gasping for breath. Always kept himself fit, Slider remembered, his own breath catching at him now. No, he *was* grinning. Bastard! Somehow, Slider accelerated.

And at last some concerned citizens were acting. Out of the corner of his eye Slider saw a knot gathered about the stalled lorry; and ahead a group of men had formed a nervous-looking but moderately determined line across the pavement. Slider shouted again, to encourage them. 'Police! Stop him!' Two in the middle of the row linked arms.

And there were a lot of people behind them, the usual rubberneckers gathering for a gape, beginning to solidify into a crowd. Bates must have seen there would be no way through, for he dodged right, down the alley between the two cinemas. 'Gottim!' he heard Atherton shout. The alley was a dead end. Slider allowed himself to slow just a fraction, so he could catch his breath. He could hear Fathom thundering up behind.

Bates ran, still lightly, damn him, down the alley before them. The larger cinema, on the right, presented a smooth wall with nothing but three sets of fire doors, the sort that can only be opened from the inside. At the end was a high, blank wall, and a clutch of overflowing wheelie bins. The smaller cinema, on the left, had a fire escape down the wall at the far end, and with a sense of inevitability he saw that Bates was making for it. Why didn't he just give up? Atherton evidently thought the same, because he yelled, 'You can't get away. You're trapped.'

Bates didn't even look back. He leapt up the fire escape like a salmon, and Slider cursed inside his head – he hadn't the breath to do it aloud.

It was an old-fashioned, black-painted iron staircase, the short flights zig-zagging between small landings. Slider started up behind Atherton, smelling the metal and a sourness of garbage on the air, feeling the handrail clammy under his hand – it had started drizzling very lightly. Atherton's nimbleness was matched now against Bates's fitness, but the accident was telling and Bates was limping again. The two made the turns simultaneously like dancers, one short flight apart. Slider was another flight behind. His breathing went through an agony point and he tasted metal in the back of his throat, and then his second wind kicked in. He reached the roof almost on Atherton's heels.

Over the parapet and on to the flat concrete. There were ventilation outlets, steaming slightly in the drizzle, a light haar which became visible like a gauze veil as a security light was triggered. It was mounted over the square brick protrusion that housed the fire door back into the cinema. Bates ran to it and tried the door, briefly and hopelessly. It would only open from the inside.

Slider stopped, turned back to where Fathom was just reaching the top of the fire escape. 'Stay there!' he shouted. He didn't want Bates dodging them all in a Dick Van Dyke chase round the chimneys and nipping back down. Atherton had stopped too, facing Bates, who backed now, slowly, away from the fire door, his eyes darting round to assess the situation. The haar was standing on his red hair like jewels. Slider could see his chest rising and falling under the close black leather. The fox was cornered and spent.

Slider walked forward towards him. 'Give it up,' he said. 'There's nowhere else to go. Come on, you know you've had it now.'

'Come quietly, is that it?' Bates said. His teeth were bared as he caught his breath, and his voice was higher and harsher than Slider remembered. 'I don't think so, Mr Plod. Not for you, that's for damn sure. If you want me, you'll have to take me.'

Slider felt a weariness that was nothing to do with his trembling legs come over him. 'Oh, don't be so bloody silly,' he said impatiently. 'You're cornered, you're nabbed, and there's nobody watching you but us, so you can drop the phoney heroics. This is real life, not a film.'

'You don't know the meaning of real life,' Bates said, backing all the while towards the parapet. 'You pathetic second-rater, do you really think you can get the better of me? You can't touch me.'

'You have friends in high places, I know,' Slider said.

'Don't think they're going to bale you out this time. You're going down.'

Bates reached the parapet, a low wall topped with flat stone slabs. He glanced quickly over to see if there was any escape that way, and began to inch along beside it. Atherton and Slider advanced steadily, adjusting to his direction. He reached the corner and glanced over the second side. Slider suddenly wondered if there was another fire escape. Bloody Nora, if he had to start running again . . .! 'For God's sake, give it up,' he said.

Atherton exchanged a glance with him. His look said it all: why didn't they just grab him? Slider opened his mouth to answer that look when he saw that Fathom, disobeying orders, was creeping up from the right, the direction in which Bates was sidling.

Bates glanced in that direction, scowled horribly, mouthed one short word of anger. He jumped up on the parapet, looking left and right for escape, staring at the next building – far too far away to jump, even for an egotistical athlete.

As one man, Slider and Atherton stepped forward. Bates dodged left, running along the parapet. As if he could read his mind, Slider knew he was going to make for the fire escape. He turned his head back to Fathom, jerked an arm towards it. 'Get back over there!'

Perhaps Bates looked round too, or reacted to Slider's arm movement. Slider replayed it afterwards a hundred times in his mind. Perhaps it was nothing but the sheerest accident. The parapet was damp from the mizzle; Bates had been limping, so he must have hurt his leg. Whatever it was, his foot slipped and he rocked off balance. His arms flailed, and his eyes met Slider's in one awful locked instant of mutual knowledge. Slider and Atherton both leapt forward, arms out, hands reaching. But Bates was gone, and there was only rough concrete under their grasping hands as they leaned over, looking down into the alley. Someone said, 'Christ!' and he never knew who it was, Atherton or Fathom. Maybe even himself. And a sound came up to them, a ghastly thud of a sort that Slider hoped he would never have to hear again.

Twenty

Time Wounds All Heels

After that, Slider felt as if his feet didn't touch the ground for weeks. There was so much to do, and so much trouble to get through. The proverbial shit storm wasn't in it. If it hadn't been for Porson standing firm at his side, Slider could never have survived it. And by the time he and Porson were both called before Commander Wetherspoon, their superior at Hammersmith, and he said, 'This is a dog's breakfast of a case. I can't make head or tail of it,' Slider would almost have been grateful to say, 'Oh, well, don't let's bother then.'

But Porson, magnificent as the Old Man of Hoy, talked and talked at Wetherspoon, and pointed out with graven dignity so many matters of simple honesty, justice and pride in the Job that Slider wanted to cheer; and Wetherspoon, who wouldn't have got where he was today without being something of a trimmer, was won over on to their side and in the end even said, 'I'm not having politicians telling me how to do my job, thank you very much.' And he went in to bat for them.

So then it was the head of SOCA, and Ormerod, the head of the Organised Crime Government Liaison Team, who was higher yet, and so on to the Commissioner of the Met, and the Home Secretary himself. There was grave internal trouble because Bates's escape could not have been managed without some complicity high up in the Met. Slider supposed that was what Pauline had been trying to warn him about. In the end there were two quite senior suspensions and an arrest of a political appointee in the Home Office just on the Bates escape alone. While Slider's heart ached that any policeman had been able to be bought like that, he had to admit that, given the size of the prize Tyler and Bates were going after, they had been in a position to make the price very attractive indeed, even to a senior Yard officer.

Through all this Tyler didn't run, didn't move a muscle, was so certain he was invulnerable and untouchable that he stayed put in his glamorous house and laughed at them.

Thomas Mark ran, but without either Bates or Tyler to protect him he didn't get far, and when they nabbed him, he didn't take much persuading to roll over. They had his fingerprints from the black Focus, the paint match from the car to the damaged bike, mud under the wheel arches matching that of the lane, and Mrs Masseter's identification. He was bang to rights for murder and perverting the course, and in the end he was glad to have the murder dropped to manslaughter and failing to report an accident in return for fingering Bates and Tyler, which he wasn't unwilling to do anyway.

'They were going to make millions out of Clydeview, and what was I going to get?' he said resentfully. 'I wanted a percentage, but they laughed at me. A flat fee, that's what they offered me. And who was doing all the dirty work?'

Slider, of his own interest, asked about Bates's plans for him.

'Oh, he was going to kill you,' Mark said indifferently. 'That was one of the things Tyler said when he got him out of jail. Kill Stonax for me and I'll let you kill Slider while you're at it. Of course, Tyler wanted you dead, too.' He looked at Slider with mild interest. 'You don't half piss a lot of people off.'

'So why didn't he kill me straight away, when he had the chance?' Slider asked.

'I suppose he liked tormenting you,' Mark said indifferently. 'He was like that. Anyway, Tyler said he hadn't to kill you before you'd nicked Dave Borthwick and charged him for doing Stonax. But you didn't charge him.'

'We knew it wasn't him, you see,' Slider said.

Mark stared at him. 'I reckon you're not as stupid as Trevor thought you were,' he said. 'But he reckoned everyone was stupid, compared to him. And he was right, most of the time.'

It was an epitaph, of sorts, Slider thought.

*　　*　　*

It took an immense amount of time to assemble all the evidence against Tyler, and to squeeze out of Vollman Zabrinski the admission that the BriTech shares were held in Tyler's name. When they were able at last to take Tyler's house apart they found a mass of equipment that he had arranged to get out of Bates's house and installed for Bates's use. He claimed he had taken it out of Bates's house for safe keeping, and since he had all the proper paperwork he at least had a workable defence for it, although a lawyer might argue that there had been no need for him to hook it all up.

One of the interesting things that emerged was that both Stonax's flat and his phone had been bugged. So they had known from his conversations that Danny Masseter was coming to see him and probably that he had received a parcel from him too. Slider considered that it might have been the imminent arrival of Stonax's daughter that had moved his elimination up the agenda. He did not air that thought to Emily or Atherton, or even Joanna.

It also emerged that Stonax had been trying for several days to get an appointment to see the Prime Minister privately and alone, and had not succeeded largely because he would not tell anyone what he wanted to talk about. That was reason enough to offer Emily for his murder. What interested Slider most about that piece of information was that Stonax had apparently chosen the political rather than the legal route to right the wrongs of Waverley B. He supposed it was simply old habit: politicians and journalists alike tend to think that the solution to everything is political.

So then there were the political ramifications to get past, and they were immense. There was no way for them at the bottom to know how far anyone else in the government was implicated, even if it was only by turning a blind eye, but hints filtered down from time to time, relayed at the last link by Porson to Slider, that it had gone all the way to the very top, both on the political and the police side. Porson hinted that this made it unlikely any action would be taken, and Tyler all along remained supremely confident that knowing where an immense number of bodies were buried would make him untouchable. If he had to leave the country again, a High Commissionership in some agreeable country was the least he was ready to settle for.

Slider himself wondered how it would be possible to put Tyler on trial, when all he had to do was threaten to finger the PM. And would the CPS even consider making the attempt if the PM was able to say that Commissioner of the Met was implicated? Slider and Atherton agreed, unhappily, that it looked as though it was another of those cases that would be buried deep and the whereabouts of the grave forgotten, which, as Atherton pointed out, made it look bad for them. They would be bound to secrecy under the Official Secrets Act, and be under surveillance for the rest of their careers, if any, to make sure they didn't spill the beans to anyone.

But in the end it was pressure from the bottom that changed things. Porson kept agitating to Wetherspoon, and Wetherspoon, marvellously shaken out of his usual servile complacency, kept poking those above him. In the end the Assistant Commissioner, who quite fancied his boss's job, leaned on the Home Secretary by reminding him that after the war the government had handed back the contaminated land to be run as a shipbuilding yard again, and who knew how many people had got sick and even died as a result? Even if they hadn't known the site was contaminated, the potential for compensation suits was beyond computation. There was a hopeful passage of play at the break-down when the Home Secretary suggested the late Trevor Bates might conveniently be blamed for everything, and the Assistant Commissioner suggested to Wetherspoon that it might be best to go that way. But Wetherspoon countered by pointing out that by now far too many people at the bottom knew too much and would not be satisfied with that, and the Assistant Commissioner told the Home Secretary that since it was impossible to get the brown sauce back in the bottle, it must be Tyler's head on a platter, or the whole Waverley B story to come out, with politically disastrous results. The Home Secretary pedalled hard on the PM's paranoia, the PM persuaded the Commissioner to take early retirement in return for a full pension and a seat in the Lords, and Tyler's fate was sealed.

Slider was dog-weary, and sick to his stomach with the game-playing, by the time it was resolved, and it was small comfort to him that they let him be in on the final arrest of Richard Tyler. Deputy Commissioner Ormerod, who had used Slider to arrest Bates the first time, insisted on it, and even laid a huge, meaty arm across his shoulders and said, 'You've deserved this. You deserve a medal, but I'm not in charge of that. But I can see to it that you're in at the kill.'

'And what happens afterwards?' Slider was driven to ask. He still didn't see how they'd ever allow him to be put on trial.

Ormerod did not pretend not to understand. 'There'll be a deal of some kind,' he admitted. 'No mention of Waverley B in return for a lighter sentence. Something like that. But we've got to be realistic. He's going down, let's be glad of that, at least.'

The words reminded Slider of what he had said to Bates, moments before he went over the top. He met Ormerod's eyes, and read in them a different certainty; and he remembered how on previous occasions, felons who had been in a position to finger the government of the day in some serious manner had committed suicide – in their cells and in inverted commas – before coming to trial.

'Tyler's finished,' Ormerod assured him. Slider tried to think of Phoebe Agnew. He thought of Ed Stonax. It was just an old-fashioned streak in him that didn't want a right by way of two wrongs. 'It's justice,' Ormerod concluded.

Of a sort, Slider amended, but only inside his head.

So Slider went along as a spear-carrier when the final drama was played out. Not that it was very dramatic. There was no kicking down of doors, of course, no raised voices. Tyler stared at them all with his feral, golden eyes, and if he was pale – well, his long, smooth face had always been unnaturally colourless.

But there was no sign of panic or fear about him. He smoothed his hair back with one long, freckled hand, and said, 'You have no idea who you are dealing with. You will be very, very sorry if you try to arrest me.'

'I'm not going to try,' Ormerod said. 'I'm just going to do it.' And he did it.

In the middle of the recital of the crimes he was going to be done for, Tyler looked past Ormerod and met Slider's eyes. 'I should have killed you when I had the chance,' he said emotionlessly. 'How could Trevor make such a mess of it? How difficult can it be?'

'Shut up,' Ormerod said. 'You're just making it worse for yourself.'

At which point, Tyler began to laugh. 'Worse? How can it be worse?'

It was the laughter Slider took away with him. Ormerod had meant well, but he couldn't really say he had enjoyed it. Afterwards, it made him feel as if he had been a spectator at a bear-baiting – not that he had any grain of sympathy or pity for Tyler, but there had been an element of voyeurism in it that he felt dirtied by. He had to comfort himself with the thought that Tyler was going to pay a penalty, whatever it might turn out to be, and Mark was in jail, and Bates was dead. It didn't bring back their victims, of course.

And when the fuss had died down, they told him, the Clydebrae site was going to be quietly decontaminated. The Waverley B House of Fun would not claim any more lives. And maybe the terns would come back.

When the arrest of Richard Tyler hit the newspapers, Sir Henry Paxton fled to America, which meant a lot of trouble trying to arrange an extradition order to get him back, and more diplomatic repercussions, because it was hard to get the Americans to pop him without knowing fully why. There was a lot of toing and froing before sufficient evidence of financial wrongdoing could be assembled not to have to mention any contaminated shipyards. But you could always get the Justice Department on large-scale fraud and wobbly accounting.

A few days after that there was a small paragraph in the paper which caught Slider's eye, reporting the death of Sid Andrew. He had committed suicide by hanging himself in the grounds of his luxury home in Northamptonshire. He had left no note, so Slider would never know whether it was remorse over his part in the Waverley B business that drove him to it, or the more general misery of realising that he was no longer a player and never would be again. But he was interested, in a mild, exhausted sort of way, to note Andrew had chosen the same suicide method as Angela Barlow.

And the next day he finally remembered to remind Hart

to telephone Reading Library and stop them harassing Mrs Masseter about the lost book; and he stood over her to make sure she did it.

By the time all this was sorted out, it was the end of October, and Joanna was so large she had to have help getting out of chairs. She had been patient with him, knowing how much he was suffering and how much he had to do and how much all the powers that be were trying to make his life hell, but in the end she said, 'It's not for me, it's for baby Derek. You know you didn't want him to be born out of wedlock. And you also ought to know that doctors' estimates of the birth date are just that – estimates.'

'I know,' he said, and saw her properly for the first time in weeks. 'Oh, darling, I'm sorry. I've made a mess of this. I've made a mess of everything.'

'None of that,' she said. 'You've done what you had to do. Now can we for Pete's sake get married before I go off pop?'

'Of course. How shall we do it?'

'I'm not walking up an aisle like this. Anyway, you have to book months in advance to get a church.'

'Register office it is. When, and who do you want to invite?'

'ASAP, and I'd like to invite everyone. Why don't we book the register office, tell everyone we know, and see how many turn up?' she said. 'It'll be self-limiting that way.'

'But what about a reception afterwards?'

She made a face. 'I hate that word. Look, let's just all go to the Tabard afterwards, and we can have a proper party some other time, after the baby's born, when I'll be in a better shape to enjoy it.'

'If you're sure,' he said doubtfully. 'I wanted you to have the wedding of your dreams. After all, you're only going to do it once.'

'I love your confidence,' she said, getting as close to him as she could for a hug. He kissed her contritely, and she comforted him by saying, 'Look, I never really saw myself done up like a meringue, with three friends bursting out of mauve satin behind me, and ten million photographs of the guests in weird configurations, and a rubber-chicken sit down, followed by a really naff band in blue dinner jackets and frilled shirts playing Tom Jones hits.'

'You didn't? I thought that was every woman's dream.'

'*You're* my dream,' she said. 'But I'm afraid what I just described is exactly what my mum and dad always envisaged for me. However, they're not marrying you, I am, so they'll have to lump it. We'll throw a monster bash after the baby gets here and let them wallow then.'

'We'll have to do something,' he said gravely, 'or we won't get the presents.'

'That's the reason I'm marrying you at all,' she said.

And in the end, it wasn't even Chiswick Town Hall and the Tabard, because man proposes and God disposes, and a couple of days before the date they had chosen Joanna phoned Slider up at work and said, 'I'm sorry to bother you, but I think I'm in labour.'

He left at once and dashed home to collect her and take her to the hospital, and sat on a hard chair for what felt like hours while she was behind a curtain waiting to be examined, then walked behind her as she was taken in a wheelchair up to the labour ward, and hung around outside for what felt like more ages while she was undressed and got into bed and examined again.

And when he was allowed back to her side, he took her hand and she said, 'I'm sorry. I couldn't hold on any longer.'

'What's to be sorry about?' he said, hoping he didn't look and sound as nervous as she did.

'You didn't want Derek to be a bastard.'

'No child of ours is going to grow up to be a bastard,' he said.

'Yes, but he's going to begin that way, poor little perisher.'

'How long have we got?' he asked. He grabbed the nurse who had been behind the curtain with her a minute ago as she went past. 'How long have we got?'

'Before baby gets here?' the nurse said. 'Oh, a couple of hours yet, I should think. First babies always take a long time.'

He dropped Joanna's hand. 'Wait here,' he said as he headed for the door.

'Where the hell d'you think I'm going?' she replied.

She was beginning to feel resentful and abandoned when Atherton and Emily arrived. 'All alone?' Emily said.

'He had to go and do something,' Joanna said, having no idea where the baby's father had disappeared to. She grimaced as another pain came.

Emily came to the bedside and held her hand until it passed. 'I'll stay with you,' she said. 'Jim might have to go back to work if it's a long time.'

'Thanks,' Joanna said. 'Did I ever tell you how glad I am you and Jim got together?'

'Oh, a few times,' Emily said.

There had been some tough days to get through, after the case was solved and the reaction kicked in, and Emily had to come to terms not just with her father's death but her father's murder. But in her grief and turmoil she always turned towards Atherton for comfort, not away from him, and through it all their relationship strengthened. And what with that, and the rounding up of her father's estate to complete, and the hundreds of requests for interviews, and the memorial service to arrange, and the book she had decided to write about him to start researching, she had decided she was not going to go back to New York. There was too much now to keep her in England. Atherton's relief had been mute but profound.

Emily's hands, Joanna noticed, were covered with scratches from playing with the cats. Greater love, she thought.

At last Slider came back, followed by a very young man in grey flannels and a tweed jacket, with a black shirt and dog collar underneath. The hospital chaplain. Joanna started to laugh. 'Really? Not really?'

'Why not?' he said, grinning sheepishly. 'Father Bennet doesn't mind.'

'But is it legal?' Atherton said. 'Sorry, Father, no offence meant.'

'It's perfectly legal,' he said. 'It's part of my duties to carry out priestly functions for patients in extremis.' He blushed as this struck everyone simultaneously as an unfortunate phrase, and he lurched in a different direction. 'But you don't have to call me Father, you know. Richard is all right.'

'I'll stick with Father, if you don't mind,' Slider said.

'And you do have to have the Marriage Authority with you?'

'I've been carrying it around in my wallet for ages.'

'Is it still all right?' Joanna asked.

'They don't go off, like milk, you know,' he said. 'Are you sure you want to marry me?'

'Of course I want to marry you. Only can we wait a sec, because I'm having another pain. Talk to Jim and Emily for a minute.'

Shortly after that, Joanna became the second Mrs Slider, courtesy of Father "Call me Richard" Bennet, with James Atherton and Emily Veronica Stonax as witnesses. Slider even had the wedding ring to hand. He had bought that ages ago, too, and had snatched it up from the bedside cabinet drawer when he collected her to bring her to the hospital – not with Father Bennet in mind, but in a sort of desperation, thinking that at least he could give it to her to comfort her for his failure to get organised in time.

And shortly after Father Bennet pronounced them man and wife, Joanna's waters broke and she was wheeled away to the delivery room.

'Just got in under the wire,' Atherton remarked. 'Talk about last-minute conversions.'

'I think that was the nicest wedding I've ever been to,' Emily said. 'And I'm thrilled to be on the wedding certificate. I wonder if they'll let us be godparents.'

Not terribly long after that – though it seemed like an awfully long time to the protagonists – Baby Derek made his first appearance on this or any stage, squashed, red and wearing what appeared to be an ill-fitting black wig.

'The teapot *with* the spout,' Joanna said proudly when they told her it was a boy.

'We're not really going to call him Derek, are we?' Slider asked her anxiously.

'I thought we could call him George after my favourite husband,' she said. Slider's name was actually George William, but he had always been called Bill to distinguish him from his father, who was also George.

They called him George, and James after Slider's favourite lieutenant, and Edward after Emily's father, since she was on the wedding certificate and they meant to ask her to be godmother. Emily cried when they told her, but they were the only tears that attended George James Edward Slider's birth.

Atherton had dashed out to get a bottle of champagne while Joanna was in labour, and had sweet-talked a nurse into putting it in the staff fridge to chill. It was interesting to Emily to watch his technique, because he had never used it on her. And so they wet the baby's head with Bollinger, in plastic cups, and none the worse for that.

And after that, there was still the monster bash to look forward to.